THE BAYOU BULLETIN

State Senator Delacroix Facing Tough Reelection Fight

With Election Day less than a month off, the battle for state senator is developing into a vigorous contest, with incumbent Philip Delacroix rumored to be fighting for his political life.

According to a member of Senator Delacroix's staff who requested anonymity, Drew Delacroix, the senator's son, has taken a much less active role in his father's campaign than in years past. "There's bad blood between those two," the source reported. "Without Drew in his corner, the senator is vulnerable."

When questioned about his son's diminished profile in the campaign, Senator Delacroix said, "Drew has always stood by me. I am proud to have his support, just as I have the support of the voters of Bayou Beltane."

Drew Delacroix could not be reached for comment.

Barbara Keiler is acknowledged
as the author of this work.

ISBN 0-373-82571-4

LEGACY OF SECRETS

This edition published by arrangement with Harlequin Books S.A.

Printed in U.S.A.

Legacy of Secrets

JUDITH
ARNOLD

Harlequin Books

TORONTO • NEW YORK • LONDON
AMSTERDAM • PARIS • SYDNEY • HAMBURG
STOCKHOLM • ATHENS • TOKYO • MILAN
MADRID • WARSAW • BUDAPEST • AUCKLAND

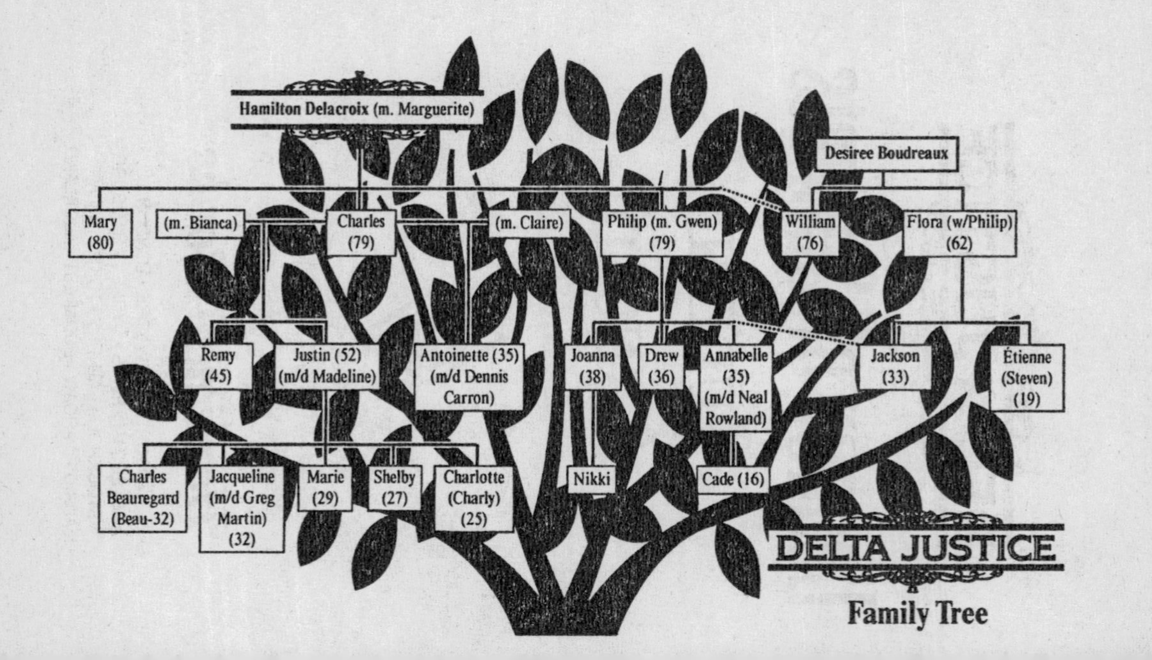

Hamilton Delacroix (m. Marguerite)
Desiree Boudreaux
Mary (80)
(m. Bianca)
Charles (79)
(m. Claire)
Philip (m. Gwen) (79)
William (76)
Flora (w/Philip) (62)
Remy (45)
Justin (52) (m/d Madeline)
Antoinette (35) (m/d Dennis Carron)
Joanna (38)
Drew (36)
Annabelle (35) (m/d Neal Rowland)
Jackson (33)
Étienne (Steven) (19)
Charles Beauregard (Beau-32)
Jacqueline (m/d Greg Martin) (32)
Marie (29)
Shelby (27)
Charlotte (Charly) (25)
Nikki
Cade (16)
DELTA JUSTICE
Family Tree

CAST OF CHARACTERS

Drew Delacroix—Philip Delacroix's only son, who followed his father into law and has spent his life trying to win Philip's approval.

Katherine Beaufort—An antique dealer from New Orleans, trying to uncover the truth about her past, and what role the Delacroix might have played in her family history.

Philip Delacroix—Drew's father. State senator and local power broker, who seems overly interested in the much younger Katherine.

Annabelle Delacroix—Drew's younger sister and Katherine's friend—a true Southern belle and owner of a bed-and-breakfast in Bayou Beltane.

Claire Beaufort—Katherine's aunt who raised Katherine after the death of her mother.

Judge Neville Alvarez—A New Orleans judge in the 1930s who arranged for the adoption of Claire and her sister.

Patrice Beaufort—Katherine's grandmother's sister, Judge Alvarez's mistress, and author of a cryptic diary that holds many secrets and perhaps some answers?

Dear Reader,

Drama. Mystery. New Orleans! Who can resist? When I was invited to write book eleven in the DELTA JUSTICE series, I was tempted. When I learned that I would get to tell Drew Delacroix's story, I was hooked.

Drew is teetering on the edge of an abyss, fighting for balance even as he contemplates how easy it would be to jump. Can a man as tormented as he be saved?

Because I'm a romance writer, I want love to redeem Drew. And because this is a DELTA JUSTICE story, rich with mystery, I want the truth to redeem him. Of course, it's Katherine Beaufort, the heroine of *Legacy of Secrets,* who gets the chance to redeem Drew. She gives him love, she gives him the truth—and she learns that while these powerful gifts may redeem a man, they may also destroy him.

Writing *Legacy of Secrets* allowed me to ponder whether the truth actually does set us free—and whether freedom is worth the pain it can leave in its wake. It also allowed me to tell the story of my heart—one in which love can somehow save the most tormented man.

Happy reading!

Judith

Judith Arnold

PROLOGUE

My woman, she drinks from the river.
My woman, she drinks from the rain.
And I drink my bourbon, and I drink the tears
Of the woman who weeps for my pain.

DREW STARED OUT at the night black water, trying to remember where he'd learned that song. An old Cajun lyric, maybe. He'd heard it somewhere, and it had fastened itself to his heart. If only he could remember.

Lately, it seemed, the only things he could remember were the things he was trying too damned hard to forget.

The shack stood on piles at the water's edge, little more than a crude enclosure at the landed end of a rotting dock. He'd taken it in payment from a penniless client a few years ago, after defending the fellow pro bono on a manslaughter charge and winning him an acquittal. Drew was a good lawyer. On rare occasions he could work a miracle. Buddy Durant had been on the receiving end of one of those miracles, and he'd wished to show his gratitude.

Drew hadn't wanted to take the shack, but Buddy Durant had insisted. In recent months, it seemed, the ramshackle twelve-foot-square building, with its crooked table and its cast-iron cot, was worth more to Drew than any money he might have been paid. What had once been a simple settlement of a debt had turned into a haven, a place for him to hide.

He could hide from only so much at his cabin on the bayou, though. He couldn't hide from himself, and he couldn't hide from the truth. That was what the bourbon was for.

My woman, she sleeps by the window.
My woman, she sleeps in her bed.
And I drink my bourbon and wait for the dawn
And pretend that I ain't feeling dead.

It wasn't working. As much as he drank, he still felt the world too keenly. The starless sky dropped down on the earth like a velvet drape, too thick for an October night. The water lapped at the pilings beneath his feet, and here and there he heard a splash, some critter breaking the surface for a breath of air. Here and there a rustle as a swallow stirred the dry leaves of a magnolia, as a coot slipped through the marsh grass. He heard the wind. He tasted the dampness of it, the spice of the foliage hanging low over the water. He felt this world stronger than he felt the bourbon spilling over the lip of the bottle and down his throat.

He felt this world, and the other world, too. The world of Bayou Beltane, the world of his family. That world was crumbling, crack by narrow crack, like an Old Masters painting; it might look grand and gracious from a distance, but as you moved closer you saw the fissures, the splits and crevices, and you realized that the grand, gracious picture was nothing but a mass of tiny, separate bits of color held together by little more than faith.

My woman, she prays to Jesus.
My woman, she prays to the Lord.
And I drink my bourbon and drown out her prayers
And my woman, she speaks not a word.

He took another long sip, then stood the bottle on the porch railing and stared out at the rippling water. His throat felt numb, but not his brain. He could suck the bottle dry and his brain would still refuse to let go.

And I drink my bourbon and drown out the prayers
And nobody utters a word...

CHAPTER ONE

"THERE'S SOMETHING WRONG with that piece," Dionne declared, glowering at the armoire that had stood on proud display in the front room of the shop for months. "It's the best thing we've got in inventory and no one wants it."

"Someone will want it sooner or later," Katherine said with a vague smile.

The armoire stood six feet tall, its mahogany veneer lovingly polished, its brass hardware gleaming. The pleated silk fabric behind the beveled ovals of glass in the two doors was clean and starched. Katherine had chosen the armoire, along with a few other furnishings from her great-aunt Patrice's estate, to sell at K & D's Antiques, the shop she and Dionne owned on the eastern edge of New Orleans's Garden District. But before the items had been put on display, she'd had each piece painstakingly restored.

If the armoire hadn't been quite so painstakingly restored, her furniture refinisher might never have found that the third drawer had a false bottom, and Katherine would never have learned that Patrice had hidden a diary in the hollow.

"I've sold too much Depression glass this week," Dionne complained, then sighed melodramatically. She was good at ranting, and always seemed to feel better afterward, so Katherine made herself comfortable in the chair behind the rolltop desk, let the computer shift into screen-saver mode, and allowed Dionne to rant to her heart's content. "You'd think folks might recall that the Depression was *not* a happy time in this country, and that Depression glass was mass-produced and handed out for free at movie theaters. But no, folks are willing to pay absurd prices for the stuff. And yet, when we have a quality piece of furniture like that—'' she gestured indignantly toward the armoire ''—they look at it, they admire it, and then they pass it up and spend their money on Depression glass.''

''We make a fine profit on the Depression glass,'' Katherine pointed out.

Dionne ignored her. She paced in the narrow aisle that ran through the front room, where the shop's antique furniture was displayed. Her route meandered among escritoires and ladder-back chairs with embroidered seats, between a working spinning wheel and an ornately carved coat tree, around settees and cedar chests. No one but Dionne could power-walk in such a constricted space. And no one but Dionne could look like a graceful lioness surrounded by the elegant century-old furnishings that filled the front room. Her braids splayed out from her face like a mane every time she reached the armoire and reversed direction. Her jungle-print blouse and gauzy wraparound skirt emphasized her exotic beauty.

''I'm telling you, that piece is haunted,'' she said. ''Folks love it, but when it comes time to pull out their checkbooks, they flee to the back room.'' The back room was where smaller items—knickknacks, folding fans, woven baskets and the ubiquitous Depression glass—were arrayed, priced and ready for sale.

''The armoire isn't haunted,'' Katherine assured her.

''You found that diary in it.'' Completing another circuit around the front room, Dionne reached the rolltop desk, planted her fists on the upper surface and leaned toward Katherine. ''There's hoodoo in that diary.''

Katherine laughed. ''There's nothing supernatural in it,'' she insisted. ''Just a lot of very tiny, crabbed writing, backward, in French.'' Merely thinking about her difficulties in translating the pages made her sigh. ''I've been deciphering it a sentence at a time, but it's slow work. I have to hold the book up to a mirror and read it in the glass. And you know my college French is *très rouillé.*''

''College French?'' Dionne snorted, her dark eyes narrowing. ''French is in your blood, Katherine Beaufort, so don't give me that.''

''I have no idea what's in my blood,'' Katherine reminded her quietly. Dionne could trace her ancestry more easily than Katherine could trace hers. Dionne was descended from slaves, and slave owners had kept meticulous records. Katherine, on the other hand, was the daughter of a woman who had been adopted at a time when the birth records of adoptees were sealed, a woman who had conceived Katherine out of wedlock and died before ever revealing who the father was.

Katherine had no idea whether she had French blood in her or not. Given her lush red hair and fair coloring, she sometimes wondered if her father had been Irish. He might as easily have been Cajun, or Creole, or any of the other ethnic groups that brewed in the melting pot that was New Orleans.

All she knew about her mother's blood was that it had contained something wild and willful. Katherine's mother had lived a troubled life and died a troubled death, leaving behind a daughter who had grown up with too many questions and hardly any answers.

''You've been trying to read that diary for months,'' Dionne reminded her. ''Any hexes in it? Any curses?''

''It's a rambling mess,'' Katherine answered, avoiding Dionne's probing gaze by studying the pattern of colorful, twisting shapes on the computer screen. Dionne was her business partner and one of her dearest friends, but Katherine wasn't yet ready to discuss all the ramifications of the diary with anyone. She was still digging out splinters of ideas and shards of thought, fitting the fragments together like a mosaic. Once she'd pieced together enough to see the larger picture, she would tell Dionne all about it. But for now...

"It's really hard to translate," she explained. "By the time I've translated half a page, I've got a pounding headache and I have to stop."

"I'll bet what's in that diary is a curse," Dionne suggested. "Your aunt cast a spell on the armoire, and once you finish translating the diary you'll be able to undo the spell and we'll sell the damned thing."

"The only spell that diary's cast has been on me," Katherine complained. "Why else would I be knocking myself out to decode it?"

Dionne swiveled around to study the armoire from the distance of Katherine's desk. "You don't think we priced it too high, do you?"

"For that quality, that workmanship and that age?" Katherine shook her head. "Maybe we priced it too low."

Dionne resumed pacing. "Twelve thousand dollars isn't exactly a bargain. But I think it's fair. If I knew any rich people, I'd convince them to buy it."

"You know plenty of rich people," Katherine reminded her. Indeed, Dionne seemed to know everyone in the city, from the blues maestros in the French Quarter to the doyennes of the Garden District. She dated street-corner virtuosos and tenured professors, and for a while last year she'd been escorted around town by a linebacker for the New Orleans Saints. Currently she was enjoying the company of a weather forecaster at one of the local news stations. Certainly he could afford the armoire. And the New Orleans Saint could have afforded a dozen at that price.

The only rich people Katherine knew right now were members of the Delacroix family. Her grandparents had been comfortably middle-class, but their only real connection to the wealthy and powerful had been her grandmother's sister, Patrice, who had been the mistress of Judge Neville Alvarez, a major judicial figure in New Orleans half a century ago. He had given Patrice money—enough money to buy some glorious pieces of furniture, Katherine acknowledged as she gazed at the armoire across the room—but mostly he'd given her pillow talk, gossip, the whisperings of a man besotted with his mistress and too relaxed after sex to censor himself.

How could Judge Alvarez have known that each time he'd left her bed to go home to his wife, Patrice had jotted down every word he'd said, backward and in French? Katherine assumed Patrice had hoped to use the information somehow. Perhaps to extort something more than money out of Judge Alvarez. Perhaps to secure his help in some mission.

She was due for another trip to the North Shore—supposedly to look at some caned chairs Philip Delacroix wanted her to price for him. But once she'd started making pilgrimages across the causeway to Bayou Beltane, all her antique hunting up in the small neighboring towns hadn't obscured her real reason for traveling there: to find out what her great-aunt's cryptic notations meant, to learn why Patrice had filled a leather-bound journal with the ramblings of an indiscreet lover, ramblings that contained references to the Delacroix, a family who had ruled Bayou Beltane like a fiefdom and whose lives had somehow come to bear on Katherine's own.

And while she was there, winnowing out precisely what the connection was between Judge Alvarez and the Delacroix, and why Patrice had cared enough to record his postcoital confessions in her diary, Katherine could look at Philip Delacroix's old caned chairs.

"So," Dionne was saying, "do you think I should talk

Lawrence into buying this thing?'' Lawrence was her meteorologist beau.

''If he truly loved you, I would think he'd buy the armoire just to prove his devotion,'' Katherine teased.

''He loves me enough to prove his devotion by buying Preservation Hall for me,'' Dionne said simply. ''Unfortunately, I don't love him.''

''I thought you did.''

''I thought I did, too.'' Dionne shrugged. ''He's too white for me. Do you want him?''

Katherine grinned and shook her head. Unlike Dionne, she rarely dated. It wasn't because she lacked her friend's easy gregariousness, though she did, or because she wasn't as strikingly pretty as Dionne, which she wasn't. Sometimes she thought it might be because she still hadn't figured out who she was, whose blood was in her veins, whether it was sinful and tormented like her mother's, whether she would wind up, like her mother and her mother's mother before her, unmarried and pregnant, rootless and alone.

Or maybe it was because she felt no compelling urge to be with a man. Now and again she would meet someone and he would stir something inside her, some softly glowing passion that with patience might be coaxed into a flame. But she didn't have patience, not for that.

And the only man of late who stirred anything in her was Drew Delacroix, Philip's son. She didn't exactly trust Philip, but at least he had pleasant manners—and some interesting antiques. His son, Drew, was short-tempered and scathing. On the few occasions Katherine had crossed his path, he'd left her churning inside. His eyes were too bitter, his mouth too hard. He was tall and lean, seemingly a paragon of robust good health. Yet he seethed with anger and unspoken resentment.

If she were a weaker soul, he would frighten her.

Instead, he merely...disconcerted her.

She knew she had to keep returning to Bayou Beltane until she could reach an understanding of what the Delacroix family had to do with her great-aunt Patrice, and thus with her. Over the past few months she had grown quite close to Philip's daughter Annabelle, who ran a bed-and-breakfast in the small town, so it wasn't as if the trips were unpleasant or a waste of her time.

But whenever she drove to Bayou Beltane, she ran the risk of crossing paths with Drew Delacroix. That risk was almost enough to make her want to toss the diary in the trash and forget about uncovering the truth.

However, she was too curious to stop trying to solve the mystery of Patrice's diary. She would keep going back, keep asking, keep searching. She only hoped she would find what she was looking for without getting burned by the heat of Drew Delacroix's wrath.

"DREW!" PHILIP HOLLERED through the locked door.

It was a small thing, that lock. Just a knob twisted, a bolt shot. Yet when Drew had it installed in the door connecting his father's office to his, the act had seemed epic.

He had asked his father to communicate with him by dialing his extension on the phone or, if the conversation absolutely had to be conducted in person, by entering Drew's office through the main door off the hall that linked the firm's offices with its library, conference room and reception area. Philip, of course, had ignored the request. He had viewed the back door that opened between the two offices as his own private access to his son. When Philip had wanted Drew, he would storm in, unexpected and uninvited.

"It was inappropriate, your barging in like that," Drew had chided once, after Philip had come waltzing into his office while he'd been in an intense discussion with a client so skittish, the sudden intrusion had almost sent her fleeing from the office. "You can't just come barging in here whenever you want. This is my office."

"It's my firm," Philip had bellowed. "I can damned well come and go as I please."

So Drew had installed the lock.

"Drew, open the door!" his father shouted.

Drew perused the contract on his desk. Let the old man shout until his vocal cords ruptured. Let him pound on the heavy oak panels until his knuckles bled. Or let him come to his senses, show some respect for his only son, and walk through the hall to the proper entry. Drew was not going to unlock that back door.

It was impossible to concentrate with his father screaming and banging on it, though. The contract's neatly printed words floated before Drew's face with all the impact and clarity of dandelion seeds on the wind. He lowered the file, pressed the heels of his palms to his eyes and listened to his father holler through the door: "Drew, damn you!"

Indeed, he thought. *Damn me.*

Silence wrapped around him. He closed his eyes and visualized his father's movements as he stepped away from the locked door, then crossed his own vast office to the hallway and made his way down its carpeted length to Drew's door. He pictured his father reaching for the doorknob. He wouldn't knock, but that was all right. He was using the correct door. Drew couldn't hope for more than that.

Philip shoved the door open the precise moment Drew would have cued him in. Clad in a beige linen suit and brown bow tie, Philip Delacroix still cut a stylish figure, although he was starting to look his age. Eighty years of hard living had ground away the edges of his features, swelled pockets of flesh beneath his eyes, dug deep lines into his high forehead and weighed down the corners of his mouth. At the moment his complexion was florid, probably from all that yelling through the locked door.

Without preamble, he tossed a thick white envelope onto Drew's desk, dislodging a page of the contract. Drew nudged the envelope aside, straightened out the papers in the file and closed it. Only then did he lift his gaze to his father. "Yes?"

"That packet needs to be delivered to Gilbert Weedon at the *Slidell Sentinel,*" Philip announced.

A year ago, Drew's response would have been to leap to his feet, pluck his car keys from his pocket and announce, "I'm on my way." Six months ago, he might have said, "No problem. I'll do it as soon as I'm done reviewing this file."

But day by day, his willingness to appease his father had eroded. He had been trying for thirty-seven years to be everything his father wanted him to be, to do everything his father wanted him to do. Thirty-seven years was a long time to keep trying in the face of failure.

He was never going to be what his father wanted. Slowly, gradually, Drew was coming to accept that no father's love should be so difficult to win, and the only reason he hadn't won it was because it didn't exist. Drew's father didn't love him, and putting his life on hold to race to a newspaper office in Slidell wasn't going to change that awful truth.

"What's in it?" he asked, lifting the envelope and testing its heft.

"That doesn't concern you. Just deliver it to Weedon."

"It does concern me," Drew said, smiling wryly. "What if it's an explosive device?"

"What in the hell would I be doing having you deliver an explosive device to Weedon?"

"Beats me. But I've read of mail bombings over the past few years, and—"

"This isn't mail. It's an envelope I'm asking you to give him."

"Or maybe it has a doll in it," Drew continued, although the weight and shape of the envelope's contents brought to mind a thick wad of currency. "A voodoo doll," he added, just to watch the color drain from his father's cheeks. For months, his father had been targeted by what Drew assumed was a practical joke. Someone had left voodoo dolls in places where Philip would find them. At first he'd scoffed, but lately, merely mentioning the dolls seemed to spook him.

Drew considered it nonsense. But the rash of voodoo incidents—strange dolls and burnt offerings that kept appearing wherever Philip happened to be—and the bad luck that had nearly toppled a few other members of the Delacroix family made his father jumpy.

"It's not a doll," Philip snapped. "It's some business Weedon and I have to take care of, and more than that you don't need to know." Philip fussed with his tie. He was clearly anxious. Drew noticed a slight tremor in his hands. "Weedon's going to be writing his endorsement of my reelection to the state senate. He needs these papers to back up his column."

"He's endorsing you, is he?" Drew leaned back in his chair and peered up at his father, rather enjoying the spectacle of his old man fidgeting.

"He's endorsed me every campaign. Why shouldn't he endorse me now?"

"I can't imagine why he wouldn't. But if he needs these...*papers,*" Drew emphasized, "to back up his endorsement, he must need persuading. After all those past endorsements, it's kind of odd." He turned the envelope over in his palm, noted the smoothly sealed flap and turned it over again. "What denomination are these *papers,* Dad?"

"Never mind." Philip whipped the envelope out of Drew's hand. "I'll have Jackson do it. I should have known better than to ask anything of you. You're supposed to be helping me with this campaign, damn it. You've helped me in every other election, and you said you'd help in this one, too, but here I am, having to take care of everything myself."

"I've done what needed to be done," Drew reminded him, struggling to rein in his temper. "I've overseen the mailings to your constituents. I've arranged for a few of your media appearances. I've set up a Web page for you, though Lord knows, you haven't got the first idea what a Web page is."

"I don't need to know. It's your job to know."

"And I've done it," Drew said, hearing an edge in his voice. "I've done enough for your campaign."

"You've done nothing, damn it! You won't even open your blasted door to your own father!" He turned and stalked to the main door. "Thank God I've got Jackson to do what needs to be done."

"Yeah," Drew muttered at his father's retreating back. "Thank God you've got Jackson." Jackson Boudreaux did all Philip's unpleasant chores. Why not run the old man's bribes for him, too?

One foot over the threshold, his father paused and glanced back at Drew. "And another thing," he said.

Drew exhaled. His breath was too sharp. Bladelike, it scraped his throat, leaving him hoarse. Was he about to be treated to the *You're a disappointment to me* lecture, or the *Tell your sister Joanna to tell her daughter Nikki to dress properly* lecture? "Yes, Dad," he said, bracing himself for whatever came.

"I won't have you harassing Katherine Beaufort anymore," Philip warned.

Katherine Beaufort. That red-haired witch had been poking around for weeks now. Months. All cool pride and sleek posture, smiling and angling her face toward his father, hanging on the old man's words, favoring him with her gazes.

Drew didn't want to harass her. In fact, he didn't want anything to do with her. She vexed him. She'd been vexing him since she'd first shown her prying, spying self in Bayou Beltane. Yakking about some old diary she'd found and asking questions, always asking questions. Not the sort of questions you'd expect of a woman seeking antiques for her shop in New Orleans.

Drew didn't trust her.

"She was in town this morning," Philip continued. "She came to appraise those chairs that have been collecting dust on the screened porch. She says they're probably close to a hundred years old and worth more than you'd think."

"They couldn't possibly be worth less," Drew muttered under his breath.

"And I might add she's a charming young lady whose friendship I treasure. But every time she sees you, you're surly and cold. I won't have it, Drew. I won't have you treating her with discourtesy."

Tension clawed Drew's stomach and drummed in his skull. He'd thought Katherine was merely a busybody, pretending an interest in the Delacroix family history and Philip's old furniture for who knew what purpose. But if she had her sights set on Philip himself... The very thought made Drew nauseous. Especially because he knew his father had difficulty keeping his trousers on when there was a pretty woman in the vicinity.

"She's too young for you, Dad," he remarked dryly, wondering what she might be after with Philip. Surely not a romance. Philip had had more than his share of sex appeal in his youth, but his youth had vanished decades ago.

Money? She wouldn't be the first gold digger to sniff

around the Delacroix family, but if money was what she wanted from Philip, she was doomed to disillusionment. Nowadays, he gave money only to people who could give him something worthwhile in return, like Gilbert Weedon and his election endorsements. What could Katherine give Philip that was worth real money? Besides the obvious, which Drew could not imagine Philip paying for, at least not with an amateur like her.

Power? With his law practice, his political career and his financial and real estate holdings, Philip had a degree of clout rivaled only by that of his twin brother, Charles. Yet Katherine didn't seem power-hungry.

She was looking for something else, something more than the old chairs on the screened porch. Antique chairs weren't enough to keep a wide-eyed, well-groomed lady like Katherine Beaufort interested in Philip.

"Her age is irrelevant," Philip retorted.

"Come on, Dad. She's almost too young for *me*."

"She enjoys my company," Philip said. "And I won't have you scaring her away."

"She's using you," Drew pointed out, watching his father's face mottle with splotches of red once more. "Lord knows what for, but she's definitely using you."

"Maybe you're just jealous because she comes to Bayou Beltane to see me and not you." Philip straddled the threshold, fumbling as he tried to stuff the thick envelope into an inner pocket of his jacket. "You treat her nicely, Drew, or you'll have me to answer to."

Drew pressed his lips together and rotated his chair until he was facing the windows behind his desk. He had always had his father to answer to, and the answers were no longer working. His father was the same man he'd always been, issuing threats, buying endorsements, treating Drew like an errand boy—and like his gravest disappointment.

Drew was tired of the condescension, the disapproval and

the bullying. His sisters had only minimal contact with Philip; the entire family had all but turned against him. Only Drew had remained loyal, but his loyalty was worn thin, fraying into loose, ragged threads.

And now he was supposed to keep his mouth shut while his father made a fool of himself with Katherine Beaufort? That confounded woman with her long legs and her glittering eyes and that hair, so thick with curls a man could lose his hands in it, lose his mind thinking about it. And a mouth that was pursed in disapproval when she saw Drew, always pursed, as if primed for a kiss.

Katherine with his father. Katherine with the old goat, the arrogant bastard. Drew's stomach twisted so tight it hurt.

He rose from his chair, moved to the door his father had left open and slammed it shut. Then he walked back to his desk, yanked open the left-hand bottom drawer and lifted out a small flask. He unscrewed the cap and tipped the bottle against his mouth.

The bourbon wasn't as intoxicating as he suspected a kiss from Katherine Beaufort would be. The liquor couldn't numb him enough to let him stop hating her.

CHAPTER TWO

THE WINDSHIELD WIPERS clicked back and forth in a slow, regular tempo, constant enough to hypnotize Katherine if she'd paid them any mind. But she ignored them, and ignored the drizzle they cleared from the windshield of the van. She devoted only enough attention to the cars around her to avoid a collision. The rest of her mental energy she channeled into reviewing the hours she'd spent that day in Bayou Beltane.

For deliveries of large pieces of furniture, K & D's Antiques used professional movers. But the piece she'd delivered to Annabelle's bed-and-breakfast that morning—a nineteenth-century stereoscope and a wooden box of slides, which Annabelle wanted to display in the parlor of her inn—Katherine could easily handle with the van. Likewise the chairs she'd picked up from Philip Delacroix's house. They weren't exquisite, and the style had been common enough at the turn of the century. But she'd be able to sell them to someone for a profit. She had told Philip last week that she was interested in buying them, and today she'd needed an excuse to see him. So now she had four dusty, musty chairs in the back of her van.

Not only had she purchased the chairs—paying less than half of what she'd charge for them, once they were cleaned and their joints were tightened—but she'd also put up with Philip. At times, he made her almost as uncomfortable as his son did. The way he looked at her implied that he was seeing not just an antique dealer, not just someone curious about the Delacroix legacy, but...a woman.

Dear God, he must be eighty years old! The mere idea of being thought of that way by a man like Philip made her queasy.

Still, his company was easier to take than Drew's, despite the fact she had to pay four hundred dollars for his weary old chairs to justify her visit.

The day had started pleasantly enough with her delivery of the stereoscope to Annabelle's bed-and-breakfast. Once the two women had viewed all the double-image slides and argued over which one was the best of the collection, Annabelle had insisted that Katherine stay for lunch. It was an invitation she wasn't about to decline. She and Annabelle had built a strong friendship in the months Katherine had been traveling to Bayou Beltane. The stereoscope was only one of many antiques Katherine had helped Annabelle to select for the bed-and-breakfast's decor.

Over mountainous plates of mixed greens and cold prawns and tall glasses of iced tea, Katherine told Annabelle about Patrice's diary. "You have to understand," she explained, "I always thought of Patrice as an eccentric character. Even in her seventies, she dressed in silks and feathers and chattered about her lovers. She was like a tropical bird. I always expected her to climb onto the porch railing, flap her arms and soar into the clouds." Annabelle laughed, and Katherine joined her for a moment before growing serious. "Of all Patrice's lovers, Judge Alvarez was the one she chose to write about in this diary. And her writings imply that Alvarez was embroiled in some intrigue involving your family sixty years ago."

Annabelle rolled her eyes. "*Some* intrigue? Which one? We Delacroix have so many intrigues to choose from."

"Well, Alvarez seemed to have been quite the wheeler-dealer," Katherine said. "I originally got caught up in the diary because he was the person who had arranged for my aunt Claire's adoption by my grandparents. Aunt Claire says she has no interest in who her birth parents were, but *I* want to know. I've tried to trace my own mother's birth parents, but every door there has been slammed in my face. If I could at least find out about Aunt Claire... I don't know." She shrugged. "It would be something. Some connection to my past. A piece of heritage to hang on to. Aunt Claire was always more like a mother to me than my own mother, anyway." She toyed with her fork, then laid it on the edge of her plate and leaned toward Annabelle. "The thing is, I've been plowing through this diary in search of information about my roots, and I've come across a few mentions of your father visiting Judge Alvarez, talking to him. Your father would have been barely out of his teens then."

"Whatever my father was doing with Judge Alvarez, I'm sure it was bad," Annabelle muttered, her tone edged in bitterness. "Even if he was a teenager... If my father had a hand in it, it would have to be ugly."

"Annabelle."

"I'm not kidding," Annabelle said. "My father is the most selfish, greedy, manipulative man I know." She ruminated for a moment, then reached some sort of decision. "You ought to talk to my cousin Shelby. She's been rummaging through some old files from my grandfather's practice. Hamilton Delacroix was the first Delacroix lawyer here in town. He groomed my father and my uncle Charles to take over his firm, but then they had a falling-out and divided the practice. If this Judge Alvarez had any dealings with my family, it would have been through my grandfather. Shelby might have a record of it in her files."

"Do her files date back that far? Patrice's diary covers a period in the late thirties."

"I'm not really sure what she's got. I just know she's

been rummaging through those papers. Shelby works in my uncle Charles's firm. Go talk to her, Katherine. Maybe she'll be able to figure out what my father was up to with Judge Alvarez."

So, after lunch, Katherine drove the few blocks across town to the offices of Charles Delacroix, where Shelby filled her in on what she'd managed to piece together from her great-grandfather's files, which had fallen into her lap a few months ago. The files contained records and personal notes that concerned Hamilton Delacroix's final trial, which he'd lost. The man he'd been defending against a murder charge had paid for that defeat with his life.

The presiding judge at that trial, according to Shelby's notes, was Judge Neville Alvarez.

"I know Uncle Philip had something to do with the trial," Shelby told her. "I'm just not sure what. I have to warn you, there's been a real reluctance among the older members of our family to even acknowledge that time in their lives, much less talk about it. If Uncle Philip had ever confided to anyone about it, it would have been Drew."

Seated in Shelby's office, Katherine closed her eyes and pictured Drew, pictured his defiant chin, his dark, brooding eyes, his lean body and long-fingered hands. Whether or not he could help her, Katherine couldn't imagine talking to him about the diary. "I'm not going to discuss this with Drew."

"It's either talk to him or to Uncle Philip himself. But if you talk to Philip, who knows what fancy lies he'll tell you? You've got half a chance of getting the truth out of Drew. He's the only person I can think of who still tolerates Philip," Shelby pointed out, then smiled slyly. "Although I hear Uncle Philip likes keeping company with you, too."

Katherine hid her disgust behind a passive smile. "He's always treated me courteously," she conceded. "And it's been worth his while. I've bought some old junk from his house."

"Junk? I thought you dealt in antiques."

"Well, you know the old line, 'We buy junk, we sell antiques.'" Katherine and Shelby shared a grin. "It's not stuff I'd have gone out of my way for, but I'll be able to sell it. And it's given me a chance to get to know your uncle."

"He's really my great-uncle," Shelby corrected her, as if eager to put as much distance as possible between herself and Philip. "I know Drew can be difficult, but he'd be your best bet if you want to find out why Philip's name keeps showing up in that diary."

"Why not Philip himself?" Katherine asked. She could handle his innocuous flirting, his lecherous grins. She could handle him a good deal better than she could handle his moody son.

Shelby shrugged. "As I said, I don't trust Philip. But then, I'm family. Maybe he'd tell you the truth...if he's sweet on you."

"He isn't—"

Shelby laughed. "Or maybe he's just taken a liking to you because his own daughters avoid him as much as possible. Talk to him, then. He might just tell you the truth. Rumor has it he sometimes does that."

Her sarcasm didn't faze Katherine. "I'll see if I can get a conversation going with him," she said. "If that doesn't work, I'll talk to Drew. Maybe," she added under her breath.

"Let me know if you find anything about Hamilton Delacroix in the diary. And I'll let you know what I find about Neville Alvarez in the old court transcripts and my great-grandfather's notes. We can pool information."

"Let's do that," Katherine agreed.

Back in the van, assuring herself that the clouds crowding the sky augered nothing more ominous than a late-afternoon rain, she had driven yet another few blocks to Philip's law firm. She hoped she wouldn't run into Drew. Like Shelby and Annabelle, she didn't trust Philip—but she distrusted Philip's son even more. She'd take her chances with the older Delacroix; she knew how to deal with him.

The receptionist told her he was in a meeting with some campaign associates. "Let me just buzz him and let him know you're here," the woman had offered, lifting the receiver of her console and pressing a button. She announced Katherine's name, listened for a minute and hung up. "You can go right into his office," she said, sounding a touch surprised.

Katherine was surprised, too. Why would Philip put aside his pressing business just to talk to her? Because she treated him more kindly than his own daughters? Or, heaven help her, because he was sweet on her?

With some trepidation, she walked down the hall to his office, where Philip himself stood in the open doorway, awaiting her. "To what do I owe this visit, my dear?" he asked, not bothering to introduce her to the two gentlemen who were waiting for her to enter before they departed from the office in a blur of suits and attaché cases.

"I didn't mean to interrupt, Philip. It wasn't that important."

"*They* weren't that important," Philip argued, waving a hand at the retreating men. "Tell me what brings you to Bayou Beltane."

She considered opening with the truth, then thought better of it. "I've decided I would like to buy those chairs."

Philip gave her a canny smile. "And you drove all the way here to tell me? You could have telephoned. Not that I'm complaining, Katherine. I'm delighted to see you."

She tried not to wince. "Well, I wanted to visit Annabelle, too."

His smile faded, less, Katherine suspected, from disappointment that he wasn't her only reason for coming than from resentment that she would have anything to do with his estranged daughter. "Annabelle, yes," he said with asperity. "The family *hôtelière.*"

It wasn't Katherine's job to repair broken families. Yet with her own family reduced to her aunt Claire and herself, not even blood relations, she wanted to believe that big, busy families ought to hold together. "Actually, Annabelle suggested I speak to you," she lied, wishing Philip would think a little less harshly of his own daughter.

"Did she?"

With a sigh, Katherine decided to stop pretending she cared particularly about Philip's old chairs. "You know about the diary my great-aunt kept. I've mentioned it to you."

"I recall," Philip said, turning from her and circling back to his desk, as if he were less than wholly interested. "You're using it to research your aunt's adoption, and you said there are mentions of the Delacroix family in it?"

She wasn't fooled. If he really weren't interested, he wouldn't remember as much about it as he did. "There are mentions of a Judge Neville Alvarez in it, too," she said, watching him closely.

His back was still to her, but she noticed the twitch in his shoulders, the sudden stiffness along his spine. By the time he rotated back to her, however, his face was set in an expression of benign indifference. "Neville Alvarez? He's long gone, Katherine."

"I know...but you knew him years ago, didn't you?"

"The legal community back then was extremely close-knit. He was a friend of my father's." He faked a smile of mild curiosity. "And you say he's mentioned in your great-aunt's diary?"

"He was a—a friend of my great-aunt, too. His name

appears quite often in her diary. I even found a mention of your name in it."

"Is that so?" Philip's gaze hardened, like molten slag chilling into metal. He stood straight, a remarkably imposing man for his age, and tapped fingers against the glossy veneer of his desk. His gaze narrowed so tightly on her it seemed almost a palpable thing. "Do you have this diary with you?"

As a matter of fact, it was in her leather tote bag, which was locked in the van. But Philip's intense stare set off tiny alarms inside her. Annabelle had warned her that Philip's involvement with Judge Alvarez could only be a bad thing. If Annabelle was right, Philip would not want Katherine—or anyone—knowing about it.

"I left it at home," she fibbed.

"You did?" He looked both disappointed and oddly thrilled.

Katherine held her face expressionless. "Of course. That's where I've been reading it. Now, shall we go have a final look at those chairs?"

"I would love to have a final look at those chairs," he agreed with unexpected enthusiasm. "I do have a few calls to make before we head out to Belle Terre, if you wouldn't mind waiting in the reception area. I won't take more than ten minutes."

"Fine," she said, forcing a smile and then hurrying out of his office. Philip made her uneasy in his own way, a way quite different from his son's. She felt Philip was lying, misleading her, trying to trick her somehow, or—she couldn't deny it—to seduce her, although he wasn't particularly aggressive in that. Drew, on the other hand, seemed quite the opposite. The hostility he exhibited toward her was *too* honest, *too* direct, and the last thing he seemed interested in with her was a seduction.

No sooner had she taken a seat in the entry lounge when

Drew swept into the building, his trench coat flapping open around his well-tailored gray suit and his fine leather briefcase beaded with raindrops. Seeing her, he halted in midstep. His eyes darkened as he shoved a damp lock of hair off his brow.

"You aren't waiting to see me, are you?" he asked, none too welcoming.

"No," she replied, just as coolly.

"My father?"

"It doesn't concern you, Drew." She could almost hear his heart thumping—or maybe it was her own. Whenever Drew looked at her, she felt flushed, her pulse skittering, her lungs struggling for oxygen.

"My father's business is my business," he drawled. One trait he shared with his father was the ability to stare at her in such a way she felt his gaze viscerally, as if it were a dagger cutting through her.

"If you must know, I'm buying some chairs from him," she said, unwilling to discuss the diary or Judge Alvarez with him. Once again she was certain she'd be safer throwing her lot with Philip than with his fierce, angry son.

Before he could question her further, his father materialized in the reception area. The two men exchanged looks that seemed to vibrate with a meaning she couldn't interpret. Then Philip said, "Let's go, Katherine."

She let him take her arm, but as he escorted her through the door to the vestibule, she glanced over her shoulder. Drew stared after her, his gaze still impaling her, honed to a keen, quiet rage.

What a day, she thought now, two hours later, as she maneuvered through the late-afternoon traffic to the Charles Street exit off the highway. The clouds had fulfilled their promise, and rain echoed against the roof of the van. The windshield wipers marked time like a metronome, but her mind moved to its own rhythm, a syncopated beat that lingered here, darted there, made her so jumpy she believed her safety belt was the only thing holding her in her seat.

She steered the van up the narrow driveway tucked between the building on Magazine Street that housed her shop and the building next door. After parking in the rear lot, she unlocked the shop's back door and unloaded the chairs from the van into the storeroom. Once she was done, she headed for the front room, where she found Dionne finalizing a sale for a customer with a gold card and a craving for Depression glass. The grandfather clock behind the rolltop desk read half past four.

"I'm fading," Katherine admitted as she helped Dionne wrap the set of pink-tinted soup plates the customer had just purchased. Dealing with the Delacroix family could be a fatiguing experience. "Do you mind if I leave early today?"

"Leave? You just got here," Dionne teased as she ran up the credit-card sale. "Did you pick up anything good?"

"Those old chairs I told you about."

Dionne curled her lip. "Those old chairs? Why, I can just picture Mistress Delacroix sitting on one of them, fanning herself while the darkies ran and fetched for her."

"The chairs aren't that old," Katherine assured her. "And I don't think the Delacroix are, either. They weren't antebellum gentry."

"All those rich white folks in those big plantation houses were."

"Don't make generalizations," Katherine chided. "You don't like it when people make generalizations about you."

"Yeah, right," Dionne muttered. "Well, if you want to hang around with the Delacroix, be my guest. Just don't be buying chairs we can't sell for a profit."

"We'll sell these, I promise. Cleaned and refurbished, they'll easily bring six hundred dollars, maybe more. And I bet we'll sell them faster than the armoire."

"In other words, they don't have a hex on them." Dionne sighed, then smiled to show Katherine she wasn't in a cross mood. "Go ahead, then, go home early. I'll close up soon, anyway, because I've got a delivery to make with the van by six. You'll owe me one, though."

"You've got it," Katherine promised, returning to the storage room for her coat. If she'd known it was going to rain, she would have driven to work, but the day had begun mild and sunny and she'd walked. She could take the streetcar home, but she hated it at rush hour, when it was jammed and sluggish. She could walk home faster.

Fortunately, her coat fell below her knees, and she always kept an umbrella stashed in the shop for emergencies. Stepping outside, she snapped it open and started down the road toward her flat, a fifteen-minute walk from the shop. The rain was cool but not cold, misting the air. Drops of moisture hovered before her eyes, lending a haze to the late afternoon and bathing the city in a soft focus. She needed the muted light, the muffled sounds. Every time her mind veered back to the conversations she'd had throughout the day, she felt as if her soul were being cracked like a whip.

Annabelle, Shelby, Philip and Drew—four Delacroix, each one so very different from the others. Could they truly all be related? Katherine had more in common with her aunt Claire, with whom she shared not a single gene, than those four had with one another.

Especially Annabelle and Drew and their father. Philip was so falsely charming, so hypocritically pleasant. Annabelle's charm was genuine and honest. And Drew...

Drew's name didn't belong in the same sentence as charm, Katherine thought with a wry smile.

By the time she'd reached her block, her feet were aching from the damp that had seeped through the soles of her leather loafers. Her coat had kept her trousers dry all the way to mid-calf, but the hems were soaked. She wanted to climb into a tub filled with hot, scented water and lie there for about an hour, until her flesh thawed and her head stopped pounding.

Her apartment was located on the third floor of a dark brick building that teetered on the border between quaint and seedy. The address, on the edge of the French Quarter, demanded an inflated rent, but since there was no elevator, the flats on the higher floors carried an affordable price, and Katherine didn't mind the climb. It was worth it to have a flat that overlooked an interior courtyard, with balconies running the building's length both in front and in back. Katherine had decorated the rear balcony outside her apartment with potted begonias and impatiens. It was almost like having her own garden.

Because of the rain, she took the inside stairs rather than the ornate courtyard stairways that linked the balconies. Her shoes left dark wet spots on the steps, but she didn't care. One of the sconce lights lining the stairwell flickered, the bulb dying a slow death, but she didn't care about that, either. All she cared about was getting into her apartment and out of her soggy clothing, escaping into the tranquillity of her own home, where the Delacroix family, its numerous intrigues and emotional upheavals couldn't touch her.

She twisted her key in the lock, shoved open the door, stepped inside—and screamed.

DREW SHOULD NOT HAVE BEEN in his office at 8:00 p.m. But what did he have to go home to? A meal growing cold on the dining room table? A conversation with his father? God save him from that.

Instead, he lingered in his office, proofreading a settlement agreement, sipping from his flask of bourbon and trying to estimate what time his father would retire for the night so he could go home and not have to see him.

Maybe he would spend the night at the cabin. He could

fire up the gas heater and huddle under the feather quilt on the narrow bed and…

And what? Keep drinking? Keep hiding? What kind of man would go to such extremes to avoid his father?

The kind of man whose father was Philip Delacroix, he told himself.

He might have been happier if the bourbon had any real effect. Some people managed to get smashed on a couple of belts; some barely had to do more than inhale the vapors rising off the top of the bottle. But Drew still hadn't found a quantity of liquor great enough to dull the pain that was gnawing at his soul. He hadn't found the amount that could make him stop caring about everything that was wrong with his life. So he kept drinking, hoping to discover the correct dosage.

He had removed his jacket hours ago, loosened his tie, unfastened his collar button and rolled up his shirtsleeves. The edges of his jaw were roughened by a day's growth of beard. His hair refused to stay back from his face. He was tired. Too tired to risk another run-in with Philip. Too tired to pretend he gave a damn whether the old man won his reelection to the state senate.

Just hours ago, Philip had chewed him out over the wording in a campaign brochure to constituents that Drew had been about to send to the printer. "Why the hell does it say I've helped the construction trades?" Philip had roared. "You know those fanatical environmentalists are campaigning against me, distorting my record, saying I'd destroy the bayou's 'delicate ecosystem' for the chance to line my pockets with some developer's money. That damned bayou's ecosystem is about as delicate as a gator's jaw—and here you are, putting out this pamphlet that says I'm in bed with the developers."

"Who you sleep with is none of my business," Drew

had muttered. ''I thought you'd want to publicize the jobs you've brought to the district.''

''Make me look like an environmentalist,'' his father had demanded. ''And don't send anything to the printer until I've okayed it. I'll see you at home.''

Not if I can help it, Drew had thought then. Now he took another sip of bourbon, prayed for it to dull his mind and smiled sourly at the hilarious thought that anyone could possibly make his father look like an environmentalist. On rare occasions, Drew could perform a miracle in the courtroom. But he'd long ago disabused himself of the notion that he could perform miracles with his father.

He heard a rapping noise, the tattoo of rain pattering against the window behind him. He ought to be using this time to rewrite the brochure; the printer was awaiting the final copy. But he didn't feel like spinning a fiction featuring Philip Delacroix as a tree-hugger.

He heard the rapping sound again, muffled yet distinct enough for him to know it wasn't rain hitting the windowpanes. As best he could tell, the sound came not from the windows behind him but from the other end of the main corridor. Frowning, he pushed away from his desk and exited his office. In the hallway he heard it again, a thumping noise reminiscent of his father's pounding on the locked oak door that connected their offices.

The reception area was lit only by the amber night-light near the vestibule door. Drew didn't bother to turn on any brighter lights. Uncertain who might be trying to get inside, he preferred not to make himself visible through the glass sidelights that flanked the outer door.

He tiptoed into the vestibule, then glimpsed a human shape through one of the sidelights. The silhouette of a woman loomed on the front step, backlit by the street lamps and silvery drizzle.

Katherine. Even with her face in shadow, he recognized

her. Even with her body wrapped in a long coat and her curls flattened by the rain, he knew her.

She lifted her hand to the door again, but he opened it before she could knock. She stood facing him, her fist raised, her eyes wide with alarm. She was drenched and bedraggled, her cheeks pale, her hair dappled with drops of water and her lips bitten raw. For a brief moment he was so taken aback by the stark anguish that dominated her face, he forgot how much he loathed her.

''Katherine,'' he said.

She lowered her hand. A raindrop slid down her cheek to her chin and clung there, unable to fall. She seemed frozen on the doorstep, too traumatized to move. He wrapped his fingers around her upper arm and pulled her inside. Then he closed the door and released her.

They stood in the dim vestibule for a moment. Katherine's hair and coat dripped water onto the carpeted floor.

Her silence grated on him. She hadn't come here to see him, and he didn't know how long he was supposed to stand before her, straining to be polite, before she asked for Philip.

A minute passed, but still she said nothing. Impatience overtook him. ''My father isn't here. It's after eight o'clock. He left hours ago.''

''I didn't come here to see him,'' she admitted, then lowered her eyes. Moisture had darkened her lashes and glued them into spikes. The rain brought out her fragrance, something faint and flowery, hinting of magnolias. Her voice was more air than sound.

What was she implying? She'd come to see *Drew?* On a rainy Monday night? Whatever for? They had nothing to say to each other, nothing to do with each other. If she was hoping to pump him for information about the family's past, the way she'd been pumping everyone else in the family—

"I meant to go to Annabelle's," she continued, her voice as pale as her face. She lifted her gaze back to him, as if searching for permission to go on. She wasn't exactly pretty—her cheekbones made her face too wide and emphasized the point of her chin, and her nose was like a child's, without a defined bridge. Yet her eyes were painfully clear. Even in the diffuse glow of the night-light he could see glints of silver and gold and green in them, glints of truth.

He nodded his encouragement.

"I—I thought maybe she—I was upset and I..." Katherine inhaled deeply, laboring to steady her nerves. "When I drove past this building, I saw a light on and I—I thought maybe you'd be here."

"Not my father," he said, braced for her admission that he was not the man she'd hoped to see.

"Not your father. You."

He reminded himself that he had no good reason to trust her. She was a busybody, insinuating herself into his father's life by buying dilapidated old pieces of furniture from him. How could Drew believe anything she told him?

The raindrop on her chin finally fell, striking her coat where it draped over her bosom. She studied his face for a few seconds longer, then pivoted and reached for the outer door. "I don't know why I came here—"

Reflexively, he reached out and touched her shoulder, refusing to let her walk out. If she asked him nosy questions, he could handle it. He could deflect her curiosity, ignore her agenda. But for some reason he couldn't stand the thought of her fleeing into the cold, wet night. "It's raining, Katherine. It's late. I'll get you a towel."

Maybe she was less than eager to leave, because she let him turn her back around. Through the thin padding that shaped her coat he felt the bones of her shoulder, slim yet firm. He tried to remember the last time he'd touched a woman, stood this close to one, teased his lungs with her scent.

It had been too long, by his own choice. Months, at least. No woman had enticed him, not since…

He frowned at the realization. Not since Katherine Beaufort had first appeared in Bayou Beltane.

Damn. He jerked his hand away, pivoted and stalked into the reception area. "We have towels in the rest room," he said, his voice tight.

"No, that's all right." She followed him into the reception area. The moisture in her hair shimmered like a net of dew as it caught the light.

"A drink, then," he offered, switching direction and heading for the hall to his office.

"No," she said vehemently.

He glanced over his shoulder at her. She was following him, frowning in disapproval.

So what if she'd smelled the bourbon on his breath? He wasn't going to apologize to her—or to anyone—for taking a nip in his office, on his own time. If she had to live his life, she'd drink, too.

"Listen," he snapped, drawing to a halt in the corridor, marooned with her in the darkness between the light leaking from the reception area and the brighter light spilling through the open door of his office. Despite the shadows he could see her too clearly, her eyes luminous with panic. "I don't know what you're doing here, what you want with me, what your story is. I know you're friends with my sister, and you've got some sort of friendship with my father. But you and I…" He shuttled his index finger back and forth between them and tried to inure himself to her soft, floral fragrance. "There's nothing here. Whatever you're looking for, you're not going to get it from me."

"My home was ransacked," she said.

"What?"

''Someone broke into my apartment and tore the place apart.''

He heard the suppressed sob coiling through her voice. She was brave enough not to let it loose. That surprised him. He'd suspected her of being pushy and stubborn, but he hadn't realized she was also uncommonly strong.

She might have come only because she was the victim of a crime and needed a lawyer. But she'd said she'd been on her way to Annabelle's. Besides, there were plenty of lawyers in New Orleans to help her through the system. Why would she have driven forty minutes from the city in search of a lawyer—especially one whose breath smelled of bourbon?

It dawned on him that her reason for coming wasn't as important as what had happened to her. Someone had broken into her apartment. ''Are you all right?'' he asked, amazed at how much her answer mattered to him.

''I wasn't there at the time,'' she said. ''I'm shaken up, that's all.''

Sighing with a surprising degree of relief, he took her elbow and ushered her into his office. They both stood blinking in the glaring light for a minute, and then he plucked her sodden coat from her shoulders and hooked it on an empty peg of the coat tree in the corner. She wrapped her arms around herself, rubbing her hands from her elbows to her shoulders and back again, as if trying to warm up. She had on a silky-looking shirt and pleated trousers that made her legs look absurdly long and sexy.

Drew gestured toward a chair and she sat. Her gaze stayed with him as he circled his desk and sat facing her.

''Someone ransacked your apartment,'' he repeated.

''I think—'' She worried her lower lip with her teeth, then found the courage to continue. ''I think it was your father.''

Drew's peripheral vision snagged on the flask, standing

beside his telephone just inches from his blotter. He was abruptly, desperately thirsty, even though he knew the booze would do him no good and would only antagonize Katherine. In general, he had no qualms about antagonizing her, but right now he didn't want her to race off to make accusations to Annabelle, who would automatically believe her suspicions that Philip would, for some reason, break into her apartment. His sister believed anything about their father, as long as it was negative.

As for Drew, he wasn't sure what he believed. His father had been in Bayou Beltane all day. Just that afternoon, hadn't he met with Katherine, right in this building? And he'd been in meetings with his campaign committee, and he'd been in Drew's office carping about the brochure. When would he have had a chance to drive down to New Orleans and ransack Katherine's apartment?

Still, it *was* Philip they were talking about. And if he felt the need, Philip would do just about anything.

"Why do you think my father did this?" Drew asked, drumming his fingers soundlessly on the desk to keep from grabbing the flask.

Katherine seemed to wrestle with her thoughts for a moment, then gripped the arms of her chair and started to stand. "I shouldn't have come to you with this, Drew."

He nearly lunged across the desk to clamp his hand over hers, holding her in her seat. That was the fourth time he'd touched her this evening. He couldn't imagine why. In fact, he couldn't imagine much of anything other than that her knuckles were as smooth and cool as buffed marble, and that if her palms were equally smooth and cool, her fingers equally graceful, he wanted them on him, touching him.

Not a good thought. As soon as he was certain she wouldn't bolt, he let go of her and settled back in his own chair. "I'm listening, Katherine. What makes you think it's my father?"

"You don't believe me."

"I didn't say that."

"I can feel it."

"Oh, so you're psychic?"

She looked about to stand again, but this time Drew was able to hold her in place with a stare. "I know you and your father are close," she accused. "I'm not sure why I thought I could trust you with this—"

"You can," he said, meaning it as much as he'd ever meant anything in his life.

Her gaze assessing, she took a deep breath, then let it out. "This afternoon, I mentioned to your father that his name had appeared in my great-aunt's diary. You know about the diary, don't you?"

Yes, he knew about the old diary she'd found, her excuse to snoop around his family because the diary supposedly contained numerous mentions of the Delacroix. He'd heard that the diary had been written in cipher, and translating it had been slow going. He hadn't wanted to know more.

"What about it?" he asked.

"Someone tore apart my apartment. I think it might have been your father—someone he hired—searching for the diary."

He frowned. That was quite an accusation. "Did whoever tore your place apart find the diary?"

"No. I had it with me. After this, I'll always have it with me." She gestured toward the leather carryall at her feet.

Drew considered her charge. "Why would my father want your diary? Does it have incriminating statements about him in it?"

"Not that I've noticed. Mostly it's full of details about Neville Alvarez's sexual proclivities."

"Judge Alvarez?" Drew perked up at the name.

"You've heard of Judge Alvarez?" she asked.

"He presided over my grandfather's last case. The one

murder case my grandfather ever lost. Everyone in the Delacroix family knows that.''

Katherine nodded. Apparently *she* knew that, too. ''Judge Alvarez facilitated the adoption of my aunt Claire. That's the real reason I've been reading the diary—because I'm trying to find out who my aunt's birth parents were. But when I mentioned Alvarez's name to your father this afternoon, he got very edgy. I don't know why. He asked to see the diary, but I lied and told him it was at my place.''

''And so you concluded that he had your apartment vandalized so he could get his hands on it.'' Drew shook his head. ''I don't suppose it occurred to you that this might have been a run-of-the-mill break-in?''

''Nothing was stolen. I don't own much of value, but none of my jewelry was missing. My CD player, my laptop computer, even the spare cash I keep in a drawer were all there. The drawer had obviously been searched, but the money was left behind. This wasn't a robbery, Drew. Even the police seemed stymied.''

''You reported it to the police?''

She nodded.

Drew cursed under his breath. ''The New Orleans police aren't known for their diligence.'' He studied her thoughtfully. Her hair was beginning to dry into a lustrous tumble of copper curls, and tinges of peach overcame the pallor of her face. Her lips were a darker shade of peach, soft and full. And her eyes... He wasn't used to anyone looking so directly at him. It was unnerving, the candor in her eyes. ''What did the police do?'' he asked.

''They sent an officer to my apartment. He walked through the apartment, taking notes and snapping photographs of the wreckage.''

''The entire apartment was turned upside down?''

She nodded again. ''Pots and pans were dragged out of the cabinets in the kitchen. The sofa cushions were yanked onto the floor. Clothing was strewn everywhere. The closets were emptied, the plants overturned. My bed was torn apart, my nightstand and desk ravaged. It looked like the aftermath of a hurricane."

He blocked out the visions her words evoked—her bed torn apart, her clothing strewn about, images that implied not hurricanes but something equally intense, something erotic. "Were there any signs of a break-in?" he asked.

"I don't know. The officer jotted things down on a pad and took his photos and said he'd file a report, but since I didn't seem to be missing anything, he said it was probably just vandalism. He told me to clean up the mess and forget about it."

"Did you?"

"No," she said. "I left everything as it was and came here. And I don't think I'll ever forget about it." A shudder seized her, and she closed her eyes. The room actually seemed measurably darker to him until she opened them again. "I feel violated, Drew," she murmured.

His mind raced. Damn, what had his father done? What could be in that diary that Philip would have done this to Katherine?

And if he hadn't done it, who had?

Drew didn't want to get involved. In his effort to break free of his father's plans and schemes, he was trying to keep his distance. He'd exerted himself not to be with Philip when Katherine was around. He'd avoided all discussions about Katherine's business in Bayou Beltane. He truly didn't want to be a part of this.

But he couldn't leave Katherine to her own devices. She'd already contacted the New Orleans police, at best a waste of time, at worst—if his father *was* involved—a grave error. Lord knew what she'd do next if Drew didn't offer his help. "Let's go," he said, shoving himself to his feet.

"Go where?"

"To your apartment. I want to see it for myself."

"You don't have to—"

"I do have to." He strode across the office to fetch her coat and his own jacket. "Besides," he began, then faltered.

"Besides what?"

He hesitated, not wanting to reveal himself, not even wanting to acknowledge that he could feel anything other than hostility toward Katherine Beaufort. And yet, at that moment, as she turned her wondrous eyes on him, he couldn't stop the truth from slipping out.

"I need to know you'll be safe," he said. "I just need to know."

CHAPTER THREE

SHE WASN'T SURE why she'd let him drive her back to the city. But there they were, Drew behind the wheel of her car, the windshield wipers sweeping back and forth and his profile blinking in and out of view whenever a vehicle passed them going the other way. She had no idea how he intended to get back to Bayou Beltane, although she supposed he could hire a cab to take him. She certainly wasn't going to drive him back herself. She hadn't even wanted him to accompany her home.

That wasn't quite true, she admitted silently. She doubted she had the courage to enter her devastated apartment alone. If she was going to have someone by her side, better that it be someone tall and broad-shouldered, someone strong enough to chase away the horror.

Drew Delacroix was tall and broad-shouldered. She had never before given much thought to his strength, but tonight...tonight he seemed strong.

Drew. How bizarre that of all the people she might have called upon, he had wound up her savior. Drew, a man with whom she hadn't exchanged more than a few words—less than half of them civil—since they'd met. Drew, whose mere presence stirred up more emotion than she could capably handle. Tall, broad-shouldered, strong Drew.

She tried to figure out why she'd driven to Bayou Beltane, rather than turning to Dionne or Aunt Claire for help. She hadn't wanted to remain inside her ravaged home, so she'd fled. But instead of fleeing to Dionne or Aunt Claire, she'd found herself on the interstate, driving toward the causeway that would carry her to the North Shore. And when she'd thought to drive to Annabelle's bed-and-breakfast, her car had all but steered itself past Drew Delacroix's glowing office window. That light-filled window had called to her, a beacon in the misty night. Even the risk that the window might be a part of Philip's office hadn't stopped her from parking and approaching the building. She'd known in some odd, intuitive way that if she could just get inside the building she would be safe.

Never would she have imagined that safety would come in the form of Drew Delacroix, the most ornery, obstinate, aloof member of the clan.

He had insisted on driving her back to New Orleans. According to him, she was in no condition to drive. She considered that opinion ironic coming from a man who'd been sipping bourbon when she'd barged in on him. Yet he seemed uncannily sober now as he slouched slightly in the driver's seat, which he'd pushed far back to accommodate his long legs, and squinted in the glare of headlights reflecting off the wet road. His hands were steady, his demeanor resolute.

In fact, the only thing that made her question his sobriety was his acting as if he actually cared about her. She simply couldn't believe it of him. She had just accused his beloved father of tearing her home apart, and his response was to appoint himself her gallant protector. Surely this wasn't the behavior of a sane, sober man.

Closing her eyes, she pictured her apartment as they would find it once they arrived. After the policeman's departure earlier that evening, she'd wandered through the three small rooms. The mere sight of the wreckage had made her shake, made her eyes well up and her stomach roil. One of her neighbors had offered to help her tackle the mess, but she'd declined. She couldn't deal with it yet. Even now, hours later, she felt queasy at the thought of the chaos awaiting her in New Orleans.

She would have expected Drew's nearness to make her even queasier. But his presence settled her. For now, she would depend on him, lean on him, let him provide safe passage through the disaster.

"So, this diary..." he murmured, his voice as dark as the world outside the car.

She glanced toward him. The headlight beams of a truck caught the edge of his profile. His nose was straight and long, his brow obscured by a thick shock of hair. His chin could have been carved out of stone. If Philip's genes were in Drew, she couldn't discern them in his appearance. Drew was so much more handsome than his father.

Now, *that* was a disturbing thought. She didn't want to think of Drew as handsome.

"What about the diary?" she asked.

"Any ideas why my father would want it?"

"None at all. Except that he might be curious about what my great-aunt Patrice had to say about his old friend Neville Alvarez."

"Maybe he was curious to read up on Alvarez's sexual proclivities."

She should never have mentioned that aspect of the diary. Not because she was bashful or prudish, but because if there was one person she didn't want to discuss sexual proclivities with, it was Drew.

"Was the old judge kinky?" he persisted.

She glanced at him again. Without any passing headlights to illuminate him, she could scarcely make out his face. She couldn't tell if he was grinning.

"If you really must know," she said evenly, determined not to let him rattle her, "the old judge was partial to unusual positions, something his wife wouldn't abide. The old judge also seemed quite given to grunting a lot during the act and talking a lot afterward. You might consider the grunting more important, but I'm reading the diary for the talk.''

Drew shot her a quick look. She still couldn't see his face, but she watched the movement of his head, the shift of his silhouette. ''And this talk includes information about an adoption?''

''My aunt Claire's adoption.''

''Why are you so interested in your aunt's adoption?'' he asked.

She remembered with a start that Drew was a lawyer. He knew how to draw out a witness with his questions. That was what he was doing now: interrogating her.

After a moment's thought, she decided she didn't mind. She didn't want silence riding in the car with them. She was jumpy enough, painfully aware that every minute brought them closer to her ransacked apartment. She would rather talk about anything—even the diary.

''My grandparents couldn't have children, so they adopted Claire,'' she explained. ''They wanted to adopt another child to give Claire a sibling. They waited a long time for a baby, but none became available. So when Claire was about thirteen, they adopted a three-year-old girl. That was my mother.''

Drew pulled into the left lane to pass a slow car, then shot her another look. ''Why aren't you researching your own mother's adoption?''

''I can't,'' Katherine said, then hesitated, trying to figure out whether she trusted Drew enough to go on. She *had* to trust him, she realized. He had taken responsibility for her safety. ''My mother grew up troubled. I don't know what might have happened to her before my grandparents adopted her. Maybe she'd been beaten. Maybe...I don't know.'' Katherine could guess, but the possibilities were too horrid to contemplate. "In any case, she was wild and reckless, and my grandparents couldn't seem to reach her."

"You're using the past tense," Drew noted.

"She died when I was six." Katherine wished she could feel some sort of emotion when she said this, but she had painfully few memories of her mother. She could remember her mother's gardenia-scented perfume, and her hair, long and wavy, the same color Katherine saw on the insides of her eyelids when she closed her eyes and faced the noon-time sun. She *thought* she remembered her mother calling her "Kitty-Kat," but she wasn't really sure if that had actually happened or she'd just imagined it.

It was all so long ago. And Katherine had probably blocked out the bad parts, which was why she was left with so little to recall.

"She'd been out partying," she told Drew. "I believe she'd been out partying the night I was conceived. I don't know. Aunt Claire said my mother loved to party." She heard bitterness in her voice, and when she swallowed she tasted bitterness. "She was in an auto accident, and she was thrown from the car. My grandparents raised me until they were too old to manage it. Then I moved in with Aunt Claire. If being a mother is about raising a child, then Aunt Claire *is* my mother. She did the hard work of raising me."

"Why don't you ask your grandparents about her adoption?"

"They've both passed on," Katherine told him. "But even before they died, they never would discuss either my aunt's adoption or my mother's. They were embarrassed. People didn't talk about infertility in those days." Katherine shrugged. "Aunt Claire still says she doesn't feel any great compulsion to learn who her birth parents were. She says the Beauforts were her parents. And they were. They raised her."

"Then why dig up the past? Why not leave it alone?"

"Because I found the diary." That was enough of an answer for her, but it clearly didn't satisfy Drew. "Patrice was my grandmother's sister. I started reading about her as she was in her youth—not the eccentric old aunt I knew, but a vibrant, passionate woman who slept with a talkative judge. It was as if a door had opened for me, my one chance to peer into the past. I have no history, Drew. As a Delacroix, you can't possibly understand what it's like not to know where you came from, who your parents truly are."

"Didn't you just say a person's parents are the people who do the job of raising that person?" he drawled, his voice tinged with sarcasm. "Wouldn't that make your aunt Claire your true parent?"

"Yes, but..." It seemed imperative to make him understand. "Don't you see? My aunt has no past, either. Except that maybe, if I finish translating the diary, I'll learn her past. If I can't learn my own history, at least I can learn hers."

"Seems to me," he murmured, almost as if he were talking to himself, "life might be easier for some of us if we could jettison our own histories instead of chasing after them." More loudly, he said, "You're going to have to give me directions to your place."

Katherine would have liked to pursue Drew's enigmatic remark about jettisoning one's history, but they were deep into the city and nearing her exit. Conversation would have to wait while she directed him through the crowded streets of the French Quarter to her block.

Conversation. She'd actually had a genuine, nondisputatious conversation with Drew. What a strange night this was turning out to be.

"Parking can be a challenge around here," she warned, but Drew managed to find a spot only steps from her building. Such luck in parking only made the evening seem even more surreal.

She wondered if Drew felt it, too. She wondered if the weirdness would continue when they went upstairs to her apartment. Perhaps they would discover everything in her home clean and tidy. Perhaps she'd dreamed the break-in. Perhaps she was dreaming this very moment, imagining the unaccustomed truce between her and Drew, the rare trust. She might wake up tomorrow with nothing but a headache and that dusty set of chairs she'd bought from Drew's father awaiting her attention at the shop.

Drew held out her car keys, but when she extended her hand, he didn't drop them into her palm. Instead he pressed them gently into the warmth of her skin, then lifted his gaze to hers. A tremulous heat skimmed the length of her spine.

After an interminable pause, he pulled his hand back. She nearly leaped out of the car. She wanted her life to be exactly the way she'd always known it. No mysteries, no crimes, and no sensations like that searing heat Drew had sparked inside her merely by brushing his fingertips against her palm.

They didn't speak as they climbed the stairs to her apartment. Taking a deep breath for courage, she unlocked her door and inched it open.

She hadn't dreamed the break-in, after all. Havoc loomed on the other side of the door, no less shocking for the fact that she'd expected it. She couldn't open the door all the way, because the coats and boots that used to reside in her entry closet were lying in a heap that blocked the door's swing. She tiptoed in, Drew right behind her, and reached for the light switch. When she flicked it on, he cursed.

It was as awful as she'd remembered, as terrifying in its thoroughness. Dirt from a potted fern soiled the rug, chairs were toppled, cabinets stood ajar and drawers tilted precariously on their tracks, open as far as they could go, their contents tumbling out. The sight of her table linens overflowing a drawer was almost obscene.

The horror she felt at rediscovering the mess was nearly as keen as what she'd felt when she'd first discovered it...except for Drew's presence. Having him with her helped to diffuse her fury. He seemed outraged enough for both of them.

Yet for all his churning anger, he remained outwardly calm. Steely, actually, as if he were caging his emotions. After his initial swearing, he picked a careful path through the debris, heading for the kitchen. He reached through the arched doorway, flicked the wall light switch and stared thoughtfully at the overturned chairs, the pots and pans on the floor, the upended canister and the rice spilling out like tiny flecks of white confetti across the counter.

When he backed away from the kitchen doorway, Katherine saw his frown. It was fierce. She would never want to be the object of such anger.

Turning, he surveyed the living room. "Whoever he was, he did quite a job of it," he observed.

Katherine nodded.

He moved through the clutter to her bedroom door, pushed it open and examined the room from the threshold. She wondered what he would think of her bed, usually neatly made but now with its sheets and blankets torn free and the mattress lying askew on the brass frame. Or the floor, strewn with silk scarves and lingerie from her chest of drawers. Or the shoes clambering out of the closet. The folding silk screen leaning against a wall. The open night table drawers, the rifled sewing basket, the mahogany jewelry box open on her bureau, its few valuable items resting placidly in their velvet-lined nooks.

Drew ventured into the room, avoiding the garments on the floor. He stared at the jewelry box, obviously puzzled that Katherine's gold brooch, her pearl earrings, her opal pendant and engraved college ring remained untouched. A common thief would have snatched them. Even though they weren't exquisite, they'd be worth something at a pawn-shop.

Shaking his head, Drew turned from the jewelry box and studied the outer wall, which backed on the courtyard balcony. "He broke in here," he guessed, circling the foot of the bed to one of the windows.

"How do you know?"

"This window isn't locked." He toyed with the brass latch. It was broken. "Can I open it?"

"Go right ahead."

He gripped the handles at the base of the window and slid it up. From the doorway Katherine watched him, trying not to respond to the strong line of his back, the flex of his arms as he shoved the window open. A wisp of night air floated in, ruffling his hair as he examined the window frame. He spent longer scrutinizing it than the policeman had. He leaned out and glanced both ways, surveying the balcony, feeling along the sill and the sash. Then he ducked his head back inside and straightened up. One of his hands was closed in a fist.

"What did you find?" she asked, her gaze falling to his hand.

He pulled the window shut, did his best to fasten the broken latch, then crossed back to her. "A button," he said, unfurling his fingers. "Is it yours?"

She plucked the button from the curve of his palm, trying not to touch him. Still, she felt his warmth on the button. It appeared to be made of a cheap metal, with a raised five-pointed star on its surface. "It's definitely not mine."

"It was caught in a crack on the window's sash outside." He took it back from her and tucked it into his trouser pocket. She heard it clink against loose change.

"Maybe we ought to give it to the police."

"I'll hold on to it for now." He removed his hand from his pocket and raked it through his hair, as if to wipe all traces of the button from his fingers. "The cop who came here should have found it. He didn't, so it's ours."

"What are you going to do with it?" Without the button to stare at, she followed the motions of his hand, his fingers combing through his hair again. He stood only a few feet from her. Just behind him she could see her disheveled bed. Another ripple of heat glided lazily down her back, making her want to arch her shoulders.

"It's our evidence now."

"Does..." She swallowed. He was much too tall, much too close for what she was going to say. She wished she could shout it from another room. "Does it look like a button from any of your father's clothes?"

He didn't flare with indignation. His gaze was so steady she found comfort in it, despite his nearness, despite the fact that he was Drew Delacroix and she had just implied that his father had caused all the destruction around them.

"No," he said quietly. He held her gaze for such a long, intense moment that she came close to believing his *no* meant *yes.*

But she had to go with his words. As difficult as it was to interpret her great-aunt Patrice's diary, it was a million times harder to translate a single look from Drew.

"I'll help you clean up," he said, abruptly turning from her and lifting a tangled pile of clothing from the floor. When he realized it was lingerie, he hastily dropped it on the crooked mattress.

"That's all right," she said, heat spreading through her cheeks. Drew's hands were too large, too masculine to be touching her silk underthings.

"I'll start in the kitchen," he said, apparently sharing her discomfort but determined to help her get her apartment back in order.

She watched him walk out of her bedroom, then watched the emptiness he'd left behind as if it were a tangible thing.

Even though she hadn't imagined that her apartment was in a shambles, she still felt as if she were dancing through a dream. Surely Drew wasn't in her home. Surely he hadn't stood in her bedroom, touched her lace-edged slip, her cream-colored bra.

Only in a dream would she be standing stock-still amid the ruins of her bedroom, thinking of how glad she was that Drew was with her. Not that she liked him, not that she had any illusions that they could ever be friends, but...

But she was glad he was with her tonight.

TWO THOUGHTS BURNED in Drew's mind, like hot coals placed on tinder, singeing and curling the fibers of wood, turning them red, making them smoke.

One was the button in his pocket. It had come from a work shirt or jacket, probably something constructed of thick denim. He'd seen such a jacket before, and he was pretty sure Jackson Boudreaux had been wearing it. Jackson was a cop gone bad, a pretty boy who loved women and wagering, and he was Philip's right-hand man when Philip was in need of some chore that no one else would do. Jackson had a way of persuading witnesses to make statements. He could coax money out of reluctant political supporters; he could line up votes at the State House when Philip, wearing his senator's hat, needed those votes. He could arrange for zoning changes, licensing agreements, all sorts of amazing things. Just last week Jackson had run that payoff to the columnist at the *Slidell Sentinel*.

Thinking about some of the errands Jackson ran for Philip made Drew want to scrub his hands with hot water and lye soap, just to get the taint of the button off his skin.

The button might not have come from Jackson. It might have come from some other jacket, some other vandal—or it might have been snagged in that crack in the sill for years, unnoticed. But Drew was going to be looking closely at Jackson's clothing for the next few days, because not only didn't he trust the man, he also didn't trust his father. It pained him to admit it, but if Philip had a mind to perusing Katherine's great-aunt's diary, he'd do whatever was necessary to get his hands on it.

Or, more accurately, he'd get Jackson to do whatever was necessary.

Drew had no trouble finding Katherine's broom—he'd nearly tripped on it when he entered her kitchen. He righted the chairs and lined them up against the wall, then swept the spilled rice into a small mound in one corner. He didn't want to be stepping on the dry kernels, grinding them into the floor tiles with his heels. Other than the rice, her kitchen wasn't in bad shape. Pots and pans were easy to gather. Plates had been removed wholesale from the shelves above the counter, but none had been broken and he could easily return them to what he assumed were their proper places.

The kitchen was easy, unlike her bedroom.

That was the other thought burning through his brain, making it smoke and sizzle. Katherine's bedroom. Her lingerie. That bit of silk he'd lifted off the floor, a slip or a nightie or one of those camisole things, as fluid as cool water between his fingers. And her bra. A lacy scrap of nothing. Touching it had conjured up a picture in his mind of her in it, her breasts smooth and plump, her nipples visible through the coy lace. He pictured her wearing it and him touching it, touching it while it was on her.

He scooped up scattered ladles and spatulas and slammed them into an open drawer, annoyed that he should even be thinking such a thing. He *wasn't* thinking it, he assured himself. The notion had simply landed on him like a spore, sent its runners into him and clung tight, so tight he was infected with it, feverish with it.

Touching Katherine. Gathering her slim body in his arms. Nuzzling the turbulent waves of her hair with his lips, cupping her bottom and moving her against him. And then easing off her shirt, touching that gossamer bra, tearing it off her. Kissing her mouth, her breasts, loving her until the only word on her tongue, the only idea in her mind was *Drew.*

He looked down at his hands. He'd picked up a bright green sponge at some point, and now he was squeezing it so hard it had lost its shape. He ordered himself to relax, to think about the button in his pocket. Slowly, his hand relented and he lowered the sponge to the edge of the sink.

He did *not* want to love Katherine. He did not want to kiss her. She'd appeared one day in Bayou Beltane, ingratiated herself with his sister and then his father, gotten the old goat's juices flowing and wound up accusing him of criminal mischief. Drew had enough trouble in his life right now. He didn't want to complicate matters with this woman.

He'd been hearing dribs and drabs about her great-aunt's diary for months. Apparently, Katherine had discussed it with his sister Annabelle and a few of his cousins, but his sisters and cousins didn't have much to say to Drew these days. They all believed he was Philip's loyal henchman, just like Jackson.

Drew wasn't Philip's henchman. He was his son, though, a son who'd tried his damnedest for his father. Not a gofer, not a sycophant, but a *son.*

It was probably too late to get Annabelle and the rest of the family to discuss the diary with him at this point. But Katherine might tell him more. If there was really something in there, something so incriminating Philip would arrange for someone to break into her apartment to steal the diary, Drew wanted to know about it.

He sorted the silverware back into its correct slots, then closed the drawer. He swept the spilled rice into a dustpan and emptied it into the trash. The kitchen was done.

She wasn't in the living room. On his way through the room, he lifted a fallen floor lamp, checked the bulb to make sure it hadn't shattered and gathered a stack of magazines that had been scattered across the rug. She didn't have much furniture, but what she had was tasteful and solid. He doubted it had come from her shop. If she could afford authentic antiques, she could afford a larger apartment in a better neighborhood than this.

He found her in her bedroom, folding a sweater. She had shifted the mattress into alignment with the box springs and made the bed. The smooth linens and the pillows propped along the brass headboard didn't keep him from picturing her sprawled out on that bed, dressed in nothing but that slinky slip and the negligible bra, her hair tousled, her eyes drowsy but bright, and a low, sultry laugh rising from her throat as she opened her arms to him.

"I'd better leave," he said, realizing that if he stayed any longer he might say something foolish—or do something even more foolish.

She glanced up at him and nodded.

"The kitchen is cleaned up. The living room didn't look too bad except for the plants and the coats from the closet. I don't want to be fussing with garments." He swore silently at his poor choice of words. He would *love* to be fussing with her garments right now—which was precisely why he had to leave.

"How will you get home?"

"I'll grab a taxi."

"It'll cost a fortune—"

He allowed himself a faint smile. "I can afford the fare."

Color rose to her cheeks and she averted her gaze, suddenly intent on placing the sweater in a drawer. "I feel indebted to you, storming into your office the way I did, dragging you down here and then leaving you to find your own way home."

"Would you rather I stayed?" he asked, then swore under his breath again. Where were these reckless words coming from?

He knew where. His heart—or, more likely, his groin. He wanted Katherine Beaufort. He wasn't sure he even liked her, but he wanted her.

"You don't have to, Drew," she said shyly. "I'll be all right."

He almost laughed out loud as he realized she'd taken his offer to stay as an act of chivalry. Oh, sure—noble Drew Delacroix, chaste of heart and pure of deed, sweeping down to New Orleans to save the damsel in distress and guard her apartment against dragons while she slept. Didn't she realize *he* was the dragon, the one she needed to be protected from?

God, he wanted her so much it hurt.

"I'm going," he said, pushing away from the door so he would be forced to stop staring at her, stop worshipping her wild hair and the natural pout of her lips, stop memorizing the slender curves of her body. Stop imagining that Katherine could mean anything but trouble to him.

"If you have difficulty finding a cab—"

"I won't." He turned from her, took a step and turned back. "Do me a favor, Katherine," he added, focusing on the window where he'd found the button so he wouldn't have to look into her wide hazel eyes.

"Anything."

No, not anything. Don't even let me ask you to do anything, chérie, *or we'll both wind up naked tonight—and sorry tomorrow.*

"Don't let that diary out of your sight," he said, then turned and stalked out of her apartment.

CHAPTER FOUR

AFTER DREW'S FOURTH monosyllabic answer in a row, the cab driver must have concluded that his passenger wasn't in the mood for idle chatter. With a final confirmation that Drew would be paying him double the fare to cover the taxi's return trip to New Orleans, the driver subsided in silence, leaving Drew to his own thoughts.

Unfortunately, Drew's first, last and only thought was Katherine Beaufort.

He had always been vaguely aware of her physical charms. True, he'd thought her hair rather an odd shade, not quite brown but not a striking red—and much too thick and wavy. She had the bearing of a headmistress: tall and sharp-edged, her horizontal shoulders rigid and her chin always held high, as if it were a dagger with which she would fend off attack. But despite her prim bearing and her chilly demeanor, he'd never denied that she was pleasant to look at.

He just hadn't liked her enough to dwell on it.

Now that he'd acknowledged his attraction to her, he couldn't *stop* dwelling on it, on her, on why, if she'd suspected his father in the break-in, she had selected Drew to confide in. Given that he was the only Delacroix who still maintained a somewhat civil connection with Philip, he should have been the last person Katherine would go to, not the first.

Maybe she knew that the few thin cords of emotion binding Drew and Philip were unraveling. Maybe Annabelle had hinted to Katherine that Drew's relationship with his father was disintegrating.

Annabelle had tried to remain loyal to Philip, but she'd given up months ago and moved out of Belle Terre, claiming she was no longer able to share a roof with the old man. "Can't you see him for what he is?" she was forever asking Drew. "I know he's our father, but he's also a bully and a tyrant. He's done bad things in his life, Drew. It isn't your fault or mine. We shouldn't have to suffer for it."

Their older sister, Joanna, had also abandoned Philip. She'd severed her ties with their father by choosing to practice law in the firm of Philip's twin brother, Charles. The rift between the Delacroix twins had endured for sixty years, and no one believed that it would ever be mended. When Joanna had taken her law degree and hung it in an office at Charles Delacroix's firm, she'd all but declared herself dead to Philip.

Drew wasn't his sisters, though. He was his father's only son, and as the only son of the patriarch, he had always operated under a different set of expectations. Whether or not Philip had ever really loved his daughters, Drew couldn't say. But as for loving his son...

Damn, but it hurt. Even now, as he gradually grew accustomed to the idea, it pained him to admit that his father had never loved him and never would. And the worst part was, Philip's rejection continued despite the fact that Drew had spent his entire life trying to win that love.

He shifted on the cracked black vinyl of the cab's rear seat and stared at the lights reflecting off the damp roadway. In less than a half hour he'd be back at Belle Terre, the pillared mansion where he lived—in a bedroom as far from Philip's as it was possible to be without inhabiting a separate address.

Drew had grown up in Belle Terre, a sickly child, not the manly lad his father had hoped for. It had seemed as if every speck of dust or pollen that wafted through the window screens quickly took up residence in Drew's delicate lungs. His childhood was a blur of vaporizers, oxygen masks, inhalators and pills. "He can't help himself," Drew's mother would plead, and Philip would snort, "He's a scrawny little weakling. I can't believe the boy is mine. No son of mine would be out of breath after a walk up the stairs."

Drew wasn't a scrawny little weakling anymore. Despite his mother's fretting and the warnings of the many doctors to whom she'd taken him, he had fought his respiratory problems. He had sprinted up the wide, curving stairs of Belle Terre, then stood on the landing, gasping and wheezing, and then sprinted down them and back up again, over and over until he couldn't breathe for coughing. When his mother told him he mustn't play strenuous sports, Drew defied her, imploring coaches to ignore her, wheedling his way onto a soccer team, onto a tennis court. When his mother finally announced that she was leaving Philip, Drew refused to leave with her. Without her to dote on him and fuss over him, he would have a chance to prove to Philip what a tough fellow he could be.

Maybe it was his single-minded pursuit of athletic success, or maybe it was just a matter of time and nature, but by his sixteenth birthday, Drew had outgrown his asthma. He'd stood six feet tall then—he added another inch to his height before he finished high school—and his torso was contoured in lean, hard muscle. He was jogging five miles every morning, dominating his opponents on the tennis court, playing football in the autumn and baseball in the spring. All the girls in his school sighed when he walked by.

But that hadn't been good enough for Philip. His son *still* wasn't good enough.

He never would be. And lately, Drew was beginning to think that perhaps it was just as well.

He dug into his pocket and pulled out the button he'd found in the track of Katherine's bedroom window. A single blue thread clung to the fastening loop. Would one of Jackson's blue denim shirts be missing a button?

Jackson Boudreaux was good enough for Philip, Drew thought bitterly. Jackson did whatever Philip demanded. It was as if Jackson's ego belonged entirely to Philip. He did as he was told, as long as Philip was doing the telling.

What would Drew do if he was able to link the button to Jackson? If Jackson had been responsible for the break-in at Katherine's apartment, the responsibility would undoubtedly lead all the way to Philip. But what on earth could his father fear in Katherine's great-aunt's diary? Why should he care about how her aunt Claire had come to be adopted?

Drew shook his head. Poor Katherine, going to so much trouble to translate the diary, having her apartment torn apart, just because she wanted to know her family roots. Didn't she realize that some roots could wrap around a person and choke the life out of him? Didn't she know that if he could only choose, he would rather be rootless than a Delacroix?

THE CAB DROPPED HIM OFF in front of his office building. He paid the driver the round-trip fare, added a ten-dollar tip and watched him pull away from the curb and disappear around the corner.

The street was dark and still. The phrase "downtown Bayou Beltane" was practically an oxymoron. By nine-thirty on a weeknight, the shops and squat two-story professional buildings had all gone to sleep. Rain no longer fell, but the air was as humid as summer. The street lamps wore haloes of moisture, and the street shimmered like a mirage.

He walked around the corner to the lot where his car had been parked all day. In the otherwise vacant lot, the Mercedes coupe stood isolated, moisture beading on its waxed veneer and making its tires gleam.

He unlocked the driver's door, tossed his briefcase and jacket onto the passenger seat and folded his lanky body behind the wheel. When he twisted the key in the ignition, the engine purred as if grateful to be awakened from its day-long slumber. Drew cruised to the open road leading north and east to Belle Terre.

The house stood in self-important grandeur at the end of a long driveway. The estate had once been a sugar plantation, but Drew's ancestry didn't trace back that far on this land. His grandfather Hamilton had been born a sharecropper's son, as poor as any newly freed slave. Only through hard work and intelligence had he risen to wealth. He'd purchased Belle Terre after he'd built his law practice into one of the most successful in southern Louisiana.

Growing up in Belle Terre, Drew had never given much thought to the opulence of the majestic twenty-five room estate, its wide porticos and Greek Revival pillars, its luxurious proportions, its stately gardens. Now, though, as he lived from one day to the next with his father in the mansion, he had become keenly aware of how huge the place was, how oppressive. He felt more comfortable in his one-room, no-electricity shack on the bayou.

He steered into the carbarn, emerged with his jacket and briefcase and followed the path to the back door off the kitchen. Lights beckoned from the kitchen windows, and as soon as he opened the back door he heard voices.

Entering the kitchen, he found André Arcenaux leaning against one of the stainless-steel counters and chattering in his dense Creole accent. A young woman Drew had never seen before sat at the table, sipping something hot from a cup and listening in rapt attention. At Drew's entrance, André paused and smiled. "This is Mr. Delacroix's son, also Mr. Delacroix," he said.

André was the cook at Belle Terre. He did things his own way, in his own time, but given his talents as a chef, he was allowed to operate without any criticism from Philip. Philip tended to treat the others on the household staff with alternating doses of contempt and rage, and other than Clovis and Mae, who'd been around forever, it seemed, most quit after a few months. Drew often didn't bother getting to know them; by the time he memorized their names, they were handing in their resignations.

He had a suspicion that the young lady at the table was a new employee. André confirmed it by saying, "Magdalena has just joined our happy ménage."

"In what capacity?" Drew asked, remembering to send the woman a smile. She looked anxious.

"General household staff. I've given her some tea. You missed dinner."

Drew's smile this time was easy. André sounded like a mother hen, clucking and scolding. "Did my father eat everything, or do you think you could spare me a scrap?"

"One scrap, perhaps." André shoved away from the counter and opened the refrigerator. "I made squab stewed with tomatoes and okra, and wild rice. You're going to want it warmed up." He turned from the refrigerator carrying a covered pot.

"Don't go to any trouble," Drew said, tossing his jacket and briefcase onto a chair and joining André at the counter, where he was pulling a plate down from an overhead cabinet. When André lifted the lid on the pot, Drew saw significantly more than a scrap of food inside. "Why did you make so much?" he asked.

André bristled, obviously resentful of the implied criticism. "I made the right amount," he retorted. "Your father had his cadre of campaign aides here for dinner, but Mr.

Delacroix had no appetite. There was another incident today."

Drew lost interest in the piquant stew, his attention fully on André. "What incident?" The break-in at Katherine's apartment? he wondered.

André glanced over his shoulder at the chalky-faced Magdalena. "One of those gris-gris dolls was left on the back porch. Magdalena discovered it and brought it inside to show Mr. Delacroix. I'm afraid he took out his temper on her, poor thing."

"I'm sorry," Drew said, immediately apologizing to her on his father's behalf. "His temper can be formidable."

"He fired me," she said somberly. "My first day, and he told me to leave."

"Consider yourself rehired," Drew said. "By tomorrow he won't even remember." Leaving André to dish a portion of stew onto the plate for him, he moved back to the table and sat facing Magdalena. "You don't believe in voodoo, do you?"

She shook her head, her eyes as round as poker chips.

"I don't, either. My father would swear to church and back that he doesn't, but someone's been trying to scare him with these things. This isn't the first voodoo token that's been found here."

She nodded and sipped her tea.

"My father likes to think he's in control of everything, but he's not even in control of his own nerves, sometimes. I'm sorry he exploded like a grenade in your face."

"If he wants me to go—"

"He never wants a housekeeper to go," Drew assured her, not bothering to add that most housekeepers quit before Philip could get around to firing them. The man was horrible to work for, exploding with alarming frequency and not caring if the shrapnel hit his employees.

The instant a better offer came along, Magdalena would

be gone, Drew was certain. She might not even wait for a better offer; she might just vanish one day, if Philip subjected her to one tirade too many.

The microwave oven beeped, announcing that Drew's dinner was ready. "If it's all right," he said, rising and lifting his briefcase, "I'd like to eat in the library."

"Would you like wine with it?" André asked.

"That would be good. Something white and dry." André usually had at least half a dozen bottles uncorked at any given time. He claimed he used them for cooking, and Drew couldn't accuse him of lying. Without a glass of wine handy, he might not be able to cook.

Drew strolled down the back hall, past the pantry and the rear stairs, past the screened porch to the cherry-paneled library at the far end of the house. He had always loved this room. Its walls were filled floor to ceiling with books—solid, leather-bound novels, complete collections of Shakespeare and Dickens and Twain, as well as old legal tomes, which had been replaced by newer editions in the firm's library downtown. The floor, covered with an exquisite Persian rug, was also cherry, as was the enormous desk. It had once been Drew's grandfather's desk, and it was so well matched to the paneling it seemed to grow from the floorboards themselves. The drapes were drawn, giving the room an almost tomblike feel as Drew switched on a lamp near the leather armchair.

Behind him Magdalena followed noiselessly, carrying a tray with his meal on it. She set the tray on the desk and smiled meekly. She looked so nervous as she backed out of the room, Drew wished he could think of a few magic words to reassure her.

The voodoo nonsense that had been plaguing Philip amused Drew in a perverse way. Someone was going to a lot of trouble to frighten the old man. Philip claimed the culprit was Jackson Boudreaux's mother, Flora. Flora and her mother, Desiree Boudreaux, lived in a shack deep in the swamp, and both were reputed to be practitioners of voodoo. Desiree allegedly could heal people with herbs and incantations, but her daughter, Flora, was a nasty piece of work. That she'd produced a son like Jackson didn't surprise Drew.

Yet why assume Flora was the one playing voodoo tricks on Philip? He had so many enemies, from his opponent in the state senate race to an old client who believed Philip's legal counsel had ill-served him. That list included the investors who'd lost money when his attempt to develop protected land was shot down by the state's Department of Environmental Standards. And even Drew's sisters, who were both furious with their father.

So many folks held grudges against Philip. Drew wouldn't put a little black-magic practical joking past any of them.

But was it just practical jokes, or something more? What would anyone hope to accomplish by frightening Philip? The old man wasn't going to back down, abandon his senate seat or stop playing power games. Maybe the perpetrator hoped to scare Philip into a coronary. His sister, Mary, had already had a heart attack, and Philip was forever popping pills and worrying about his blood pressure.

Sighing, Drew shook his head to clear it of that unsolved puzzle and surveyed the old law books lining the shelves behind the desk. He had never before cared to research adoption law in Louisiana, but now… Call it curiosity. Curiosity about precedents set, about judgments handed down. Curiosity about whether any of those judgments might have borne the signature of Judge Neville Alvarez.

Drew pulled a book from a high shelf, lugged it to the desk and settled himself in the chair. The wine was crisp and light, having none of the nearly toxic bite of the bourbon he'd drunk earlier. The stew smelled glorious, but he wasn't terribly hungry, at least not for food.

He was hungry for a woman whose hair was the same lustrous shade as the cherry-wood walls around him. A woman whose determination to learn the truth was so admirable he wanted to match it with his own determination. A woman who wore silk next to her skin. A woman who claimed to be on a quest to discover who she was, but who seemed to know herself better than anyone Drew had ever met before.

KATHERINE ARRIVED at Annabelle's bed-and-breakfast shortly before one. Annabelle had insisted that Katherine come for a late lunch, and Katherine—feeling less than safe and confident in New Orleans the day after her home had been ransacked—gladly accepted the invitation.

Besides, she'd spent the morning finalizing a huge sale—a turn-of-the-century secretary desk, hutch and matching claw-foot chair—to one of her regular customers in the Garden District. When Katherine had learned of the pieces' availability, she'd called Miriam Carpentier, positive that Miriam would want the set. Miriam had indeed wanted it, and as soon as the pieces were restored, Katherine had had them trucked over to the Carpentier house.

She'd made a client happy, and she'd made K & D's Antiques a tidy profit. And considering she'd accomplished all that on less than two hours of solid sleep, she was entitled to drive across the lake to have lunch with Annabelle.

She told herself the previous night's insomnia had resulted from the break-in. But it was a different sort of break-in that most disconcerted her, a break-in that even the installation of a more secure lock on her bedroom window couldn't have prevented.

Drew Delacroix had broken into her mind. And she couldn't get him to leave.

All night long, she'd lain in her bed—the bed a thug had torn apart in his search for her great-aunt's diary, if that had indeed been his target—and thought about Drew's large, male hands touching her lingerie. She'd lain on fresh sheets—unable to sleep on the old linens—and thought about Drew's fingertips brushing her palm as he placed her key in it. She remembered the way his eyes had seared her, the way he'd stared at her in the close confines of the bedroom, the way her pulse had charged ahead for no good reason. She remembered the sharp expletive he'd uttered the instant he'd glimpsed the demolition of her apartment.

Never before had she considered a man's swearing so chivalrous.

Had she simply not noticed before last night that he was profoundly good-looking? Or had she noticed and refused to acknowledge it, because he had always seemed relentlessly antagonistic toward her?

He hadn't been antagonistic last night. He'd been...well, not quite friendly, but *involved.* As if she mattered to him. As if her obsession with an old diary wasn't laughable. As if her yearning to know at least something about her aunt Claire's ancestry made sense to him.

He would never keep her awake all night again, though. She would never let him. If there was one thing she didn't need in her life, it was a damnably handsome man, especially one who acted as her savior. She didn't want a savior. She must have been mad to have gone to him last night. She *had* been mad, and justifiably. What woman wouldn't be a little bit crazy after learning that her home had been torn apart by a prowler?

Next time—though she prayed fervently there wouldn't be a next time—she would save herself. She wouldn't run to a man for help.

A couple, clearly in love, were leaving the bed-and-breakfast as Katherine approached. The man and woman eld hands and whispered together, oblivious to the rest of ne world. Katherine stepped aside and left the front walk lear for them; she was sure they would have walked right nto her if she hadn't.

Smiling, she resumed her stroll up the path to the veranda nd inside the front door. In the parlor, she spotted someone olding the stereoscope to the light from the window and iewing a slide through the twin lenses. Tall and trim, he vas clad in dress-cut khaki trousers and a tailored brown hirt. His dark blond hair was long enough to cover the ollar of his shirt in back.

She didn't have to see his face to know. She hardly had see his back. Just his stance, the way he held his shoulers, the way he planted his feet...

Drew.

He lowered the stereoscope, bent toward the table to seect another slide from the box, and hesitated. He must have limpsed her peripherally, because he straightened up and otated to face her. "Hello, Katherine," he said with forced ordiality.

His eyes were cool, his mouth shaping a tentative smile. Ie didn't seem thrilled to see her, but he also didn't seem urprised.

"I'm here to have lunch with Annabelle," she said.

"I know." He lowered the stereoscope to the table and emoved the slide from its ornate bracket. He placed the lide in the box, closed it, and crossed the parlor to her. Iis tie, a lightly patterned brown-and-beige silk, was lightly loosened. He must have come here from his office. 'Annabelle told me."

"Then you're leaving?" she asked hopefully.

He smiled, a flash of white teeth and unexpected dimples. 'No, I'm not leaving," he drawled.

Annabelle bustled out of the kitchen, wiping her hands n a towel and grinning at her good friend and her older

brother. "Hi, Katherine! I hope you don't mind that I i
vited Drew to have lunch with us."

Actually, Katherine minded a great deal. She'd be
looking forward to some giddy, hearty girl talk, somethi
to take her mind off last night's trauma. With Drew prese
girl talk was unlikely, and getting her mind off last nig
was impossible.

She opened her mouth to protest, but Drew sent her
quelling look. Not that she would submit to any comma
of his, spoken or silent, but when she shifted her gaze
his sister, Annabelle looked so sweetly beseeching Kat
erine had to swallow her objections. With a reluctant sig
she followed Annabelle into the kitchen, Drew behind he

Annabelle seemed to have too much energy. S
bounced around the room, arranging plates of cold cu
lettuce and tomatoes, relishes and fresh-sliced Frenc
bread. "It's do-it-yourself po'boys," she announced, di
ging into the refrigerator for a pitcher of iced tea. "Dre
would you get the napkins, please? They're over on t
counter, in the silver napkin rings."

Drew obediently fetched the napkins from a counte
Katherine glared at Annabelle. "I hope you aren't plotti
something," she murmured under her breath.

"I'm sorry, Katherine, but..." She grinned, looking an
thing but sorry. "Well, Drew told me he had some thin
he'd like to discuss with you, and I mentioned to him th
you were going to be here for lunch, and then, well,
occurred to me you two could meet here and discuss it."

"If Drew wants to discuss something with me," Kat
erine said, loudly enough for him to hear, "he can conta
me himself. He doesn't have to crash my lunch dates."

Annabelle's grin faded. "Oh, Katherine, I didn't thi
you'd mind. It's my fault, really—"

"It's my fault," Drew broke in, his gaze hard on Kat
erine, although he was speaking equally to both wome

"You're right, Katherine. I should have called you directly." He set the napkins down on the table and started for the door.

"Now, you get right back here, Drew," Annabelle scolded. "When was the last time you ate a decent lunch? Most days you'll just grab a beignet and eat it at your desk. And like as not wash it down with bourbon. Sit down." She pointed to one of the chairs. His withering look failed to deter her. "I mean it, Drew. Sit."

He glanced at Katherine, and she almost laughed at the helpless plea in his eyes. "You'd better do as she says," Katherine said. "She sounds serious."

Scowling, he lowered himself into the chair. Katherine took the seat across the table from him. Annabelle poured the iced tea and then sat and beamed at her two guests in turn.

"Aunt Mary is alive and well," Drew muttered to his sister. "No need for you to step in and take over."

"Aunt Mary?" Katherine asked Annabelle.

"Aunt Mary is the official family matchmaker," Annabelle explained. "I am most definitely *not* a matchmaker."

"Good thing," Drew grunted.

"I'm sure that if matchmaking was on your agenda," Katherine added, "you would have found a woman better suited to your brother's personality. And you certainly wouldn't have attempted anything that ridiculous with me. You know I'd never stand for it."

"I know, I know!" Annabelle sounded more than a bit defensive. "I'm not trying to bring you two together! Believe me, I'm not that crazy!"

"Good," Drew and Katherine said simultaneously. Startled, Katherine glanced his way and found him looking at her. They both averted their eyes.

"Drew said he wanted to see the diary," Annabelle told her.

Katherine turned to him again and found his gaze stead and level on her. "Great-Aunt Patrice's diary? You war to see it?"

"Yes," he said.

"Last night you didn't express any interest in seeing it."

"Last night?" Annabelle perked up. "What are you talk ing about, Katherine? What happened last night?"

Katherine and Drew both ignored her. "Last night I wa worried about you. Today I'm more worried about the di ary. Will you let me see it?"

She hadn't let anyone see it. She'd talked about it to he closest friends. She'd revealed bits and pieces of its con tents. Given the rigors of translating it, she scarcely knev more than bits and pieces of it herself. But she hadn't ac tually shown it to anyone. The story it had to tell was to personal, too significant. Too essential to her life.

If she were ever to show it to anyone, Drew would hardl be the first in line. Last night notwithstanding, she didn' trust him. He'd come through for her once, but he was stil a cold, gruff man, and there were so many people sh trusted more than him. Dionne, or Annabelle, or even An nabelle's sister, Joanna, or their cousin Shelby, or her ow aunt Claire, who insisted she had no interest in the diary.

Katherine would never show it to Drew. How could sh possibly trust a man who could set her nervous systen humming with a mere touch? How could she trust a ma who looked at her the way Drew Delacroix looked at her

"All right," she heard herself say. "You can see it."

CHAPTER FIVE

AS SOON AS KATHERINE agreed to let Drew see the diary,
er emotions went into flux. It was a good idea. It was a
orrid idea. She'd be wise to let him view Patrice Forêt's
nemoirs; she was a fool even to consider it.

He had done nothing to qualify as the first member of
he Delacroix family to see the diary. He had never solicited
Katherine's friendship, never cultivated any sort of rela-
ionship with her. He had no right to gain access to her
reat-aunt's secrets.

Or else he had all the right in the world simply *because*
e hadn't cultivated a friendship with Katherine. He was
mpartial, someone whose interest in her extended only to
rotecting her from Philip and his henchmen.

Katherine took a few dainty bites of her po'boy before
iving up, too tense and confused to put forth the effort
eeded to chew and swallow. She sipped her iced tea and
vatched Drew consume his sandwich. He ate heartily, pur-
osefully, as if he intended to grow a few inches taller in
he next several days. Like Katherine, he added little to the
onversation.

Thank heavens Annabelle was willing to play the role of
onvivial host. But then, it had been her maneuvering that
ad brought Katherine and Drew together at her table. The
east she could do was regale them with tales about her
oneymooning boarders—the starry-eyed couple Katherine
ad barely avoided colliding with on the front walk—and
bout the trio of retired schoolteachers who were using

Bayou Beltane as their home base during a week of antiquing. "I told them all about your shop, Katherine," Annabelle reported. "One of them says she would never look twice at anything that isn't French Provincial, and I told her she wouldn't find much of that at K & D's. But the others definitely intend to browse through your store. One of them is apparently a fanatic about Depression glass."

Katherine managed a smile. "She'll find plenty of that in our back room."

"That's what I told her. The way those retired teachers keep fussing over Cade and Ty..." Annabelle launched into a cheerful monologue about her son and stepson and her husband, Jake, while Katherine picked at her food and Drew devoured his.

His plate empty, he wiped his hands on his napkin, dabbed his mouth and looked across at Katherine. As soon as Annabelle paused for breath, he asked, "Are you free this afternoon?"

Katherine mulled over her answer. Yes, she supposed she could be free that afternoon, given how profitable her morning had been. But to spend a free afternoon with Drew...

Well, perhaps they wouldn't spend the entire afternoon together. He'd have a look at the diary, discover that he couldn't easily skim the backward writing and send her on her way. She'd already told him he could see the diary, and she wasn't about to let it out of her sight, so if he wanted to study it, he would have to accept her presence as part of the deal.

His eyes remained on her, rephrasing his request silently. *Can we manage this? Can we be comfortable in each other's company for an hour or two? We did it last night, more or less. Can we do it again?*

"Yes, I'm free," she said.

"You have the diary with you, right?"

"At all times." Her foot nudged the tote bag under her

chair. It was slightly larger than a purse—large enough to hold everything she normally carried in her purse, plus the diary, the mirrored powder compact and French dictionary she needed to read it, and the notebook in which she wrote the translation.

Drew rose to his feet and nodded toward his sister. "If it's all right with you—"

"It's fine with me," Annabelle said too eagerly, shoving back her chair and grinning first at him and then at Katherine. Katherine recalled Annabelle's claim that her aunt Mary was the family's official matchmaker, but the way Annabelle smiled roused Katherine's self-protective instincts. She considered Annabelle a friend! A friend wouldn't attempt to set her up with a man, even if that man was the friend's brother.

Actually, that seemed exactly what a friend would do.

Katherine took a deep breath to still her nerves. Later, when Drew wasn't around, she would ask Annabelle not to meddle in her social life again. For now, for Annabelle's sake, she supposed she could endure an afternoon with him.

After thanking Annabelle for lunch, Drew and Katherine left the bed-and-breakfast. The afternoon sunshine was bright, giving his hair a golden sheen. Despite his business attire, he had the look of a beach bum, his skin sunburnished, his untrimmed locks tossed by a breeze and his step surprisingly light, as if he had nothing to worry about.

Katherine knew he had plenty to worry about. An untroubled man wouldn't sit alone in his office after hours, drinking bourbon. But his problems weren't her concern.

There was no question of his driving her car for her today. She climbed in behind the wheel before he could even suggest it, and then realized he'd never intended to. He strode right past her car, unlocked the sleek Mercedes coupe parked in front of hers by the curb and got in.

She must have imagined his warmth last night. Well, not

warmth, she amended, pulling away from the curb and falling in behind him as he drove down the street. Drew Delacroix didn't *do* warmth. His emotions ranged from cool to arctic. Last night she'd detected a slight thaw on the top layer of his permafrost personality, but she suspected it had had less to do with her than with his fear that his father might be complicit in the ransacking of her home. She mustn't misconstrue his solicitousness as genuine caring.

His office was only a few blocks from Annabelle's inn. He drove into a small, private parking lot around the corner from the building's front door, and she followed him into the lot, parking in a space marked for visitors. He waited for her to lock her car, then led the way to the front door and inside.

The receptionist looked up and smiled, obviously recognizing Katherine. "Is Mr. Delacroix expecting you?" she asked pleasantly.

"No, he's not," the younger Mr. Delacroix answered for Katherine. As if afraid she would linger in the reception area for a chat, he cupped his hand around her elbow and steered her gently but firmly down the hall to his office. Once inside, he shut the door and released her.

"Are you afraid your father will see me here?"

"My father's out this afternoon," Drew said, moving directly to his desk. "He's on the stump today, shaking hands and kissing babies."

Katherine was aware that Philip was a state senator, up for reelection. She tried to gauge Drew's expression for a hint of how he felt about Philip's campaign; his tone was sardonic but his face was benign. "What about you?" she asked. "Don't you have clients to see?"

Drew shook his head and gave the knot of his tie a sharp tug to loosen it. "I rearranged my schedule."

Around her aunt's diary? Had he really been that certain she would agree to let him look at it that afternoon?

Warily, she approached the desk and set her tote bag on a chair. "Before I show it to you," she said, determined to assert herself, "I'd like to know if you figured out whose button it was."

She didn't have to clarify which button she meant. He lifted the small star-embossed button from his pocket, making her wonder whether he carried it around with him the way she carried the diary around with her. "I've got an idea whose it is," he said, turning the button over and over in his hand, "but I haven't seen him today." He raised his hand nearly to eye level and stared at the button for a moment, then dropped it back into his pocket and gazed expectantly at her.

He really was startlingly handsome, especially when he wasn't scowling. He must have been scowling the many times their paths had crossed before last night, because during all those times she'd been immune to his charcoal-gray eyes, his chiseled features, his athletic physique. He wore his clothing well, soft cotton shirts that draped smoothly over his torso, trousers that emphasized the length of his legs, sleeves that he was right that minute unbuttoning and rolling up to his elbows, making her far too aware of his bony wrists and sinewy forearms.

She didn't want to be aware of his wrists or forearms or anything else about him. She wanted him to scowl, so she could regain her immunity to him.

She traced the angle of his gaze to her tote. He seemed eager to get down to business, and she shared that eagerness. The sooner he saw for himself the nearly indecipherable scribblings on the pages, the sooner he would give up. Then she would be able to go away and build her resistance back to where it ought to be.

She pulled the diary from the depths of the tote and handed it to him. He ran his fingers lightly, almost reverentially, over its worn leather surfaces. Katherine relaxed a bit, pleased that he was treating the book with appropriate respect. He opened it gingerly to the first page and scowled, but even scowling he looked inordinately handsome to her.

"You can read this?" he asked.

"Very slowly. With a mirror." She poked around in her tote and pulled out her compact. When she worked on translating the diary at home, she usually positioned herself on the floor in front of her open closet door. She had a full-length mirror hanging from the back of the door, and if she propped the book up and sat next to it, she could read the pages in the glass. "I also brought a French-English dictionary with me, in case we need it." She dug the paperback from her tote, followed by a spiral-bound notebook with a pen clipped to the cover. "And here are my translations to date."

"That's quite a carryall you've got," he joked wryly. "Are you going to pull a magician's bouquet of silk flowers out of it next?"

"I've pulled out everything you need to know about," she said, opening her compact and standing it on his desk.

He turned the fragile pages carefully, frowning at the minute backward script, until he reached the ribbon that marked how far she'd gotten in her translation. "This must be torture to read," he murmured.

"Only an idiot would bother." Or someone obsessed, she added silently as she flipped open her notebook. "I should also point out that it's not chronological."

He shot her a puzzled look. "It's a diary. Diaries are supposed to be written chronologically."

"Not this one. It seems as if she'd just open to a page at random and begin writing. I tried translating from the back page, but that wasn't the earliest entry. Neither was the first page. She jumped all over the place."

Drew lowered the book to his blotter, next to the compact, and carried one of the visitors' chairs around the desk so he and Katherine would both be able to sit facing the mirror. "Why do you think she wrote it that way?"

"To try the patience of future generations," Katherine muttered, taking the seat he'd brought and opening her notebook. "I believe she skipped around the diary for the same reason she wrote it backward and in French. She didn't want it to be easy to read. She wanted anyone who found it to be totally confused."

"I'm totally confused and I didn't even find it. Why would anyone keep a diary that would be so hard for the diarist to write—and then to read? What's the point of that?"

"I think—" Katherine sighed "—she was keeping this diary for the purpose of possibly blackmailing the judge."

"For money?" The notion apparently intrigued Drew. He sat down in his swivel chair next to her and thumbed through the diary again. "I imagine Alvarez was rich, but—"

"Great-Aunt Patrice wasn't interested in money. If she were, she would have married a wealthy man and been done with it. I think she wanted leverage with him. He was married and he was powerful. She probably stashed the diary away like a nest egg, figuring it would be there if she ever needed it. Maybe she wanted something other than money."

"Interesting." He glanced at the page marked by the ribbon, then turned the book toward the compact and held it open. "What does it say about my father?"

She flipped through her pages of notes, looking for references to Philip Delacroix. "Here's one entry," she said, skimming her notes. "Judge Alvarez told Patrice he'd gone to dinner at Belle Terre with Hamilton. Here..." She ran her index finger down the page, searching for the text. "Here it is. 'Neville dined at Belle Terre—Hamilton and

Marguerite, their daughter, Mary…' Is that the family matchmaker?'' she asked, glancing up.

''That's her.''

With a nod, Katherine resumed reading. '''Mary, and his three sons, twins Charles and Philip and their younger brother, William. The twins and Mary all favor their mother as much as their father, but young William has nothing of either parent in his face.'''

''Gossip,'' Drew grumbled. ''No wonder it's taken you so long to translate. This is boring.''

''Wait, let me continue. 'Although Charles and Philip have identical features, Neville says there is a glint in Philip's eye, a sense that he is always planning his next move. ''Have you ever known a man like that?'' Neville asked me. ''A man, not yet twenty, able to see his way to checkmate by the third move.'''''

''My father doesn't play chess,'' Drew commented.

''I believe the judge was using a metaphor.''

''Thanks for clearing that up,'' he said archly. ''Anything else about my father?''

''Yes, there was another mention.…'' She leafed through the pages, trying to find it. ''Here—this was some time after the dinner party. 'Neville tells me we must be discreet. He says young Philip Delacroix, the son of his friend Hamilton, has seen us together last week. Neville's wife has been in Shreveport nursing her ailing cousin, and so Neville and I went out to dine. How this young Philip could have seen us I cannot say, but Neville is quite upset. So upset he…''' Katherine tapered off, embarrassed.

''So upset he…what?''

Sighing, she read the rest of the sentence. '''So upset he could not perform without a great effort on my part.''' She sighed again. ''There's a lot of that.''

''A lot of great effort?''

"A lot of emphasis on how well they...*performed.*" Katherine couldn't bring herself to look at him.

"I'm an adult, Katherine. I think I can weather it." He arranged the book in front of the mirror. Only a small circle, less than half the page, showed up in the mirror. "How are we going to do this?" he asked, peering into the circle.

"You'll have to hold the mirror up, line by line," she told him, demonstrating by lifting the mirror and angling it more effectively.

"I wonder why Neville was so upset about my father seeing him with his lover out on the town. I mean, Dad was barely out of his teens. What could he have done?"

"Told his father, maybe? Your grandfather was a highly esteemed attorney. He could have used the information against Alvarez."

"But they were friends."

"Maybe Philip threatened to go to Neville's wife."

"That sounds like something he'd do," Drew agreed grimly. He squinted at the writing in the mirror, moved his lips slightly and mumbled to himself, struggling with the French. "*Écharpe en soie.* The judge gave her a silk scarf."

"He liked giving her gifts," Katherine told Drew. "Ten pages back, he gave her a brooch."

"Was ten pages ago before or after the silk scarf?" he asked. "In real time, I mean."

"I don't know. Keep reading—out loud, please, so I can write it down."

"Let's see how much of my school French I remember." He leaned toward the mirror and proceeded to translate, stumbling over a word here, a word there. "'My judge is...was hungry tonight,'" he read, a line denting the bridge of his nose as he focused on the tiny script. "'*Oui, il a faim*...for his lady.' For Patrice or his wife?" he asked, glancing at Katherine.

"Patrice. He was never hungry for his wife, according

to her. She does tend toward purple prose," Katherine warned, beginning to dread this exercise. If Judge Alvarez was hungry for his lady at the start of this entry, his lady would undoubtedly be elaborately describing their "performance" before she got around to writing about more interesting topics.

Resigning herself to a spate of florid phrases about lustful deeds, Katherine jotted the translation into her notebook as Drew turned back to the mirror. He read a bit in French, under his breath, then let out a low whistle and translated the words for Katherine. "'Neville tied my wrists to the bedpost with the silk *écharpe*—the scarf he brought me. Ah, my lover. He brings me such practical gifts.'"

Katherine felt her cheeks grow hot. She hunched over her pad, writing furiously so she wouldn't have to think.

"'He tells me he has always wanted to love me this way, and of course I agree. He tells me he wants me to...*crier*, to cry out, and I do, because it excites him so.'"

Katherine wrote even more furiously. When she was translating the diary in private, she found her aunt's erotic entries almost laughable, because her memory of Patrice was of an eccentric old woman, her face lacy with wrinkles and her tiny body wrapped in garish silk caftans. The only time Katherine had ever seen Patrice cry out, it was because Katherine was speeding her tricycle down the walk to the street.

As a young woman in the throes of passion, surely Patrice could have cried out to excite her man. But hearing such passages read in Drew's low, husky drawl embarrassed Katherine. He kept his gaze fixed on the mirror, yet she felt his attention on her, his awareness of her as strong as hers was of him. Their chairs were separated by a couple of feet, their arms by inches. Her cheeks bloomed with heat as he continued.

"'He likes it that I cannot move, because...because of

the *écharpe* that...that holds my hands above my head. He is an...*étalon*.' A stallion?" Drew asked.

"A stallion," Katherine confirmed, then cleared her throat and wrote it down. "I'm sure this isn't what you were hoping to find in the diary—"

"Ah, but it's fun," he said, a wicked smile teasing his mouth. She glimpsed his dimple and resented it, resented the dark masculinity of his voice. He wouldn't be a stallion, she knew. He wouldn't gallop through the act, snorting and whinnying. He would be...a man. Strong and passionate, waiting for his woman, neither riding her nor carrying her but moving with her, collaborating.

She coughed to cleared her throat again. "The judge always talks after sex," she said, gesturing toward the mirror. "That's when the good stuff begins."

"It depends on one's definition of the good stuff." Drew did Katherine the favor of keeping his eyes on the mirror. "'We...sweat like...like animals, my Neville and I,'" he read. "'My hands are numb, but my body is...full...full with him.'" Drew leaned back and shook his head. "She might have embarrassed herself more than him if she went public with this diary."

"Why? He was married. She wasn't."

"The writing is execrable."

"She wasn't a poet. She was a woman."

"A woman with numb hands and a full body." He angled his head and studied her out of the corner of his eye. "Are you thirsty? I could get you a cold drink."

"No, thank you."

"You look flushed."

"I'm just a little warm. This office is stuffy." She proceeded to unfasten the French cuffs of her blouse and roll up the sleeves. "Keep reading, Drew. I believe the execrable part is over."

He bent back over the mirror. "'We drink sweet wine in bed, and...as ever...Neville tells me of his day....'"

Now that Katherine didn't have to listen to Drew read about sex, she allowed herself to appreciate his fluency in French and his willingness to strain his eyes on the tiny print reflected in the mirror. With him reading, she could write more rapidly, and they made progress. Over the next half hour, Drew translated and Katherine recorded Alvarez's description of jury selection for a murder trial over which he was presiding.

By the time Drew reached the next entry, Katherine did want a cold drink. He summoned a secretary and requested iced coffee for them both. When the secretary carried in a tray with two tall, frosted tumblers of coffee, she also handed Drew several message slips. Katherine was surprised that he considered the diary important enough to have his secretary hold his calls.

In the next entry—after some overheated prose about making love in a doorway, standing up—Patrice wrote that she and Neville discussed the irony of Patrice's sister being barren when so many girls who should have remained virtuous wound up in trouble instead. Desperate to help her sister adopt a child, Patrice asked Alvarez if he'd found a baby for the Beauforts. "'I reminded him of his promise,'" Drew read. "'I reminded him of the pregnant woman he had told me about, the daughter of a friend. She is in Baton Rouge to spare her reputation, a fine woman in such a condition. So many *scandales* in this family Neville knows so well. But this is a fine girl, wealthy and white. How can she get herself into such a predicament? It is so wrong, Neville says, a girl from such an excellent family.'"

Less than an hour after he'd mated with his mistress in a doorway, he was criticizing a fine girl for having gotten pregnant out of wedlock. If Katherine had been alone, she would have laughed out loud at the judge's hypocrisy. But she was with Drew, and every word, every mention of fine girls and pregnancies, sweat and crying out became burdened with extra meaning. The iced coffee cooled Katherine's throat but not her blood.

"Is there a rest room I could use?" she asked, longing to splash some cold water on her steaming cheeks.

Drew lowered the book and rubbed the back of his neck. "Over there," he said, pointing behind him. She saw a door near the windows and started toward it, but he stopped her. "Not that one," he said, rising and smiling contritely. "Over here." He pointed out another door along the same wall. "That one leads to my father's office. This one is my rest room." He courteously crossed the room, opened the door and flipped on a light switch for her.

She stepped inside, shut the door and sighed. The beige-tiled room was small and crowded, not just a sink and commode but a stall shower crammed into its narrow confines. Katherine moved to the sink, cupped her hands with cool water and let it spill onto her cheeks. Then she reached for a towel, wiped her face dry and checked her appearance in the vanity mirror above the sink.

A mirror. Much bigger than the tiny compact's reflecting surface. She surveyed the sink fittings, wondering if there was a way to prop the book up so Drew could see it in the vanity mirror.

She opened the door and beckoned to him. "Would this mirror be easier to work with?"

He was still standing, massaging the nape of his neck and mussing his hair in the process. Her fingers flexed involuntarily, as if they yearned to rub the knots out of his neck for him, to ruffle the silky strands of his hair.

No, she didn't yearn for that, not with Drew. Even if he had inspired a twinge of lust in Katherine by reading carnal passages in the diary, it meant nothing. She knew the dangers of indulging in lust. She didn't need Judge Alvarez's

pious lectures about the shame of fine girls getting int
trouble. She wasn't even all that fine; she would never wan
to risk anything that might get her into that sort of trouble
Especially with Drew Delacroix.

He approached the bathroom, carrying the diary wit
him, and quickly contrived a way to prop the diary agains
the faucets so that two pages at a time were fully visibl
in the mirror. "Great idea," he said, lowering the lid of th
commode and gesturing. "Have a seat."

Katherine sat as delicately as possible on the molded
plastic lid. She adjusted the knees of her pleated woo
slacks and crossed one leg over the other. Lifting her pa
and pen, she chuckled. "I feel like a stenographer in hell,'
she said. "The ultimate punishment—to take dictation in
lavatory."

"At least you get to sit," Drew pointed out, proppin
his arms on the sink and peering into the mirror. "Wher
were we?"

She glanced at her notes. "The family and its scandals.'

"Right." He perused the page, then translated, "'I think
my Neville will at last get Lorraine and Brice...*petit enfant*
Little baby. I do not wish for a silk scarf to bind my wrists
I wish for my sister to have a child.' Who are Lorraine an
Brice?" Drew asked.

"My grandparents."

"So this baby is going to be your aunt? The one wh
raised you?"

"If we ever get to an actual adoption," Katherine answered with a nod.

Drew turned the page and scanned it. "This is a new
entry," he said, then proceeded to work through it. It begar
with yet another steamy description of sex—on the floo
this time, with Patrice on her belly and the judge on top o
her, so heavy he left her breathless, which made it hard fo

her to cry out, but he loved to hear her cry out and she did her best....

The plastic seat dug into Katherine's bottom, and her pen scratched rapidly across the lines of her notebook. Beads of perspiration gathered along her hairline. Drew's leg was an inch from hers, his shoulders strong and broad as he braced himself on the sink.

He was too close, but in the tight confines of the bathroom she couldn't distance herself from him. She should never have suggested they move their operation in here. For that matter, she should never have agreed to let Drew see the diary.

To her great relief, he finally made his way beyond the sex to the subsequent pillow talk. According to Patrice, the judge complained about his wife, how cold she was, how repressed. He discussed the importance of passion in a man's life. He explained that a wise man knew how to rule his passions, but a fool allowed his passions to rule him. He mentioned the murder trial over which he was presiding. *"Quelle affaire brutale!"* the judge was quoted as exclaiming with a sanctimonious flourish. "'Because of passion,'" Drew translated, "'a woman is dead. Her murderer shall hang for it. I must see to it that he does.'"

Frowning, Drew straightened up. "That's wrong."

"What?" She stopped writing. "You translated something wrong?"

He chuckled and shook his head. "If your aunt is writing the truth, Judge Alvarez committed a serious judicial impropriety."

"He's committing all sorts of improprieties," Katherine observed. "Why not judicial ones, as well?"

"I guess a judicial impropriety tends to stick in a lawyer's craw."

In other words, Katherine concluded, the sexual improprieties apparently *didn't* stick in Drew's craw. The back of her collar felt damp from perspiration. It was much too warm in the windowless bathroom. She needed more iced coffee. Or just plain ice.

"Besides the obvious fact that a judge shouldn't be discussing an active trial with his sweetheart," Drew explained, "he shouldn't be promising to see a defendant hanged before the defendant has even been found guilty. A judge is supposed to remain impartial throughout the trial. Not that many of them do, but to go about revealing such extreme bias is outrageous."

"Why do you suppose Patrice wrote it all down? She wasn't an idiot. She knew Alvarez was doing bad things. She wanted a record of them, just in case." Katherine ruminated for a moment. "She was planning to use the diary for leverage. Getting a baby for Lorraine and Brice Beaufort was something she really wanted to do—and something she felt Alvarez could help her to do. My theory is, she was keeping a record of his dirty deeds in case he didn't come through with a baby."

Drew shrugged. "Maybe. Though I wonder why, if your grandparents wanted a baby so much, they didn't just go to an orphanage and adopt one. Every nun in New Orleans in those days probably knew of a girl in trouble. If your grandparents had gone through the usual channels—"

"They wouldn't have," Katherine corrected him. "They were ashamed of their infertility. My grandmother told me it was a terrible embarrassment, something my grandfather couldn't admit to. They had to find a baby secretly, from some place other than New Orleans, and present it as their own, so no one would know."

"That's ridiculous," Drew muttered.

"Yes, of course it was ridiculous. But that was the society they lived in. They weren't rich, but they were very status conscious. And my grandfather was an exceedingly proud man."

Drew gazed at her, his eyes dark and glittering. "All that tuff the judge said about passion... I can understand that ind of passion. I can't understand yours, Katherine."

"My—my passion?" Her mouth was parched. She pictured the half-consumed tumbler of iced coffee she'd left n his desk and sighed.

"Why are you so passionate about this diary?"

"Why do you think your father tried to steal it?"

He didn't bother to answer. "It would seem there are etter uses for passion."

Her fingers fumbled the pen. It slipped out of her grasp nd dropped to the floor.

He bowed to pick it up and handed it to her. He looked ompletely unruffled, but there was no sign that he was easing her, no hint of a smile, no tantalizing dimple at the orner of his mouth. He gazed at her for an endless second, hen turned back to the mirror. "Okay. Where were we?"

"The murder trial," she said, her voice as raspy as sandaper.

Drew read more cryptic passages about the trial, and then new entry that dealt with a secret tryst in Grand Isle, where the lovers ran through a sex manual's worth of positions and seductions in the sea-scented room of an inn. Then another entry, during which the lovemaking was folowed by a discussion about the nice white girl in a family way whose father had sent her to a convent in Baton Rouge until her baby was born.

"'Her father was distraught,'" Drew translated laboriously. "'He is...a good friend of Neville's. A fine man, an ttorney, watching his family...fall to pieces. A woman whose youngest brother has the calling and is preparing for eminary, and two other fine brothers. Her father is a lawer, and she comes from great wealth....'" He fell silent.

The air hung heavy in the room. Katherine waited for him to continue, and when he didn't, she lowered her pen and looked up at him. He was staring at the mirror, his eye stark, his complexion losing color. His hands were fiste against the sink, and his body was so still he had to hav stopped breathing.

"Drew?" she asked quietly.

He said nothing.

"Drew, what is it?"

"Aunt Mary." His voice was hushed, but it echoe against the hard tiles of the room.

"Aunt Mary? Your family matchmaker?"

"Oh, God." He closed his eyes and shoved away fro the sink. The diary snapped shut and tumbled into the basi

"Drew?"

"That fine white woman having a baby in the conver in Baton Rouge," he whispered, "is my Aunt Mary."

CHAPTER SIX

"YOU CAN'T KNOW THAT for a fact," Katherine said.

"Not for a fact, no." He lifted the diary out of the sink, wiped a drop of water from the leather binding and handed it to her. "I can't know it for a fact, but I can know it for the truth." Inside his chest his heart felt frenzied, like a wild bird trapped in a cage, batting its wings against the bars and trying to escape. But he held himself calm. He would not let Katherine see how shaken he was.

She stared at him, obviously bemused. He handed her the book and stalked out of the bathroom. In his desk, in the lower left drawer, he had a bottle of bourbon. And if ever he needed that bottle...

No. He wouldn't drink in front of her. He wanted her to believe he was completely in control, utterly self-possessed. He wanted her to think highly of him. God only knew why he cared, but he did.

Not surprisingly, she followed him out of the lavatory. "I don't understand," she said. "Where did you get such an idea? Are there passages in the diary that you were translating in your head and not sharing with me? The pages we just went over..." She opened the book to the place the ribbon marked, where Drew had stopped translating. "I may not read French as well as you, but I'm sure I would have recognized Mary's name if it was written in the book."

"It isn't," he acknowledged, mustering the courage to face Katherine. Her eyes were as clear as the purest water.

He could dive in and drown in them. He wanted to. H wanted to gather her to himself and go under, sink down seal himself away from the surface of the world.

"Then how did you reach such a conclusion? Where' the basis for it?"

He wasn't sure he could explain. It was so patently ob vious to him, as ordinary—and extraordinary—as gravity Like gravity, he felt it without having to think about it.

Asking her simply to believe him wouldn't work. "Th family," he began, pointing toward the book in her hands "A lawyer father who happens to be good friends wit Neville Alvarez. A younger brother who's studying for th priesthood. Great wealth."

"Do you think the Delacroix are the only family tha would fit that description?"

"I think..." *I think your eyes are too beautiful,* h wanted to say. *I think your hair is phenomenal. I thin closing myself up inside that tiny bathroom with you mad me inhale too much of your scent, and now I'm drugge with it.* "I think my father would be likely to steal the diar if the pregnant woman was his sister."

"Why? Is he an overprotective brother?"

"Everybody wants to protect Aunt Mary," he said. Aun Mary was tall and gangly and hopelessly sweet. No matte who wasn't talking to whom in the Delacroix clan—an that usually comprised a large percentage of the family— Mary talked to everyone. No Delacroix would ever delib erately give her offense. None of them would ever allo her to venture into harm's way. She was the family's an chor, its pillar, its guardian angel.

Why hadn't her brothers protected her back then, whe she'd been pregnant? Where had her father been whil she'd been engaged in a premarital affair? Why hadn't th men who loved her taken better care of her?

"You could be wrong," Katherine argued. "In fact, yo

probably *are* wrong." She extended the diary to him. "There's nothing in here—"

"It's in here." Drew tapped his chest with his thumb. "Do you think only women have intuitions? I have an intuition about this. I just know..." He sighed. How could he explain something that had no explanation? "Never mind."

"No, I won't 'never mind.'" She touched his arm. Her fingers spread gracefully over the brown cotton of his shirt. He stared at her hand, felt its delicate pressure through the fabric and wondered whether she pitied him. He must sound deranged to her. Perhaps she'd suggest that he seek psychiatric help.

But even if she thought he was a lunatic, she wasn't afraid of him. If she were, she wouldn't be touching him so consolingly, her fingertips moving gently on him, her face just inches from his as she peered up at him.

He didn't dare to speak or to move. Strength seemed to emanate from her touch. Strength and heat and something more.

"I know there are other passages in the diary about the *petit enfant,*" she said. "And passages about Alvarez's dealings with your family. Maybe you're mixing them all together."

Her hand still rested on him, her fingers still curved around the muscle in his upper arm. Her fingernails reminded him of pearls, round and shiny with an opalescent glaze. Her hair smelled like lilies.

He was mixing everything all together, all right: passages about the *petit enfant* with passages about crying out in ecstasy, passages about trials and *scandales* with passages about silk scarves and sex. He was mixing the erotic tale of illicit lovers with the wide-eyed, copper-haired woman standing beside him right now, her lips pursed as they always were, her gaze beckoning, her fingers lightly stroking his arm through the sleeve of his shirt.

Her touch didn't comfort him, but he wanted it, wanted *her*, wanted her more with every anguished beat of his heart.

"Yes," he murmured, bringing his hands to her cheeks and angling her face. "It's all mixed up."

"Drew?" She searched his face, silently questioning.

There was only one answer, and he gave it without words. He expressed himself with his fingers dancing against her smooth cheeks, with his body leaning toward her, his mouth descending to take hers.

She didn't resist, didn't withdraw. All she did was sigh as their lips met. Hers were as soft as they looked. They shaped to his, shy yet willing. He knew his manners; he mustn't devour but must take small sips, tiny bites, even though he was starving for this woman, ravenous for her.

A soft, desperate sound escaped her as he plunged his fingers into her hair. The diary slipped from her hand and hit his desk with a thud. She lifted both hands to his shoulders, clung to him, closed her eyes and opened her mouth, inviting him to take her as greedily as he wished.

He couldn't believe that this enchantress, this seductress, this magnificent woman was Katherine Beaufort. He couldn't believe the busybody whose presence in Bayou Beltane had irritated him for so many months would lure his tongue into her mouth with such ease, teasing and tasting, tilting her head so he could help himself to more. He couldn't believe that Katherine could grip his shoulders so eagerly it was like having her entire body gripping his.

He wanted her body taking him, tight around him, holding him inside her. He wanted her as aroused as he was, and he urged her against the desk so she couldn't back away from him when he pressed his hips to hers.

She shuddered. Given the way he moved against her, she

had to realize the effect she was having on him. Instead of breaking from him, she skimmed her hands along the nape of his neck and shifted her legs, allowing him to press closer.

He could die smiling from such pleasure. "Let me..." he whispered, sliding one hand down her back to her waist and lower, to align her hips with his. "Katherine, I want..." He didn't have to tell her with words. His body spoke for him, rocking against her in a slow, deliberate rhythm that made her moan.

Sinking onto the edge of his desk, she tore her lips from his and hid her face in the hollow beneath his jaw. He listened to her ragged gasps and felt his heart beat, fast and fervent, against her cheek.

Attempting to calm them both down, he combed his fingers gently through her hair. The rippling strands coiled around his knuckles. He had never realized curly hair could be so sensual.

"I can't do this, Drew," she whispered. As she spoke, he felt her lips brush against him like dainty kisses.

He didn't plead, didn't argue. She *could* do this if she wanted. And she wanted. She wouldn't be standing in the snug circle of his arms, taking comfort from him, if she didn't.

"I don't—I don't even like you." A dazed laugh punctuated her claim.

"Does that matter?" he asked, even though he knew damned well it did. For him as well as for her. He wasn't his father; he believed a man ought to care about a woman if he was going to take her to bed. And Drew did care about Katherine. At least he'd cared about her yesterday evening, when he'd seen the destruction at her apartment. And now that he knew she wasn't playing up to his father, trying to woo the old man for some nefarious purpose... Yes, Drew was sure he cared about her.

"Drew." Sighing, she pushed away from him. He reluctantly took a step back, giving her room to escape. She moved around to the other side of his desk, using it as a barrier—as if it could keep him from her. He could vault over it in a single leap without straining himself.

The only barrier he would respect was the one he saw in her frightened eyes. She was suffering regrets. She considered their kiss a mistake. She didn't want him, after all.

He had an ego to protect, and he immediately went to work constructing his own defenses. "I don't know what got into me," he said brusquely, meeting her alarm with chilly poise. "It's been a long day, and that diary puts ideas in a person's mind. It won't happen again, I promise you." He lifted the offending diary, passed it across the desk to her and then turned from her to stare out the window. The least he could do was let her compose herself without his eyes on her.

Evening had fallen. The sky was washed in rose, lilac and mauve, and cars had their headlights on in the dim twilight. How long had he been working on the diary with Katherine?

Not long enough—and far too long.

"I'd better go," she said quietly.

"Yes. You'd better." He heard ice in his voice.

Her footsteps were barely audible on the carpet. The click of the latch as she opened the door nearly escaped him. The snap of it shutting was no louder, yet it echoed with deafening force inside him.

KATHERINE DIDN'T START breathing again until she was out of the building. She stood on the corner, letting the cool air of the encroaching night close around her. Then she started to shiver.

Whatever could she have been thinking of, to let Drew Delacroix kiss her like that?

She *hadn't* been thinking. She'd only been feeling, and responding. Responding to his lithe physique, his height and posture. Responding to the desire burning in his gaze, the electrifying pleasure of his hands on her face, in her hair, his mouth crushing hers.

He definitely wouldn't be a stallion. He was much too subtle, much too masterly. His mouth was too eloquent, his hands too gifted.

She had never been so turned on by a kiss before.

Maybe it wasn't just Drew, she pondered as she walked around the corner to the lot where she'd left her car. Maybe her intense response had been her own doing more than his. For all the restraint she exercised around men, maybe this time her mother's genes had risen up inside her, making her wild and wanton, too excited by a man's passion to care about the consequences.

She had spent her entire life trying not to become what her mother had been. She had carefully avoided looking for love in the arms of men. She'd found the support and security she needed with her grandparents and her aunt Claire, with her friends and her work.

Yet the longing was still there, no matter how well she suppressed it. And one kiss from Drew, one glorious, demoralizing kiss, had been enough to set it free.

She'd felt much safer when she was hating him. Maybe she'd hated him because she'd known, on some subliminal level, how dangerous he could be if she ever let herself stop hating him. More dangerous than the burglar who'd ransacked her home. More dangerous than any truth she might find in the pages of her great-aunt's diary. Drew could break Katherine's inhibitions, her self-defenses, every shred of protectiveness she relied on to avoid ending up like her mother.

Drew could do that, and the possibility scared the hell out of her.

LIGHT FILLED THE WINDOWS of the library as Drew strolled the path from the carbarn to the back door. That new maid Magdalena must have forgotten to draw the curtains—if she was still in his father's employ.

The air was heavy with the scent of fading flowers and overripe fruit as autumn shifted closer to winter. He would much rather have been filling his lungs with Katherine's lighter, more delicate perfume.

Hell and damnation. Everything in the universe reminded him of Katherine right now. And she'd said, "I don't even like you."

Give her three points for sincerity, he thought grimly. Give her one hundred and three points for brutality.

He shoved open the kitchen door and grunted a greeting to André, who was busy garnishing a platter of sliced roast beef with sprigs of parsley before it made its way to the dining room. Drew kept on through the kitchen and out into the back hall, heading straight for the library. He didn't want to force his way through a heavy meal and a stilted conversation with his father. What he wanted was solitude, to wrestle his libido back into line and analyze the notion that had mixed him up enough to think Katherine would be receptive to him.

Aunt Mary. The family diplomat, the childless matriarch. The only woman he'd been able to turn to after his mother had left. The kind confessor, the bestower of unconditional love. The grand dame of the Delacroix clan.

He simply couldn't imagine her in the throes of passion.

Opening the library door, he nearly stumbled into Jackson Boudreaux, who appeared to be about to leave. This was a surprise. Philip's meetings with his lackey always took place at the office, with Jackson skulking in the back door to avoid being seen. His father must be in a particularly magnanimous mood, Drew thought.

Philip was seated at the desk, a snifter of brandy in his

hand and the *Slidell Sentinel* open in front of him. He peered up over his reading glasses and gave Drew a smug grin. "Mighty nice endorsement Gilbert Weedon gave me in today's edition."

An endorsement worth every penny Philip had paid for it, Drew thought caustically.

"That's all, Jackson," Philip muttered. "You can go."

"You said there'd be something in it for me if the endorsement came through," Jackson reminded him.

"Not now."

"You said—"

"I said, not now." Philip glowered at him. "Go."

Drew entered the library and stepped out of Jackson's path, allowing him room to exit. Jackson acknowledged Drew with a scowl, then glanced over his shoulder at Philip. "I'll see you tomorrow," he warned. Clad in twill work pants and a white shirt, Jackson lifted the blue-denim jacket he'd been clutching in one hand and shoved his arms through the sleeves. The jacket was a classic dungaree style, with button-down breast pockets, tapering seams and tabs at the waistband, adjustable to make the jacket fit more snugly over the hips.

The tab nearest Drew was missing its button. A small tuft of torn threads marked the spot.

Drew clamped his mouth shut and took another step back. He listened to his respiration, listened to the beat of his pulse in his ears, listened to his father's cackling laughter as he rattled the broad pages of the newspaper. Drew focused on each sound, memorized it, relied on it to keep him from saying anything to Jackson.

Still scowling, Jackson left the library, closing the door behind him. Drew counted to five before turning to his father. The man was preening, so confident of his own triumph that Drew nearly choked on his anger. Philip Delacroix had just been in this room with the man who had broken into Katherine's apartment. Jackson had to have done it at Philip's behest.

Philip must be desperate to get his hands on the diary. Was he really so anxious to spare Aunt Mary's reputation? Yes. He would consider Aunt Mary's history important—not for her sake but for his own. His campaigns were based on old-fashioned morality and family values. Lord spare him from the voters if they ever caught on to what a hypocrite he was.

"Dad, I need to talk to you," Drew said.

"This sounds serious," Philip said, his grin expanding as if to say that nothing Drew needed to talk to him about could be the least bit significant. He leaned back in the leather chair and took a sip of his brandy. His bow tie was still neatly tied, his shirt crisp despite the late hour. He removed his half glasses and set them on the newspaper, then eyed his son with mild boredom.

Drew's jaw ached from clenching it so tightly. "Did Aunt Mary ever have a child?" he asked.

Something flickered in Philip's eyes, a glint of panic that he erased with a blink. When he opened his eyes again, they were devoid of light. "Don't be ridiculous."

"I'm never ridiculous." Drew approached the desk but refused to sit in the chair across from his father. He wanted the advantage of his height as he questioned Philip. "Did she ever have a baby?"

"Of course not."

Drew ignored the bland denial. "Did she have a baby fifty-eight or nine years ago, out of wedlock, at a convent in Baton Rouge?"

His father was no longer looking at him. "Where is this coming from, Drew? What nonsense has possessed you?"

"Not nonsense, Dad. A desire for the truth."

"There's nothing—"

"Look at me," Drew demanded quietly.

His father took a sip of brandy and set down the snifter. But he refused his son's request and continued to avoid Drew's unwavering gaze. "Don't you order me around. Your question is disgusting. It doesn't deserve an answer, but I've given you one."

"Not an honest one," Drew said, still quiet, his emotions banked.

"Why would I lie about such a thing?"

"To protect Aunt Mary, maybe."

"Ah, so you're willing to grant me a capacity for brotherly kindness?" Philip seemed to be looking everywhere but at Drew, which only stoked Drew's certainty that the old man was lying.

"Or maybe to protect the father, whoever he was."

"This is none of your business."

"It's my family!" Drew bellowed, hoping to jolt a response out of his father. He pounded the desk with his fist. "I'm tired of your lies, Dad. I deserve to know the truth!"

At last he won a response. His father shoved himself to his feet and met Drew's gaze, his eyes ferocious, burning with fury. "You don't deserve anything. The truth isn't yours to own. People are entitled to their lives, their mistakes and their privacy. Don't you come in here suggesting ugly things about your aunt Mary. She's a good woman, always was, and she'll die a good woman, and you have no right to be accusing her this way!"

"Whether or not she had a baby, she'd still be the best damned member of this family," Drew retorted. "I'm not accusing her—"

"Implying that she would have done such a thing! In a Baton Rouge convent! For heaven's sake! You said this is your family. Then show some respect for it. Your family deserves as much."

"My family," Drew reminded him, his voice hoarse from his attempt not to shout, "is built on lies. Lord, what a fine, respectable family we are!'' A bitter laugh escaped him. ''Your brother William turns out not to be a Delacroix by birth. And Annabelle—your own daughter—was forced into her first marriage by you, even though she was pregnant by another man. Thank God she stopped living a lie and found herself where she belongs, with Jake.'' Drew shook his head. ''It's all lies, Dad. Too much of what has gone on in this family is lies. I'm sick of it.''

''So be sick of it!'' Philip shouted. ''Do you really think I care whether you're sick or not? Get out of here, if you're so sick of it.''

''You're willing to add me to your list of enemies? The last ally you've got in this family? You don't have many friends left, Dad. You could count them on your fingers and still have your thumbs free. You shouldn't be so willing to give me up.''

''A son who shows no respect for his father—''

''What is there to respect?'' Drew clawed a hand through his hair in frustration. Was there not a single honest bone in his father's body? A single honest impulse? ''Just add my name to the list. I'll curse you behind your back like they do. I'll plow through your old records, looking for evidence against you. I'll start leaving gris-gris for you. Give me a chance to send you one of those voodoo dolls, Dad. I'll remember to stick a pin in it first.'' He shook his head again. ''You've got enemies from one end of the spectrum to the other. I guess you don't mind having one more.''

Philip snorted. ''Flora Boudreaux is a fool, and she's leaving me those bits of voodoo just to bug me. You want to bug me, too? You want to be as big a fool as she is? Go ahead, be my guest.''

''Flora.'' Drew shook his head. ''It amazes me to think she's your enemy, too. You've got so many people lined up against you. Your daughters can barely stand to speak to you, your brother and all my cousins won't have anything to do with you. And a mean-spirited nobody who lives in the swamp keeps sending you bad-luck voodoo charms. I know what you did to my sisters, Dad. I know why they've turned against you. But what did you do to Jackson's mother? How'd you wind up getting her to hate you?''

''My relationship with Flora—''

''Relationship?'' Drew pounced on the word so quickly he wasn't even aware of what he'd found until the impact echoed in his mind. Flora's mother, Desiree, had been acquainted with the Delacroix family for generations, and Philip employed Flora's son to do his dirty work. But how could Philip use the word *relationship* to describe himself and Flora? ''What relationship?'' Drew asked, his voice hushed but taut.

His father grew pale. ''Get out,'' he snapped.

''What relationship?''

''Get the hell out of here.''

''What relationship?''

Philip closed his hand into a fist and swung at Drew. Younger and more agile, Drew easily deflected the blow, clamping his hand around his father's wrist and holding it with steely firmness. Across the width of the desk they glared at each other, father and son trapped in a maelstrom of hatred.

''What relationship?'' Drew asked, softer than a whisper.

Philip gave him a withering look. ''What other kind is there?''

''You slept with her?''

''Don't be an idiot, Drew. Do you think I'd have anything to do with a lowlife like Jackson otherwise? Do you think I'd let that man into my life if he wasn't—*ow!*''

The old man winced as Drew's fingers tightened mercilessly around his wrist. Drew didn't particularly want to hurt him. He wasn't even aware of what his hand was doing. Alarm bells were clanging in his head, deafening him. He was shaking with rage, insane with it.

Then he remembered to breathe. Air filled his lungs, hurting and healing all at once. His hand went limp and he dropped it, then fell back a step from the stranger—his father—standing on the other side of the wide cherry desk.

Jackson. Jackson Boudreaux. The man who would do whatever Philip asked of him, the way a loyal son would.

Jackson Boudreaux, Bayou Beltane's crooked cop, the handyman who fixed any problem Philip had that couldn't be fixed legitimately, the thug with dirt on his hands and stains on his soul.

Jackson Boudreaux was Drew's brother.

He couldn't remain in the room with his father. He couldn't remain in the same house. He raced out of the library, staggered up the stairs, charged down the hall to his suite and locked himself inside. The bedroom was neat—Drew liked orderliness—and he knew where everything was, including his own private supply of bourbon.

He pulled a new bottle from the top shelf in his dressing-room closet. He gave the cap a sharp twist, and the seal broke with a crackle. He unscrewed the cap, caught a sharp whiff of the stuff and felt his throat squeeze shut.

No. He would not drink. Drinking wouldn't change the fact that his father had lain with Flora Boudreaux and sired a child with her, a son—the son he'd always wanted, the son who had grown up to be just like his father, manipulative and corrupt.

Jackson was the son Drew could never be, the son Philip had always dreamed of. Jackson Boudreaux.

He lurched into the spacious bathroom, across the polished marble floor to the pedestal sink, upended the bottle and watched the bourbon stream out in a chugging flow. It turned the white porcelain gold, then vanished down the drain. Gradually the last of it seeped away, leaving the sink white again, leaving Drew standing in silence.

Jackson. Oh, God. Jackson Boudreaux was his father's son.

Drew couldn't stay at Belle Terre. He had to get out. Like his sisters before him, he had to escape from Philip's tyranny, his depravity. Drew couldn't stay here another night.

He walked in measured steps back into his dressing room and pulled a suitcase from a shelf. Slowly, methodically—if he didn't think through each movement and choice he would surely fall to pieces—he packed the suitcase with jeans and khakis, shirts and underwear, a sweater, a necktie. He stripped off his office attire, stalked back into the bathroom and cranked the shower faucets to a hot spray. Plumes of steam rose above the curtain. He stepped into the tub and prayed for the water to purge him, to wash away whatever taint his father might have left on his skin. Washing the taint in his soul would be impossible.

Turning off the shower, he toweled himself dry, donned clean jeans and a fresh V-necked sweater, brushed his dripping hair back from his face and packed his toiletries into a leather case. He added the toiletries to his suitcase, zipped it shut, pocketed his wallet and donned a fall-weight leather jacket.

Then he left. He lacked any idea of where to go. All he knew was that wherever he went, it had to be far away from Philip Delacroix.

CHAPTER SEVEN

"LOOK, I'M NOT GIVING YOU any advice," Dionne insisted.

Katherine wedged the receiver between her chin and her shoulder, freeing her hands so she could clear the table while she continued the phone conversation. "That's exactly what you're doing," she argued as she pulled a stretch of plastic wrap from its box. She'd made herself a spinach salad with mushrooms and a crumbled hard-boiled egg tossed into it, but the appetite that had abandoned her the moment she'd seen Drew at Annabelle's had yet to return. "You're giving me advice, Dionne."

"All right, then," Dionne conceded cheerfully. "If you insist, I'm giving you advice. Stay away from those Delacroix men. Rich white folks can't be trusted."

"That's a racist remark," Katherine scolded, though she was smiling.

"Yeah, well, it isn't directed at you. You're not rich."

Katherine would have laughed if she weren't so drained. The emotional residue of her afternoon with Drew lingered inside her, simmering in her blood.

She didn't need Dionne's warning; she was smart enough to keep her distance from him. She knew he'd kissed her only because he'd been in a state of turmoil and she'd been handy. He would have kissed anyone who'd been standing in his office. His passion had had nothing to do with Katherine.

Acknowledging that truth broke her heart.

She was more troubled by the notion that Drew could

break her heart than by his kiss. Why should she feel such despair at the thought that he'd turned to her not out of love but out of convenience? Why was her heart breaking over the fact that he harbored no personal feelings for her?

Because his kiss had felt personal at the time. Because she'd *wanted* it to be personal. Because she wanted to be wild and wanton with him, to forget her responsibilities and drop her guard and let him sweep her away. She had never before allowed herself to desire anything like that, anyone like him—and now she would never get what she desired. She ought to be grateful, but she felt only a keen disappointment.

"I'm telling you," Dionne prattled on, "if you let that Delacroix boy fuss with your aunt's diary, it's going to bring bad luck. Look at the armoire, right? Has that piece sold yet? No, it hasn't. And I'll tell you why—"

"There's hoodoo in the diary," Katherine recited, then sighed when she spotted a small mound of spilled rice hidden behind the flour canister on the counter. "Dionne, I've got to go."

"I'm just telling you—"

"You're just giving me advice. But you're wasting your breath. Nothing is going on between Drew Delacroix and me—he just helped me translate a little of the diary."

"You've got that faraway voice." Dionne clicked her tongue. "I know that voice. That voice means you're thinking about long, hot nights and lazy kisses."

"No." She was thinking of fierce, greedy kisses and Drew's arousal pressing between her legs. She was thinking about the way her self-protective instincts had fled her when he'd gathered her in his arms. "Don't lecture me, Dionne. Okay? I know better than to let Drew Delacroix get close to me."

"I'm almost reassured," Dionne said, sounding anything

but. "I'll see you at the shop tomorrow. I'll have a whole new set of lectures for you then."

"I can't wait," Katherine muttered, then forced a laugh. She knew Dionne's intentions were kind. And in the course of their friendship, Katherine had certainly given Dionne plenty of unsolicited advice concerning romance. In fact, she'd probably given Dionne more advice than Dionne had ever given her, since Dionne had so many more romances.

After bidding her friend goodbye, she hung up, then pulled the canisters away from the wall and cleaned up the overlooked pile of rice. All evening she'd been finding reminders of the previous day's mayhem—items misplaced, clods of dirt from her potted ferns ground into the rug, a leather glove under the sofa, a box of note cards caught behind the night table. Her landlord had installed a new lock on the window sometime during the day, and it gleamed silver, looking out of place against the painted window sash.

She tried not to let the vestiges of the previous evening's mess depress her. She had enough to worry about with the current evening's mess.

Drew. His kiss. His yearning. His ability to awaken a yearning just as powerful in her.

She couldn't want him. She mustn't. She shouldn't even let him near Great-Aunt Patrice's diary again—except that it was too late. He'd already seen it and drawn his own conclusions.

What was that old saying of Aunt Claire's? Something about how impossible it was to stuff the toothpaste back into the tube once you'd squeezed it out. That adage seemed appropriate to Katherine's life right now. Drew had seen the diary, and he'd kissed her, and that toothpaste was never going to go back into the tube.

The buzz of her doorbell broke through her melancholy thoughts. She glanced at her wristwatch—eight-forty—and decided that if her caller wasn't a neighbor checking in on her or asking to borrow an egg, she wouldn't open the door. She wasn't in the mood to invite anyone in—particularly if the visitor hadn't even had the courtesy to phone ahead.

She crossed the living room to the door and squinted through the peek hole.

Drew.

Retreating from the door, she closed her eyes. Why had he come here? She didn't need his help tonight. Her home hadn't been invaded—and it wouldn't be, unless she opened her door to him.

Had he come expecting to kiss her again, hoping that this time she might not come to her senses as quickly as she had at his office earlier? Surely if all he'd wanted was a convenient body to hold on to, he could have found a woman in Bayou Beltane. He didn't have to drive all the way across the lake to New Orleans.

The doorbell buzzed again. She sighed. If she didn't let him in, he'd likely find his way around to the inner courtyard and up the stairs. Her bedroom window hadn't posed much of a barrier to whoever had broken in last night. Drew could easily break the new lock, if that was his aim.

But he wouldn't force anything. He'd backed off in his office. And she'd been as much at fault as he for that kiss.

She released the safety chain and opened the door. "Can I come in?" he asked, hovering on the threshold.

A quick glance told her too much. He was dressed in faded jeans, a sweater and a battered leather jacket. His jaw wore a faint stubble of beard, his hair fell every which way, and a small suitcase stood on the floor beside him. His eyes were as flat as glass, and just as transparent. She could see right through them to the fear and anguish raging inside him.

She didn't smell bourbon on his breath, or the bright mint of mouthwash implying that he'd tried to cover up the smell of liquor. "Yes," she said, stepping aside and gesturing with her hand. "Come in."

He lugged his suitcase into the apartment and closed the door behind him. Then he leaned heavily against it, rolled his head back and stared at the ceiling. "I'm sorry, Katherine. I didn't know where else to go."

"It's all right." Something terrible had happened. Something so terrible she didn't have to worry about fending off his advances or obeying Dionne's admonitions about rich white men. Drew was more than preoccupied—he was possessed. He hadn't come to her because she was convenient—heaven knew, the drive across Lake Pontchartrain was hardly a convenience. He had come because he didn't know where else to go, and he believed she would open her home to him.

She backed up, giving him time and room to collect himself. After a long minute, he lowered his suitcase to the rug. Then he lifted his hands to his face, rubbed his eyes, raked his fingers through his hair and groaned. "That's not true," he murmured. "What I just said now—it's a lie."

"Oh?"

"I could think of other places to go. I could have gone to Annabelle's or Joanna's. But they're my sisters, and I didn't think—I can't talk to them about this."

About what? Katherine wondered. *And what makes you think you can talk to me?*

"Or I could have gone to my cabin. It's really more a shack, out on the bayou. I drove halfway there before I realized I couldn't bear to be alone. Not tonight."

Oh. In other words, he *had* come to Katherine in the hope of resuming what he'd started with her in his office. He'd traveled all this way because it beat spending the night alone.

Dionne was right on both counts: the diary carried a curse, and Katherine ought not to trust the Delacroix men.

"I'm afraid you'll be disappointed," she said, swallowing her own disappointment. "I don't intend to offer you my company tonight."

He straightened up and stared at her. A faint, bemused smile crossed his lips. "I didn't mean it that way," he said quietly, his eyes losing some of their panic and allowing in a glimmer of contrition. "I just don't want to be alone, Katherine. We don't have to talk. We don't even have to be in the same room. I..." He let out a long, weary breath and massaged the nape of his neck with his hand. Then he lowered his arms and regarded her somberly. "I'm sorry, Katherine. If you want me to leave, I'll—"

"No." She spoke automatically, but when she paused to reconsider, she knew in her heart that she wanted him to stay. He hadn't come to her for sex. One objective look at him told her as much. A man who would drive as far as he had for a seduction would have shaved, at the very least.

"I've been..." He shook his head and started again. "I learned something this evening. I'm...kind of a wreck." He moved toward the sofa, then paused and glanced at her. "Can I sit?"

"Of course. Would you like something to drink?" She prayed he wouldn't ask for anything alcoholic.

"A cup of coffee would be nice."

"A cup of coffee." She hid her relief behind a nod and abandoned him for the kitchen. While her hands measured scoops of coffee and chicory into her coffeemaker, her mind measured the man in her living room. What could have happened to him? Had he gotten confirmation that his aunt Mary had, in fact, given up a baby for adoption? Could such news devastate him so completely?

If that was the reason for his apparent shell shock, Katherine could reassure him. She could tell him that if his aunt had offered her baby for adoption, she had given Katherine's grandparents the most generous gift of their lives.

Drew's aunt Mary should be honored for her deed, not scorned. What might have been viewed as a *scandale* sixty-odd years ago had in fact been an act of selfiess love.

While the coffee brewed, Katherine tiptoed to the doorway and spied on Drew. He sat on the sofa, his knees spread, his elbows propped on his thighs and his chin cupped in his hands. His eyes were closed. She read tension in his brow, desolation in the hunch of his shoulders, the tumble of his hair. Once again, he was causing her heart to break—but this time it was breaking not for herself but for him.

Dionne's warning echoed in her mind: *Stay away from those Delacroix men. Rich white folks can't be trusted.* Katherine wasn't sure she could trust Drew, and under ordinary circumstances she would be wise to stay away from him. But last night hadn't been ordinary, and he'd given her his unconditional support. Tonight she would do the same for him.

By the time she'd arranged a tray with two cups and saucers, a sugar bowl and a pitcher of cream, the coffee was ready. She filled the cups and carried the tray into the living room. Drew opened his eyes and stood as she approached. Once she'd lowered the tray to the table in front of the sofa and sat, he resumed his own seat. She handed him a cup of steaming coffee and he flashed her a grateful smile.

She waited for him to speak, but he remained silent as he stirred a spoonful of sugar into his cup and sipped. He lowered the cup to the table and stared at it, as if mesmerized by the patterns of the steam rising from the drink. Finally, he asked, "Is this cup an antique?"

She laughed. "No, it's just old." Her cups were a whimsically mismatched set that she'd picked up here and there—castoffs from Aunt Claire, items purchased with spare change at rummage sales, souvenirs she'd bought on an antiquing jaunt through New England several years ago. The cup he was using had spiderweb cracks veining its surface, but it wasn't old enough to be an antique. If it had been, she would have had it for sale in her store.

"It tastes good," he said, then took another drink. "It's strong."

"It'll probably keep you up all night."

"I don't expect to be getting much sleep tonight."

She eyed him warily, her suspicions once again aroused. If he had any intention of spending the night not getting much sleep because he was busy making love to her... No. The bleakness of his gaze, the harsh angle of his jaw informed her that whatever might keep him up all night had little to do with her.

She sipped her own coffee, savoring the sharp tang of it on her tongue, finding in its rich aroma the courage to question him. "Is it about the diary, Drew?" she asked gently. "About your aunt Mary?"

He turned to her. Beyond grief she saw a desperate need in his gaze, and a profound fear. "No," he said. "It's not about Aunt Mary."

"Do you want to talk about it?"

"No." Then he laughed sadly. "I don't even want to think about it. But I can't stop. I can't rid my brain of it."

"What can't you rid your brain of?"

He looked away.

Impulsively, she leaned forward and covered his hand with hers. Just as impulsively, it seemed, he rotated his wrist and wove his fingers through hers. He didn't squeeze, didn't cling. His hand simply nestled into hers, warming her as he took warmth from her.

She was about to give up on ever getting him to talk, when he said, "I know who broke into your apartment."

She struggled not to flinch. His hand remained steady and snug around hers, his fingers barely moving as he turned and met her gaze. He had the most amazing eyes she had ever seen. As dark and dangerous as smoke, they disturbed and attracted her at the same time.

"My brother," he said.

"Your what? You don't have a brother." If Annabelle had had a brother besides Drew, she would have mentioned him to Katherine.

He nearly smiled, yet there was no joy in his expression. "I found out tonight that I do. His name is Jackson Boudreaux."

Katherine opened her mouth and then shut it. Oh, God. He had a brother. His father had another son, one neither Drew nor his sisters had known about. "How did you find out?" she asked.

"My father told me."

"And you believe him?"

Drew allowed himself a bitter laugh. "For once in my life, yes."

"Does Annabelle know? Or Joanna?"

He shook his head. "I haven't told them, and I'm sure my father hasn't, either. They wouldn't have kept it from me if they knew."

"But you're keeping it from them." Katherine had no right to challenge his decision, but she wanted to keep him talking. When he fell quiet, he seemed so hopelessly lost.

"I just found out. Just this evening. I didn't want to tell anyone, but...I couldn't be alone right now. I just didn't think I could—I don't know, I didn't think I could handle it by myself. I didn't know what to do. So...I came here, Katherine. I'm telling you."

It was a privilege she wasn't sure she deserved, a responsibility she wasn't sure she could accept. Yet Drew had chosen her for a reason—apparently one he himself couldn't identify, but a reason nonetheless. Some urge had

›rought him to her, some hope of receiving compassion, if ıot salvation, from her.

"Do you think your father's revelation has anything to lo with my great-aunt's diary?" she asked. "I mean, you hink your brother..." He winced at the word, and she hastly chose a new one. "You think this is the man who broke nto my apartment."

"I saw his jacket this evening. It was missing a button, ust like the button I found in your window frame." Drew noved his thumb aimlessly against hers, tracing a wavering ›ath down to her wrist and up again.

"Do you think he broke in because there's something hat concerns him in the diary?"

"No."

"Then why would he—"

"I don't know!" Drew groaned, obviously exasperated. Ie slid his hand from hers and turned once again to stare ›ff into space. "I don't know," he repeated, this time oftly. "All I know is that this man—this son of a bitch...)h, God," he whispered, half a prayer and half a curse. 'I've known him all his life. He's a punk. A piece of cum." Drew lowered his head to his hands, closed his eyes ınd shuddered. "I don't know anything, Katherine. Not ınymore."

She wanted to take Drew in her arms and cradle him ıgainst her bosom, rock him like a baby and swear that :verything was going to be all right, that she would take :are of him. She had never had strong maternal instincts, ınd she certainly didn't feel maternal toward Drew. But he wanted to comfort him, to promise him good things, to ›rotect him against all the hurt in the world, all the mistakes ›thers had made, mistakes that would leave their scars on ıim even though he'd done nothing to bring them upon ıimself.

"I need air," he said abruptly, shoving himself to his

feet and striding across the room to the door that led outside onto the courtyard balcony. Katherine stood, turning in time to see him step outdoors. She gave him a few minutes alone and then moved toward the door, halting before going outside. She didn't want to encroach on his solitude.

He stood gazing down into the paved courtyard below. She observed the arch of his back, the length of his legs, his feet planted squarely and his forearms propped against the railing. One of the lamps lighting the balcony cast an amber light over his hair, locating the gold highlights and bringing them to life.

She gave the doorknob a twist, then hesitated, hearing his voice. He was singing, his voice as hushed as a breath of warm autumn.

"My woman, she opens her body," he sang. "My woman, she opens her eyes...and I drink my bourbon and walk from her bed...though she's lonely and lovely and wise..."

It took Katherine a long moment to recall where she'd heard the song before. "It's an old lullaby, Kitty-Kat," she heard her mother whisper. "Just an old bit of blues about a no-good man."

Katherine's vision blurred, her eyes filling with tears. Not only for Drew but for herself, for the mother who had sung such a mournful song to her child, teaching her that men were no good.

When Drew sang it, though, Katherine felt the pain of the man in the song, not the sorrow of the woman.

Quietly, she pushed the screen door open and joined him at the balcony railing. He fell silent but didn't glance at her—a good thing, since her eyes were still damp. "Sing the rest," she said.

"I've got a lousy voice."

"You have a beautiful voice." She could recall only one voice more beautiful—her mother's. Like her mother, Drew was weeping by singing, opening his heart through the music. Katherine didn't want him to stop. She wanted to stand beside him as he sang, to be close to him while he grieved.

He gave her a long, pensive look, then returned his gaze to the inlaid bricks of the courtyard below them. "And I drink my bourbon and walk from her bed," he sang, "and a piece of my soul, it just dies."

His voice dissolved into the night, haunting her with the power of the words, the loss they conveyed, the anguish they hid. And she felt as if a piece of her soul had just died.

IF ANYONE HAD ASKED HIM why he'd gone to Katherine, he would not have been able to explain. He asked himself, and his answer came to him in the words of that old Cajun song. He had no reason to believe Katherine was lonely like the woman in the ballad, but tonight wasn't about reasons, about logic and rationales. Tonight was about a lovely, wise woman and the man—Drew—who honestly didn't believe he would survive the night without her.

She stood beside him, gazing at the maze of stairs that connected the balconies from floor to floor. "My mother used to sing that song to me," she said.

"Really?" He remembered her telling him that when she was six, she'd lost her mother in an automobile accident. The song must have stirred more sadness in her than in him.

"My mother didn't know too many lullabies," Katherine said.

"That's a ghastly song for a child to hear before she falls asleep."

"I loved it when she sang it to me. She would sit on the edge of my bed and stroke my hair, and then she'd lean toward me, smelling of gardenias, and say, 'That's men for you, Kitty-Kat. They love you and then walk away. They love their liquor more.'" Katherine paused, then shook her head and smiled sadly. "Then my mother would kiss my forehead and walk away from me. Off to find herself her own liquor and one of those men."

"Do you miss her?"

"No." Katherine shrugged. "Maybe, sometimes. I miss what she could have been."

He had noticed her shoulders before, their horizontal rigidity, their solid strength. Tonight they looked fragile, though, more slender bone than muscle. He had learned early in life never to lean on anyone, and he supposed that she must have learned that lesson, too. "I lost my mother," he told her.

"I'm sorry, Drew."

"Not the way you lost yours. She walked out on my father. She took my sister Joanna and moved to California and never came back. Joanna did, but not my mother."

"Why did she only take Joanna?"

"She wanted to take Annabelle, too. But my father played some sort of mind game on her and he got to keep Annabelle in Bayou Beltane."

"And you?"

Drew contemplated his answer. "I refused to go with her. I was so angry with her for leaving. She was rejecting my father, so I rejected her." He stared into the air in front of him, as if he could find answers in the molecules. "Years later, while I was visiting her and her second husband, she told me she'd left because my father had a mistress. Not just an affair, a mistress of long standing." *Flora Boudreaux,* Drew realized with a spasm of pain in his gut. *Jackson's mother, Flora.* Had Drew's mother known that Jackson was Philip's child? Had she known and never told Drew? Had she betrayed him with her silence, as well?

"My mother had a tendency to smother me," he went on, refusing to buckle under the weight of this new insight.

"I was a sickly kid, and my father resented me for that, and my mother doted on me. Her doting only made my father's resentment worse. So when she walked out on us—I know, she was just walking out on my father. But to a young boy, it felt like she was walking out on everything, taking a sledgehammer to our family and leaving the shards behind." He exhaled. If ever a man needed a cigarette, this was the time—and he didn't even smoke. "My loyalties were with my father. I reckon I bet on the wrong horse."

"You were a child. You couldn't have known which side to take. You shouldn't even have been put in that position."

"Shouldn't," he murmured, the word bitter in his mouth. His entire history was compiled of *shouldn'ts.* When Katherine took his hand again, he knew he shouldn't look at her, but he did. When he looked at her, he knew he shouldn't want her. But he did.

If he were his father, he would ignore the *shouldn'ts* and take what he wanted. But he would rather fall on a machete than resemble his father in any way.

He eased his hand from her clasp and closed his eyes so he wouldn't have to see the flicker of hurt in hers. He ached to tell her that he wasn't rejecting her, that if there was any one thing that could make this night endurable, it would be her body, her sex, her deep, throaty sighs, the taste of her tongue in his mouth, the friction of her hands on his skin. It would be her, naked and vulnerable, giving herself to him.

And as she gave, he would take. He would be just like his father.

"I'm not going to touch you," he said abruptly, turning toward the screen door, wondering whether he should grab his suitcase and flee.

Her heard her breath catch. "Fine," she said, the single syllable locked in ice.

If only he could make her understand. "I don't want to hurt you, Katherine."

"Good. I don't want to be hurt." She stalked across the narrow balcony and through the screen door.

Wonderful. By trying not to hurt her, he had hurt her. He was cursed, he truly was. Doomed to be venal and self-centered, just like his father. Just like his brother, Jackson Boudreaux.

Reluctantly, he crossed the balcony and went inside. She was bent over the coffee table, gathering their cups onto the tray. Her hair spilled down around her face like ribbons of flame.

"Katherine—"

"It's late," she said without looking at him. "You've been through a lot. We're both tired." One of the cups rattled against the saucer, as if her hands were trembling when she held it.

He wanted to move closer, to take the rattling cup from her, to take her in his arms. That alone was reason enough for him to remain where he was, on the far side of the sofa. "I don't need you making excuses for me," he said. She straightened up, and the entire tray seemed to be shaking.

He wasn't going to let her drop it, with all those charmingly mismatched pieces of china on it. Two long strides brought him to her. He managed to lift the tray out of her grip without touching her. Before he could say anything more—and insult her even further—he pivoted and carried the tray into the kitchen for her.

"What do you want from me, Drew?" she asked, sounding too close.

Turning, he found her filling the kitchen doorway. She could have been half as tall and she would still present the most formidable barrier he could imagine. He didn't want to go past her. He didn't want to push her aside, or avoid her, or wish her away.

He wanted *her,* and it was a raw, physical, selfish, savage vant. Not the sort of want a man ought to feel for a woman e scarcely knew, a woman who deserved better, a woman vho had let him into her home out of the goodness of her eart.

His heart had no goodness in it. "What I want from ou," he confessed, "is more than I'd ever have a right to sk for."

The blunt answer seemed to take her aback. "Well," she aid, then faltered. "Well, what are you going to do?"

"If it'll make things easier for you, I'll leave."

"And go where? Home?"

"I don't know where my home is anymore," he said. 'Belle Terre isn't my home. The shack on the bayou—"

"You can stay on the couch if you want." She turned nd walked back into the living room, freeing him from the rison of her kitchen. Yet he remained where he was, lisening to her open and close drawers, listening to the vhoosh of cushions being tossed, the creak of old springs nd hinges as she tugged the sofa open into a bed.

He transferred the cups to the sink. From the living room ame the snap of a linen sheet being unfolded, the puff of pillow being jammed into a case. He rinsed the cups.

If he could get through tonight, he would return to Bayou Beltane tomorrow. He would head directly to the office of is brother-in-law, police chief Jake Trahan, show him the utton he'd found in the window frame and demand that ake arrest his detective, Jackson Boudreaux, and turn him ver to the New Orleans police. Who the hell cared if Jackon was Drew's brother? Who cared if Flora Boudreaux, vith her voodoo dolls and her vicious moods, had slept vith Drew's father? Who cared why Philip had wanted Katherine's aunt's diary so badly he told Jackson to steal t? Who cared why Jackson was willing to break laws for Philip?

Drew knew why. He knew what it was like to want a father's love badly enough to commit immoral acts to win it.

And Drew did care. He cared to know why his father had done what he'd done to Katherine's apartment, to Drew's mother and his sisters. And to Drew.

Damn it, if he didn't care he wouldn't be here, looking for comfort from Katherine, aching for something he had no right to want.

How on earth would he endure a night in her living room, knowing she was on the far side of the wall, in her bed? In a nightgown, one of those silky little things like the lingerie he'd found on her floor last night. Her hair rippling across the pillows. Her body warm and lithe, her arms empty, her eyes and her body closed to him. *Lonely and lovely and wise,* he thought.

He would endure it because he had to, because even being so close to Katherine and unable to have her was better than spending another night in the same house with his father.

CHAPTER EIGHT

IN THE MORNING, he was gone.

Whether he'd actually gotten any sleep overnight, Katherine couldn't say. He'd made use of the sofa's fold-out bed, but the linens indicated that he'd had a restless time of it. The sheet she'd so carefully tucked around the corners of the mattress had been tugged loose. The blanket was tangled and the feather pillows lay lumpy and uneven, one at the center of the mattress and the other propped vertical against the sofa cushions. On the coffee table she found a note, written on a page torn from the message pad she kept beside the phone in her kitchen.

Katherine,

I wish I could have stayed to say good-morning. I wish I could have stayed to thank you for tolerating a desperate man in a frantic state of mind. I wish for so many things, and more than a few of them have something to do with you, but perhaps it would be best if I keep my wishes to myself.

This morning the world looks marginally better than it did last night. I have business to attend to, ruins to pick through, wrongs to remedy. By the time you read this, I will have gone back to Bayou Beltane, because running away from home seems like a childish way to deal with my life.

Please accept my gratitude. Someday, perhaps, this

will make sense to you. Someday it might even make sense to me.

Drew.

She reread his letter. His penmanship was a marvel of angles and slashes, his words a marvel of implied emotion.

She read the note yet again. *I wish for so many things, and more than a few of them have something to do with you…* She ached to know what he wished for, what those many things were that had to do with her. Did he wish for her comfort, or her body, or both? Did he wish for her great-aunt's diary to explain his father to him?

In any case, she probably ought to be glad he intended to keep his wishes to himself. She didn't need a man in her life, especially one who had such difficult problems to clear up in his own life. She ought to forget about his wishes—and about him. She ought to forget about his dark, dangerous eyes and his lean body, the sex appeal that emanated from him in potent waves, the pain that stretched his voice into a limber incantation when he sang about leaving a woman's bed and dying a little bit.

She ought to set out to do what she'd been doing all along—keep reading the diary until she was convinced Drew's aunt Mary was really Aunt Claire's mother—and then put the matter to rest.

Her own bed was as rumpled as the sofa bed. Far too aware of the man on the other side of the wall, she'd suffered her share of insomnia last night, and she was going to pay the price today. Two cups of strong black coffee did little to burn off the fog of drowsiness from her brain, and chewing on a croissant seemed like too much effort, so after a couple of bites she tossed the roll into the trash. She donned a simple black skirt and a green sweater set, clipped her hair back from her face with a couple of barrettes, checked the window locks as if she actually believed the landlord's flimsy locks could keep out an intruder, and left for work, dutifully carrying her leather tote with the diary and her translation inside.

The day was mild, almost balmy, and she decided to walk to the shop. She hoped the hum of traffic and the shimmer of sunshine would energize her. By the time she reached Magazine Street, she was feeling moderately animated, despite the fact that the past two nights had been among the most bizarre in her life—nights that had both involved Drew Delacroix.

"You look like hell," Dionne said as Katherine entered the shop. Dionne's affable smile failed to prevent the words from stinging.

Dionne, naturally, looked wonderful. She had on one of her gauzy confections—a flowing skirt paneled in mauve and forest green and a blouse in a busy pattern featuring both those colors. She had gathered her braids at the nape of her neck and tied them with a scarf of the same fabric as the blouse. Her eyes were clear and focused.

"Isn't there a law against telling your best friend the truth before 10:00 a.m.?" Katherine set her tote on the chair behind the rolltop desk. "For the next half hour, I want you to convince me I'm beautiful."

Dionne ignored the request. "What happened? Was there another break-in at your apartment?"

Yes, Katherine almost said. Drew had broken in and ransacked her emotions. "It's just some Delacroix stuff," she answered vaguely. More than wanting Dionne to lie to her, she wanted to lie to Dionne. But lying came no more easily to her than to her friend.

"What kind of Delacroix stuff?" Dionne asked. "What have those folks done to you now?"

"Nothing." In spite of her fatigue, Katherine smiled. "Drew thinks he knows who tried to steal my diary," she added, turning on the computer.

"Really?" That brought Dionne up short. "Who? Why?"

"The *who* part is involved," Katherine answered, still opting for vagueness. "I'd rather not bandy about accusations until Drew knows for sure. As for *why*... I think I'm going to have to finish translating the diary to figure that out."

"Why do I have the feeling," Dionne asked, giving Katherine a canny stare, "that you're translating the diary more for the sake of the Delacroix family than for your aunt Claire?"

"Why do *I* have the feeling you're going to bug me about this until I scream?" Katherine shot back. "Let's drop it, Dionne. We've got customers."

The customers were three robust silver-haired women. It didn't take long for them to reveal that K & D's Antiques had been recommended to them by the proprietor of the bed-and-breakfast where they were staying across the lake. These were the antique-hunting retired teachers Annabelle had told Katherine about.

"My word, look at this glorious cabinet!" one of them squawked, and all three—even the French Provincial fanatic—swooped down on Great-Aunt Patrice's armoire, chattering and gushing over its beauty. Katherine and Dionne exchanged a silent look; Dionne held up one of her hands to show Katherine that she'd crossed her fingers.

After praising it to the skies, the three women analyzed the armoire in the context of their homes' decors, and with great regret concluded that it would not work in any of their houses. Dionne rolled her eyes while Katherine directed the threesome to the back room, where the Depression glass was on display. Two hours and three hundred and eighty dollars later, the retired teachers packed up the trunk of their car with glassware, silver baby spoons and a framed silhouette of a pretty plantation belle with ringlets and a delicate nose.

The armoire remained unsold.

"I've had it," Dionne announced, her indignation balanced by the glint of humor in her eyes. "We have got to break the spell of that damned piece."

"What do you have in mind? A visit to a black-magic practitioner?"

"A visit to your aunt Claire," Dionne declared, lifting her woven straw purse from under the desk.

"Now?"

"It's nearly lunchtime. We're allowed to close for lunch."

"Yes, but—but Aunt Claire is at work."

"It's nearly lunchtime for her, too," Dionne pointed out as she adjusted the hands on the cardboard clock sign they hung in the door when they closed the shop during the day. The sign read Will Reopen At One-Thirty.

Katherine had no objection to visiting Aunt Claire for lunch. She just wasn't sure she was in the right state of mind to behave like a well-mannered niece, not when she was so distracted by thoughts of Drew.

Everything reminded her of him. The slant of the late morning sun. The ache of weariness at the nape of her neck and in her leg muscles, souvenirs of her inability to find sleep last night. The low, fierce pulse of her blood through her body whenever she recalled his eyes, the strong arch of his back, the heartbreak in his smile, the even deeper heartbreak in his voice wrapping itself around a song: *And I drink my bourbon and walk from her bed...and a piece of my soul, it just dies.*

She and Dionne rode the streetcar through the Garden District and west to Tulane University, where Claire Beaufort worked as a reference librarian in the main library. Students swarmed along the paths and across the lawns of the campus, taking advantage of the balmy autumn day The foliage was tinged with gold and copper, and couple walked hand in hand, just a few years younger than Kath erine but seemingly of an entirely different generation.

What was it like to be twenty and in love? she wondered Surely it was much easier than to be twenty-seven an shredded inside, trusting a man, yet distrusting him; exas perated with him, yet longing to ease his sorrows; knowin that to care about him would be a foolish mistake, yet car ing, anyway.

Unable to produce college IDs, Katherine and Dionn were stopped at the library's front desk. They gave Claire' name to the receptionist, and within five minutes Kather ine's aunt appeared in the anteroom, smiling with surprise "What are you two troublemakers doing here?" sh chided.

"We've come to take you to lunch," Dionne announced

Claire didn't argue. She had known Dionne ever sinc Katherine had introduced them nearly a decade ago, whe Katherine and Dionne had befriended each other thei freshman year at Tulane. Like so many other undergradu ates, the two girls had lived in a dormitory and subsiste on pizza and chips. But Claire had always watched ove them, taken them to her flat for home-cooked meals, ad vanced them the occasional ten-dollar loan and, in genera made them feel safe and pampered without lecturing ther too often on the evils of drugs and drinking or the treacher of boys.

Tall, slim and fast closing in on her sixtieth birthday Aunt Claire was the sort of woman people called "hand some." It was a euphemism for plain but dignified, Kath erine believed. Claire's hair had faded from black to slat gray, and her chin had grown pointier, her lips thinnin over the years. There was nothing objectionable in her ap pearance, but nothing striking in it, either. As another pai of obviously lovesick students strolled past, Katherine wondered whether Aunt Claire had ever known love.

Probably not. In her teens, when Katherine became infatuated with boys, swooning over this one and that with barely a minute to catch her breath, she'd often asked Aunt Claire for advice. Aunt Claire was the only mother figure Katherine had, and Katherine had interrogated her relentlessly about sex and romance and the mysteries of love. Claire always seemed one step removed from it all.

"But weren't you ever in love?" Katherine would ask when Claire would give one of her phlegmatic bits of advice about keeping one's head and never letting passion run the show.

"I am not a passionate person," Claire would always reply. "And given what passion did to your mother, I count my blessings."

Claire recommended a coffee shop a block from campus. Over Katherine's and Dionne's protests, she insisted that they would be her guests for lunch. They all ordered po'boys and iced tea, and while they waited for their food to be served, Katherine and Dionne obediently answered all Claire's questions about their health, Dionne's parents and the shop.

The minute their bulging stuffed sandwiches arrived, Dionne took over. "Speaking of the shop, we wanted to talk to you about that armoire that used to belong to your Aunt Patrice."

Claire nodded. "A lovely piece, once you had it refinished."

"We can't sell it," Dionne said.

"Dionne is too impatient," Katherine argued mildly. "I know we'll sell it eventually. It's just that it's a large, expensive piece—not the sort of thing a person would buy on impulse."

"It's haunted," Dionne declared.

Claire's eyebrows rose. She drank some iced tea, then smiled. "I don't truck with that nonsense, Dionne. And you're too sensible to believe such things, either."

Katherine shot Dionne a triumphant grin, but Dionne wasn't discouraged. "It's because of the diary that was hidden inside it," she explained. "Katherine won't let it alone."

At that, Claire rolled her eyes and sighed. "I wish you would, Katherine. *I* don't care about who gave birth to me, for heaven's sake. Brice and Lorraine Beaufort were my parents."

"Aunt Claire..." Katherine set down her sandwich and fixed her aunt with a steady gaze. "Remember I told you some months ago about the Delacroix family, up on the North Shore?"

"Yes. I'd heard of them long before you ever started mentioning them, dear. They're an old, powerful family in Louisiana. And you've become friendly with that young Delacroix woman who runs the bed-and-breakfast."

Katherine nodded. "That young woman's brother thinks you're his cousin."

Claire flinched. She, too, lowered her sandwich, and Katherine noticed a fine tremor in her hand as she reached for her iced tea. "Me? A blood relation of the Delacroix?"

"Drew believes his aunt Mary is your birth mother."

"And this diary Aunt Patrice kept—does it confirm that?"

For once, Katherine actually sensed an interest in Claire about the diary. "I haven't found definitive proof yet. But the birth mother came from a family Judge Alvarez knew, and the family structure seems to match his aunt's generation of the Delacroix family. I don't think Drew would invent something like this. There's so much going on in his life, this is the last thing he'd want to contend with. Yet he's convinced of it. He thinks his father tried to steal the diary, maybe to conceal that his father's sister gave birth to you—''

''Stop.'' Claire's voice was as hard and solid as a slap. ''Why in the world should I—or, for that matter, you—care about what this...this Drew fellow thinks? I don't want to know any of this, Katherine. I know who my parents are. Lorraine and Brice Beaufort.''

''Did she tell you someone broke into her apartment?'' Dionne asked Claire.

''She mentioned it. And she suggested whoever broke in was searching for the diary. But for heaven's sake, there are other reasons someone might have broken in. You know what it's like in that part of town. Some drug addict was probably searching for cough syrup in her medicine cabinet. Or for spare change. Or it could have been a prank. Last year, one of the fraternities made its pledges break into houses, steal a can of beer from the refrigerator and then sneak back out without getting caught.'' She pursed her lips. ''Needless to say, that fraternity is still on probation.''

''I don't believe this was just a prank,'' Katherine argued. ''Neither does Drew.''

''And Drew is all-knowing? He's the supreme expert here?'' Claire scowled.

Katherine felt her cheeks warm. What *was* Drew? Why should she believe so strongly in his theories?

The button. He'd found that button in her window frame. The button had been torn from the jacket of his brother.

''I want to know, Aunt Claire,'' Katherine said quietly. ''I *need* to know. If Drew is wrong, I'll keep going through the diary until I learn the right answer. If you'd rather not know, I won't tell you. But it's something I need to find out.''

Claire's anger seemed to ebb. ''Of course,'' she murmured, reaching across the table to squeeze Katherine's hand. "I wish you didn't need this, but if you do, you do. We all have different needs, I reckon."

Like passion. The thought was so unexpected, so sudden Katherine stifled a gasp. Unlike her aunt, Katherine needed to acknowledge at least one traceable aspect of her genealogy—and she needed passion. Whether it was the wildfire of her mother's blood burning inside her, or simply her aunt's faith that everyone had different needs, Katherine knew she needed passion. She needed that sharp, deep twist of emotion. She needed to be held the way Drew had held her in his office, and to be kissed the way he'd kissed her. She needed to know that kind of fulfillment at least once in her life.

If that meant she was wild and evil, so be it. If it meant she would wind up as her mother had wound up—well, she could only pray she would survive her own passion. Just as she wouldn't lock away her curiosity about Great-Aunt Patrice's diary, Katherine wouldn't lock away her heart.

"WHERE IS JAKE?" Drew asked Annabelle. "I called his office this morning and he wasn't in. I have to talk to him."

Annabelle handed him a pile of folded towels, lifted the second pile stacked on top of the dryer and led the way out of the laundry room, through the kitchen to the supply closet on the second floor of the inn. "He was at a meeting up in Slidell this morning," she told him. "He was coordinating an investigation with their police department. Hand me the towels just a few at a time, please." She arranged her stack of towels on an empty expanse of shelf.

Drew presented her with the top couple of towels, still warm from the dryer. The advantage of Annabelle's being married to Bayou Beltane's police chief was that Drew could discuss his suspicions about Jackson with someone to whom he had a personal connection. The disadvantage was that he couldn't go to the police without his sister learning about it.

"It's nothing important," he lied, handing her another towel. "When will he be back?"

"He's probably back by now." Annabelle took a few more towels from him and frowned. "What's going on, Drew? Have you been drinking?"

"No."

She studied him closely in the shadows of the linen closet. "No," she echoed. "You haven't been drinking. But you look a mess. The rings around your eyes are darker than a raccoon's, and you missed that patch with your razor." She stroked the edge of his jaw near his left ear. He heard her fingernail scratch on the stubble. "Your clothing is rumpled—and it's too casual. You always dress more neatly, even when you aren't working. What's going on?"

"I rushed this morning." And dressed in clothing he'd tossed into his suitcase last night. And shaved in his private bathroom at the office. And nearly sliced his neck open remembering when Katherine had been enclosed in the tiny room with him, gazing up at him with her gemlike eyes and her wistful half smile while he translated scenes about tying a woman with a silk scarf and making her cry out in ecstasy.

"Would you at least tell me what it's about?"

"Jackson," he said, tossing her a bone to chew on.

"Jackson Boudreaux?"

Drew nodded and handed her the last of the towels.

"He's a good-for-nothing. Jake would like more than anything to have him off the force."

"Just one more reason why I've got to see Jake. So, you think he'd be back by now?"

"Drew." Annabelle cupped her hand over his forearm, forcing him to meet her gaze. "What is it? Did Dad do something worse than usual? Or did he have Jackson do it for him?"

"Both." Before he could say anything more, Drew kissed Annabelle's forehead and stalked down the hall to the stairs. Shoving his hand into his pocket, he felt his keys, some loose change and the button he intended to show Jake, Drew's evidence against his brother.

Let Jake tell his wife about Jackson. Drew couldn't do it. He couldn't bear to watch Annabelle's eyes fill with tears of shock and dismay. He couldn't bear to watch her overflow with anger and bitterness. Perhaps selfishly, he couldn't bear to listen to her tell him how wrong he'd been to remain loyal to their father, to continue working in his law firm and living in his house.

Drew already knew his loyalty had turned him into a fool. He couldn't bear to let his sister rub it in.

KATHERINE FOUGHT the late-afternoon rush-hour traffic across the causeway to Bayou Beltane. Perhaps she should have telephoned first to find out if Drew was even in town, let alone at his office. She had with her the ever-present tote, packed with Patrice's diary, the French dictionary that Drew didn't seem to need and the pocket mirror.

She also had his note. In it he'd said he was going back to Bayou Beltane. He'd said he had wrongs to remedy. She prayed that he'd chosen the proper remedies, that he hadn't done anything rash.

If anyone was acting rashly it was Katherine, weaving in and out among the cars clogging the causeway in her dogged journey to Bayou Beltane, to Drew. But ever since Dionne had dragged her off to see her aunt, she'd understood something essential about herself: she was her mother's daughter. The wildness was in her. She'd managed to deny it for twenty-seven years, but she couldn't deny it forever, not as long as Drew was in her life.

She had no idea what she'd do when she saw him. Throw herself into his arms? Ha! If she did that, she'd surely scare him away. Last night he'd been in no condition to think about anyone but himself, anything but his own personal calamity.

Yet he had been thinking of her, and again this morning. He'd been thinking of sparing her his distress by leaving her apartment before she awakened.

And when he'd kissed her... He'd been thinking of her then.

It had nothing to do with love, she reminded herself as she steered off the highway and onto the side road into Bayou Beltane. Love was the last thing she wanted from Drew. He was too mixed-up, his life as tangled as a ball of yarn after a litter of kittens had been at it. But passion... She wanted Drew's passion, just one more tiny taste of it, just enough to know what had made her mother the way she was.

Drew's window wasn't the only one filled with light as she drove down the street past the building that contained his father's law offices. Philip might be in the building, too, and Katherine didn't want to see him. She wondered if Drew could still work side by side with his father when their relationship was such a tortured mess. Philip's behavior and the revelation of his long-held secret had demoralized Drew. How could he continue in the firm?

She parked in the lot around the corner from the front door, climbed out of her car and inhaled the warm air, so much cleaner and sweeter than in New Orleans. If Philip happened to be in and Katherine couldn't avoid him, she would be polite. They'd had dealings; she couldn't shun him, even if he'd broken his son's heart. It wasn't her business to intervene in their strife.

Squaring her shoulders, she crossed the street and entered the building. The receptionist looked up and obviously recognized Katherine. "Mmm...which one do you want to see?" she asked.

Her lack of professional polish caused Katherine to smile. "Drew, please."

"Lucky for you. Philip isn't in." She lifted her phone and pressed a button on her console. "Drew, Katherine Beaufort is here. Would you like me to send her down to your office?"

A long silence ensued. The receptionist swiveled a quarter-turn away from Katherine, the phone pressed to her ear. Katherine didn't know whether Drew was haranguing her for presuming that he'd want to spare a minute for Katherine, or whether he was weighing his decision. With each passing second, Katherine grew more anxious.

She tried to signal the receptionist that she was going to leave. Who had she been kidding, imagining herself prepared for any activity resembling passion, especially with a man like Drew? How could she believe he would want to waste an ounce of energy on her? He'd run to her last night because he hadn't been thinking. Now he was thinking.

Unable to catch the receptionist's eye, she backed slowly toward the exit. The receptionist suddenly rotated forward in her chair and lowered the phone. "He says you can go to his office," she said solemnly.

Her grave expression didn't bode well. Katherine should have fled, but that would be cowardly, so she took another deep breath, squared her shoulders again and nodded to the receptionist. Then she walked down the hall to Drew's office, rapped lightly on the door and eased it open.

He stood at his desk, his gaze locked on her as she filled the doorway. His hair was as mussed as it had been yesterday, his eyes shadowed. He had on the same faded blue jeans he'd worn to her place last night, but she knew he must have washed at some point during the day, because the hint of beard darkening his jawline appeared only about eight hours old. And he'd changed his shirt. This one was pale blue, with his initials monogrammed above the pocket. He had no tie, and his sleeves were rolled up a few turns.

If she hadn't been so distracted by his gaze, by the enigmatic curve of his lip— Was it a smile? Was he happy to see her?—and the lean contours of his torso, she might have contemplated the strangeness of his dressing so casually for work. But perhaps he hadn't been working. Perhaps he'd come to the office to clean out his things, or to confront his father, or to...*pick through the ruins,* as his note to her had put it.

His eyes mesmerized her. They held a warning and a promise, and she wasn't sure she should heed the warning or accept the promise.

"Maybe I shouldn't have come," she said.

"It doesn't matter. You came." As simple as that.

She stepped into the office and closed the door quietly. She remained near it, though, just in case she needed to beat a swift retreat. "Are you all right?"

"I've reported your break-in to Annabelle's husband," he told her, eluding her personal question. "He's the chief of police."

She nodded. "I know."

"I showed him the button from Jackson Boudreaux's jacket, and he said he'd question Jackson. I don't know if he's done that yet. Jackson's been off work for a few days. He's been running a lot of errands for my father, now that the election is approaching." Drew's voice was flat and impassive. That this Jackson Boudreaux was his half brother, his father's secret child, didn't register in his tone.

It registered in his eyes, though. Shadows swirled in them like leaves in a breeze, mottling the light.

"Have you talked to your father?" she asked.

He laughed without smiling. "And told him what? That he's a son of a bitch? He already knows that."

"But—" She faltered, unsure of whether she had the right to question him. He'd come to her last night, though. He'd brought his pain to her, and she'd accepted it. That gave her certain rights. "Have you moved back into your house?"

"No." His eyes grew darker yet.

She wanted to cross the office to him, but she sensed little welcome in him. "Have you talked to Joanna or Annabelle?"

"Not about Jackson."

"Drew." More deep breaths. More squaring of shoulders. And then she dared to stride toward him. "Drew, what are you going to—"

The sudden sound of shattering glass froze her where she stood. Behind Drew, the window splintered into a thousand shards as a rock came flying through. Before she could scream, Drew was next to her, pressing her against the wall by the door, shielding his body with hers. The rock ricocheted off the back of his chair and hit the carpeted floor.

"Drew—"

He covered her mouth with his hand. His body was large and strong against hers. She heard his respiration, unnaturally slow and even as he glanced over his shoulder at the window. Something else came flying through the jagged hole in the pane. Katherine caught only a vague glimpse of something white and oddly shaped soaring into the office.

Turning back to her, Drew pressed her harder into the wall, pressed himself harder into her, pressed his hand more firmly against her mouth.

The object fell to the floor with a muffled thud. Drew's breaths grew deeper, steadier. But his heart was pounding.

She felt it through his shirt, through her sweater, felt its rapid drumbeat. Hers beat in the same crazed tempo.

Neither of them moved for a long time. They only stood there, snug against the wall, facing each other, eyeing each other above Drew's silencing hand. Katherine tasted his touch on her lips.

At last he relented, let his hand drop and took a step back. Without him holding her, she felt wobbly, but she willed her legs steady. She wasn't going to stumble and swoon in front of him.

"What was it?" she whispered. Fear froze her vocal cords.

He gazed at her for a moment longer, as if to assure himself that she was safe, and then stalked across the room. She followed cautiously, halting when she reached his desk and saw the floor on the other side strewn with bits of razor-sharp glass. Drew walked straight through it and hunkered down next to the pale object that had followed the rock through the window.

It was a cloth doll, lumpy but clearly designed to resemble a human. The face and hands were a pink shade, the legs tipped in black, and the body had the outline of a white blazer and trousers inked onto it. At the neck was a small brown bow, resembling one of Philip's dapper bow ties. A mouth had been drawn on the face, a bright red O, and the eyes were also round and gray.

Protruding from the doll's chest, exactly where its heart would be, was a sharp silver pin.

CHAPTER NINE

DREW COULDN'T CARE LESS about the doll. It was the damned broken window that bothered him.

And then he raised his eyes to Katherine, and he forgot all about the window.

She was pale, her eyes round, her lower lip caught in her teeth. "Don't touch it," she whispered, glancing at the doll only long enough to let him know what she was referring to.

He would never have figured her for someone who gave credence to witchcraft. She seemed much too sensible, a bit obsessed about her roots but otherwise solid. Not the sort to be traumatized by a silly prank.

"There could be glass on it," she explained. "You might cut yourself."

He let out a long breath and straightened up. So she wasn't spooked by a bit of voodoo. She was pallid and wide-eyed because she was worried about the broken glass—or, if he let himself believe it, because she was worried about him.

"I'd better call a glazier," he murmured, staring down at the doll. When he moved his head he noticed glints on its surface, tiny slivers of glass. Katherine had protected him from cuts, all right.

"A glazier?" She frowned. "Don't you want to call the police?"

"No."

"Someone hurled a rock through your window." She

pointed to the fist-size stone lying on the carpet, as if she felt he needed proof.

"Someone hurled a rock through my window so she could hurl that doll through my window."

"She?"

"Or he." But Drew suspected what his father did: Flora Boudreaux was behind the voodoo stunts that had been plaguing Philip for months. The police—Jake—had already been called about a couple of past incidents at Belle Terre, and Flora was at the top of their suspects list. If word of this got around, Philip—and by extension the old man's reelection campaign—would become the butt of bad jokes. Not that Drew should care, but old habits died hard.

Drew wondered whether Flora's badgering of his father was in some way related to the intimacy they'd shared so many years ago, whether Flora was trying to get at Philip because of Jackson. Did she want Philip to acknowledge Jackson publicly as his son? All the voodoo dolls in the world wouldn't scare him into jeopardizing his position that way.

Drew walked to his desk, bits of glass crackling against the soles of his shoes, and lifted the telephone receiver. He punched a button, waited, and then spoke. "Darlin', could you call a window repair service? I've got a broken window here." Before his receptionist could question him, he hung up.

He thought to reassure Katherine with a smile, but when his gaze found hers he couldn't smile. She looked so solemn, so indignant. So unexpectedly beautiful, with all that fiery hair rippling around her face and her pugnacious chin thrust forward. Drew had never been particularly taken by compliant, docile women. At the moment, *compliant* and *docile* were the last words he'd use to describe Katherine's attitude.

"Do you have enemies?" she asked.

At that he laughed. "Are there snakes in the bayou?"

"Then who do you think did this? Which enemy?"

Ignoring her earlier warning, he plucked the doll from its bed of broken glass and shook it off. The seams were crookedly stitched and the details as clumsy as the work of a toddler, but he had no doubt whom the doll was supposed to represent. Drew hadn't worn a bow tie since his senior prom.

"It's my father," he said.

"Your father did that?" She gestured toward the broken window.

"My father was the target. Whoever did this picked the wrong window, that's all."

"I imagine he has even more enemies than you."

Drew shrugged. As the shock of this black-magic bombardment wore off, he realized he didn't want to think about his father. He wanted to think about the way Katherine had felt in his arms just minutes ago, her back pressed into the wall and her front pressed into him. He wanted to think about what it would be like to make love to her against a wall, standing up.

"Drew, this could all be connected," she continued earnestly. "First my apartment is broken into, and now this criminal act here...."

"No." He dropped the doll onto his blotter, then circled around the desk to her. He took her hand in his—not because he was aching to touch her but because he didn't want her succumbing to paranoia, chasing conspiracy theories. "Someone's been sending my father little voodoo calling cards for a while. This was just the latest. It has nothing to do with your apartment."

"How can you be sure?"

"Does anyone know you're here?" he asked. Her hand was icy in his.

She gazed down at their hands, as if she had also noticed

the difference in temperature. "Just the receptionist. Unless..." Her voice faltered.

Her hair was too close to him. Close enough that he could see the varying hues of it, gold and russet and pale brown, like leaves turning in autumn. Close enough that he could see the convoluted curl and twirl of each strand. Close enough that he could smell her hair, smell her, fill his lungs with her soft, feminine scent.

"Unless what?" he murmured.

"Unless someone followed me here." She lifted her face, depriving him of his close view of her hair but rewarding him with her eyes, as bright and luminous as sunlight reflecting off the water. He was so mesmerized by the glitter in them, he almost forgot to pay attention to what she'd said.

Unless someone followed her here. And why shouldn't someone have followed her? His father wanted that blasted diary. If he would send Jackson to tear apart her flat in New Orleans, why wouldn't he have someone follow her?

Drew honestly didn't think the doll had anything to do with Katherine. But of course she could have been followed. Especially in Bayou Beltane, where the man who wanted her diary, the man who obviously feared its contents, could easily have tracked her to this office.

"We'd better get out of here," Drew said, abruptly releasing her and turning back to his desk. He gathered the papers he'd been going through, and the doll, and stashed them in a deep drawer of his desk, which he locked. His father didn't have a copy of the key.

Ah, what a fine father-son relationship they had, Drew thought bitterly, glancing over his shoulder at the lock he'd installed on the door separating his father's office from his own. What a marvelous family it was, when a son would exert himself so mightily to keep his father locked out.

After a quick check of all the desk drawers to make sure

they were locked, he returned to Katherine, touched his hand to her elbow and ushered her to the door, snatching his leather jacket from the coat tree on his way. "Where are we going?" she asked in a hushed voice.

"Shh." He hurried her down the hall to the entry, where he paused to speak to the receptionist. "If someone comes for the window, have them take the measurements for a new pane and then board it up. We've got to leave."

"Okay," she said with a worried smile. She appeared on the verge of questioning him further, but he denied her the chance by hustling Katherine through the door and outside.

The sky was still pale with late-afternoon light. Drew held her under the overhang, in the door's shadow, and stepped forward to survey the street. Maybe her paranoia was contagious, because he shared her concern that she might have been followed. He glimpsed the bulky leather tote, her hand fisted around the straps, and then scrutinized the street again. No sign of his father, Jackson or any of the other lackeys Philip had at his beck and call.

Drew took Katherine's free hand and sprinted with her around the corner to the parking lot. "My car—" she began.

"Leave it." He opened the passenger door of his coupe and helped her onto the low seat. "If someone's following you, they'll see your car parked here and assume you're in the vicinity." He climbed in behind the wheel, revved the engine and shot out of the lot.

"Where are we going?" she asked again.

"To my cabin," he said, flicking his gaze toward the rearview mirror. In the downtown district at rush hour, with cars swarming along the streets as lazily as no-see-ums in the summer, it would be hard to tell if anyone was following his sports car, but once he reached the empty back roads, he would know if someone was on his tail, or Katherine's.

He wondered what stick of dynamite might be hidden in her aunt's diary to make his father—or anyone else—want to follow her. He wondered whether she was being followed at all, or whether her words had triggered an overreaction in him. He wondered whether the voodoo doll *had* been intended to scare him rather than Philip, whether Flora actually thought she could scare him as much as she'd scared his father. He wondered what he could have had in mind when he'd resolved to take Katherine to his ramshackle cabin on the bayou.

He knew what he had on his mind: her hair, her eyes, the feel of her body tight against his...and the narrow bed in the cabin.

He told himself to think about something else, fast.

"Maybe we ought to translate some more of that diary," he said.

"Maybe." Next to him, she seemed to unwind a little. She loosened her hold on the tote's handle and stretched her legs beneath the glove compartment. "I shouldn't have come to you," she murmured, staring resolutely through the windshield at the blurring scenery. "I don't know why I did."

He glanced briefly at her. Her profile was delicately etched, her hair a cloud of curls that contrasted with the sharpness of her nose and chin, the elegance of her cheekbones. The way she kept her head motionless, her eyes carefully avoiding his made him suspect that she knew exactly why she'd come.

He wished her reason was as clear to him as his own—and he wished his reason for welcoming her arrival wasn't what it was. He had no right to sweep her off to his cabin, where she wouldn't be able to escape him. Where they would be enclosed within those snug walls, surrounded partly by snake- and alligator-infested water and partly by jungle-dense woods. Without light or heat. With nothing but a few pieces of furniture including that blasted bed, and Katherine's great-aunt's diary, and its descriptions of hot, hard sex.

How had this happened? How had Drew become so obsessed with Katherine? She wasn't his type—except that when he tried to remember the kind of woman who *was* his type, he thought of a tall, slim, headstrong woman with fire in her eyes, a woman who came to him and pretended she didn't know why. A woman who didn't want him to cut himself on razor shards of glass.

The car had left the town center for a two-lane blacktop. Drew checked the rearview mirror again. No one.

"I think we're safe," he said, knowing damned well that the way he was feeling toward her was anything but safe for either of them.

She twisted in her seat to glance out the back window. Then she twisted back and sank into the upholstery. "You know who threw that voodoo doll into your office, don't you."

The sun blushed, a soft red sphere lighting the treetops as it dropped below the forest that flanked the horizon. "I've got an idea," he allowed. "Maybe we could go visit her. She lives with her mother on another part of the bayou."

"Who is she?"

"Jackson's mother," he said, trying not to choke on the words.

Katherine sat taller and looked directly at him. "Why would she be harassing your father?"

The idea of Flora Boudreaux's link to him made him feel physically ill, even after he'd had twenty-four hours to get used to it. "We could ask her."

"Will she answer if we do?"

He laughed sourly. "Who the hell knows what she'll do? Her mother, Desiree, is a good woman, but Flora is a nasty piece of work. She won't tell us anything she doesn't want to. But—'' he switched on his headlights as the sky faded to a velvety blue ''—if she's out to get my father and I tell her I'm not on my father's side, she might talk to me. The enemy of my enemy and all that.''

Katherine lapsed into silence. He rolled his window down an inch so he could listen to the wind. The scents of warm earth and dying leaves wafted into the car and mingled with Katherine's fragrance.

''Maybe,'' she said abruptly, her gaze once again fixed on the road ahead, ''I came here for the same reason you came to me last night, and I came to you the night before.''

He sighed. He still hadn't figured out why he'd gone to her, except that it had seemed like the only safe, sane thing he could do. Last night, when the ground was heaving and splitting into chasms beneath his feet, he had known she would offer him shelter, a place where he might take a step or two without losing his footing.

Had the ground shifted beneath her, as well? ''If you're looking to me for stability,'' he warned, ''you came to the wrong man.''

She chuckled but still refused to look at him. ''I know, Drew. Believe me, I know.'' She brushed a wind-tossed curl of hair back from her face. ''I hinted to my aunt Claire today that she might have Delacroix blood in her.''

''That must have thrilled her to tears.''

''She didn't take it badly. She was mostly just stunned.'' Katherine absently ran her fingers along the straps of her tote. ''I'd love to be able to find proof one way or the other, to put her mind at ease.''

''If she finds out she's a Delacroix, I doubt it's going to put her mind at ease.'' He eyed her skeptically. ''Your mind, maybe. Hers? Not likely.''

''Don't you think there could be one of those great, passionate reunions if we brought my aunt Claire and your aunt Mary together? I've read about birth children finding their birth mothers. Sometimes it's a beautiful thing."

"I would have considered it much more beautiful not to know about my birth brother," he muttered.

"Would you?"

No, he thought. Ignorance wasn't bliss. In his life, in his family, ignorance was doubt. Knowing was better than not knowing, even if knowing hurt like broken glass grinding in his heart.

Up ahead on the side of the road stood a small convenience store. Drew pulled into the unpaved lot and turned off the engine. "Do you want to wait in the car?"

"What are you getting?"

"Supper."

She unfastened her seat belt and climbed out.

In the shop they bought cellophane-wrapped sandwiches and bottles of soda pop. The bottles of bourbon and whisky lining the shelf behind the cashier's counter caught Drew's eye, but he resisted the temptation. He'd learned long ago that there wasn't enough liquor in the world to get him drunk, and tonight he was going to need a sharp, clear mind. Even the thinnest cushion against reality might make him forget who he was, who Katherine was, what they were running toward, and what truths might be awaiting them when they finally got where they were going.

He added a bag of pretzels and two Bosc pears to the pile of food on the counter and responded tersely to the garrulous clerk, who seemed far too eager to get a conversation going.

"Gonna be chilly tonight, don't you think?" the girl chattered. "There's a real nip in the air. You can tell winter's just around the corner."

With a nod, Drew collected his change and the bag full of food, thanked the clerk and beckoned Katherine out of the store.

"How will we get to this woman's house?" she asked once they were settled back in the car. "Flora, you said? Can we drive there?"

"We'll rent a boat. My cousin Remy runs a swamp-tour business on the bayou. We can rent a boat from him."

"Do you want your cousin knowing?" she asked.

"Knowing what?"

She frowned, piecing together a reply. "About the broken window and the voodoo doll."

"No need to discuss it."

She let out a long breath, then mustered her courage. "Do you want him knowing that you're bringing me to your cabin?"

He sent her a quick, assessing look. What exactly were her expectations about this trip? Did she know what he imagined whenever he thought about having her alone in his cabin? Was she imagining the same thing?

No. She was thinking only about voodoo and her diary, her aunt's legacy and Philip's eagerness to steal the book before she found out what that legacy was. And maybe she was thinking about Drew's brother, and Drew's safety, and the shattered glass on his office rug.

A few threads of light basted the dusk sky together as he steered into the parking lot beside the building housing his cousin Remy's Willow Island Swamp Tours. While he gathered the bag containing their dinner, Katherine climbed out of the car and surveyed the nearly empty lot. The air was heavy with the scent of murky water and dense foliage, a smell Drew knew better than he knew the floral fragrances of the gardens surrounding Belle Terre. The perfume of the bayou was warm and musky, a green, shadowy fragrance that made his cabin hideaway even more precious to him. Remy knew Drew had a place somewhere on one of the waterways, but Drew had never told him where. He didn't share his place with anyone.

Yet he was going to share it with Katherine. Because he was afraid for her, he told himself. Because he wanted to solve the mystery of her great-aunt's diary before his father stole the damned thing. Because he could no longer remain calm in the face of so many lies. Because he hoped the truth might bring him peace.

Nothing more than that, he silently vowed. Bringing Katherine to the cabin was nothing more than a search for the truth.

He locked his car and ushered her through the gift shop, where Remy ran his swamp-tour business. Remy wasn't there, but his assistant, Claudia, stood behind the counter, running up a credit-card sale for a customer. She glanced up at Drew, smiled in recognition, and then finished dealing with the customer.

Drew waited for the man to leave before approaching the counter. "Can I bother you for a boat?" he asked, setting the bulky paper bag on the counter and digging into his hip pocket for his wallet.

Claudia eyed Katherine, then turned back to Drew. "Overnight?"

He smiled thinly. "I reckon that depends on how bright the moon is." Boating through the narrow runs, some of them choked with marsh grass, others harboring alligators, wasn't an activity Drew cared to perform without adequate light to guide him. If he couldn't make it from his cabin back to Remy's dock before dawn, it wouldn't be because he wanted to spend the night with Katherine. What he wanted with her could occur as easily at high noon as at midnight's darkest moment.

And what he wanted with her wasn't going to happen in any case. The stress fractures undermining his life would only get worse if he added lust to the mix.

They would translate the diary. Eat their sandwiches. Maybe track down Flora, who lived with her mother on a different branch of the bayou, and see if she might be able to explain the doll that had flown through his office window less than an hour ago.

Claudia passed him a rental form to complete and processed his credit card. The paperwork took only a couple of minutes. Claudia knew better than to banter with Drew. She was a pleasant enough young lady, but Drew suspected she was somewhat intimidated by him. Whenever he stopped by Remy's place for a boat, he was rarely in the mood to make chitchat with anyone. In general, he headed for the cabin to get away from society, not to indulge in conversation. The cabin was his retreat.

He signed the charge slip, pocketed his receipt and accepted a key from Claudia. "Take number four," she said. "It's at the end of the dock. Easier to get out."

Drew thanked her, hoisted the bag of food into his arms and motioned with a nod for Katherine to follow him. They left the gift shop and strolled down the dock to boat number four, a sleek aluminum craft with an outboard motor. Drew helped Katherine down into the bow, then passed her the bag. He untied the ropes, leaped lightly into the boat and ignited the outboard motor. He kept the throttle low even after they were well clear of the dock.

He wasn't in a huge hurry to reach the cabin. Once they arrived, he would be alone with her, in the lingering twilight, with only a few sandwiches and the diary to distract him. The longer the trip took, the more time he would have to breathe in the humid evening air, to let the damp breezes wash over his face, cleansing him, cooling him down.

She sat in the path of his vision, as if she were his landmark, the goal he was aiming for. Her hair rippled in the wind as the boat glided through the water, and her eyes were bright, taking in the scenery. She let one hand trail through the water, her fingers sifting through the current and sending twirling eddies back to the stern.

"Keep your hands in the boat," he cautioned her. "There are hungry creatures with sharp teeth living in the bayou."

She jerked her hand out of the water. Her eyes glittered silver and her hand shimmered with moisture. She said nothing, only smiled slightly. "Maybe I'd have been better off on dry land," she said. "Even if your father was on my tail."

"My father's more dangerous than a gator," Drew told her, not bothering to add that she might have been safer with his father *or* a gator than with him.

No. He wasn't going to think that way. He'd spent most of his life learning to control himself. He hadn't been born an athlete, but he'd built himself into one through discipline and willpower. He'd learned to ignore his doubts, to swallow his anger, to lock all his unanswered needs into a little box and store them in the cellar of his soul. Sometimes his control would slip, and he would drink too much, rage too much, need to run away to the cabin until he'd regained his grip on himself. But he wasn't going to loosen his hold, not tonight. Not with Katherine.

The house Flora shared with her mother loomed into view around a bend in the bayou. Odd blossoms and twigs hung drying in clusters from a clothesline strung across the porch. Desiree Boudreaux was a practitioner of the healing arts, using her herbs and potions to cure folks of whatever they didn't trust with their doctors. But Desiree's daughter practiced other arts, black arts that had nothing to do with healing.

The old woman sat on a rocking chair on her porch, her hair tied beneath a colorful scarf and her bird-thin body wrapped in a shapeless dress. Well past ninety years old, Desiree appeared ageless, her eyes sharp, her skin dry in the balmy evening. Late October was a pleasant time to enjoy the night on the bayou. The frogs still sang, but mosquitoes and gnats no longer hovered like blood-thirsty clouds above the water, and the air no longer carried the oppressive wet heat of summer.

Desiree's gaze fell upon the boat as Drew steered it close to her dock. "Is that you, Drew Delacroix?" she asked without standing.

"It's me." He throttled the engine down to idle. "Is Flora home?"

"What do you want with her?" Desiree's voice lilted; her gaze was incisive, cutting through the thickening gloom.

"Just to talk." To ask her how she could have produced a son with his father. To ask her why, since Philip had fathered her son, she was pestering him with her silly voodoo stunts. To demand answers, to tell her he was on a quest for the truth and he wasn't going to let her stand in his way.

"She's not here," Desiree said, leaning forward in her chair, her feet flat against the porch planks. "Who's that with you?"

"A friend."

Even in the twilight, he could see Desiree's frown as she assessed Katherine, who sat motionless in the boat's bow seat, her hands folded in her lap and her eyes shuttling expectantly between Desiree and Drew. "I didn't know you had any friends," Desiree taunted.

Drew laughed, despite his suspicion that Desiree wasn't joking. She had been connected to his family and this bayou for longer than Drew had been alive, and he accepted her words as he would those of a loving but critical grandmother. "All right, then," he conceded. "She's not a friend. She's a foe. Desiree, allow me to introduce you to my foe, Katherine Beaufort. Katherine, this is Desiree Boudreaux."

"How do you do?" Katherine called politely across the

few feet of water that separated the boat from Desiree's rocking chair.

"He could be trouble," Desiree warned her, gesturing toward Drew with a gnarled hand. "His father is trouble."

"I'm not my father and he isn't me," Drew interjected, "any more than you are your daughter or your daughter is you."

Desiree couldn't argue with that. She turned back to Katherine, her eyes narrowing, darkening. "I've heard about you," she said. "The red-haired lady who asks questions."

Katherine pursed her lips. She might have heard unspoken condemnation in Desiree's words. "She asks good questions," Drew said, defending Katherine. "Do you know when Flora will be back?"

"That's not a good question," Desiree retorted. "I don't know. Why do you want her?"

Something hardened in Drew's chest, chilling into stone. "My father told me about Flora," he said. "He told me about Jackson. I know, Desiree. I know that much of the truth."

"Then you know enough."

"No. I need to know the rest."

"You won't find answers here," she said, shoving herself to her feet with a strength that belied her age.

"Flora is sending voodoo dolls to my father. She broke a window—"

"Whatever is broken in your life, Drew Delacroix, your father broke it." Desiree sounded weary all of a sudden, her voice weighed down with her years. "Your father broke it," she repeated, then turned and stalked into her cabin. The door snapped shut behind her, leaving only the chair, now still, and the drying herbs swaying on the string above it.

As he reached for the throttle, Drew glimpsed Katherine

staring at him. Living up to her reputation, the red-haired lady asked a question. "So you really believe it was Jackson's mother who threw that voodoo doll into your office?"

"I'm certain it was her."

"But why would she do that?"

He shifted the engine into gear, keeping the speed low so the motor's rumble wouldn't overpower their voices. "The more I know," he admitted, "the more I realize I don't know."

"You aren't going to find anything about Jackson and Flora and voodoo in Patrice's diary."

"What makes you so sure of that?" He steered across the river, navigating through marsh grass and feeling his eyes adjust to the encroaching night.

"It was written sixty years ago. Long before any of this happened with your father and Flora."

"You heard Flora's mother," Drew reminded her. "Whatever's broken, my father broke it. He probably started breaking things more than sixty years ago."

"You think my aunt Claire's adoption had to do with Flora? I don't understand." She sounded utterly bemused.

"I don't understand, either," he assured her, finding the branch in the bayou that he was looking for and piloting the boat down it, away from the part of the swamp where Desiree lived with her daughter Flora, away from his cousin's boat rental business and into a more remote section of the bayou, the region where his shack stood, where no one could find him. The precious, private part of his world that he'd never shared with anyone.

He would share it tonight, with Katherine. She would share her diary and its secrets with him, and he would share his cabin and its secrets with her. And maybe, somehow, some of the countless questions that plagued both of them would lead to answers, and another piece of the truth would make itself felt.

CHAPTER TEN

SHE WASN'T SURE WHAT she'd expected. Electricity, at least.

There was no electricity in Drew's cabin. The only light they had came from a kerosene lamp on the table at the center of the tiny single room, the only warmth from a propane space heater, which he'd turned to the lowest setting.

Sitting in the rustic darkness with him was like drifting into a dream. The entire evening—from the moment she'd climbed into her car after work and headed north across the causeway for no better reason than that she had to see Drew—had felt like a dream. The broken window, the doll, the journey to the lake, the boat ride to that exotic old woman's house, and now here…

All a dream. A strange, potent reverie in which her body was energized not by oxygen and the nutrients in the sandwich she was eating but by passion, by the hope of learning things she'd never even considered before.

"Does Desiree Boudreaux know you well?" she asked.

Seated across the narrow table from her, his face glazed with a layer of amber from the lamp burning between them, Drew reached for his can of soda. "She knew me before I was born."

Because it was too dark to look at anything else in the cabin, Katherine looked at Drew. She studied the angles of his face, the sinew shaping his forearms, the ridge of his knuckles, the muscles in his neck moving as he took a sip of his drink and swallowed. "She knew my father. She knew my grandfather."

"Was she teasing you, or does she really have a low opinion of you?"

A dry laugh escaped him. "The latter."

For some reason, Katherine wasn't surprised. Nor did she expect him to defend himself or ridicule the woman's judgment. "Why does she think poorly of you?"

He settled back, the joints of his wooden chair creaking slightly. Through the thin, cracked walls of the cabin she could hear a contrapuntal chorus of frogs and crickets and the rhythmic lapping of water against the dock that extended out from the shack. "She has her reasons," he said cryptically.

Before tonight, Katherine might not have cared what those reasons were. But everything was different now. The dream seemed more laden with truth than anything that had come before. "What might those reasons be?" she pressed him.

He swallowed another drink of soda, then set down his can and eyed her in the golden light. "I was Philip's son," he said. "I supported my father. I stood by him."

"Surely a man can't be condemned for that."

"It depends on who his father is. In this instance, anyone who would support a man like Philip Delacroix doesn't deserve much respect." He sighed, shifted again and scowled as the decrepit chair whined beneath his weight. "Besides that, I drank too much."

Katherine pursed her lips. She had heard about his drinking from Annabelle and his cousins. She'd seen evidence of it on an occasion or two. His indulgence in alcohol had always made her uneasy, probably because her own mother had had a weakness for that particular poison. "I notice you're talking about it in the past tense."

"Yes."

"You've stopped drinking?"

"I quit."

She supposed the shock he'd had would be enough to drive a sober person to drink—or a drinking person to sobriety. "Just like that?" she asked. "Cold turkey?"

"I'm not an alcoholic, Katherine. I drank too much, but I don't have the chemistry for addiction. I'm not going through withdrawal now."

She hadn't expected him to speak so frankly. But why not? Things between her and Drew had changed drastically over the past several days. He was a man who had sung a Cajun lullaby in her presence. Who had revealed the truth about his father to her. Discussing his body chemistry with her didn't seem so odd.

A light wind tested the walls of the cabin. Katherine couldn't feel it seeping inside, but a draft caused the flame tipping the lantern's wick to shiver inside its glass chimney. "This isn't exactly the sort of abode one associates with the Delacroix family," she said.

"That's probably why I like it." Drew stood, gathered the wrappings from their sandwiches and tossed the trash into a small wastebasket beside the narrow cast-iron cot that stood against one wall. The mattress was made up with linens, a woolen blanket and two plump feather pillows. Katherine wondered how often Drew slept here, whether he could sleep more soundly on that cot than on the sofa bed in her apartment.

She shouldn't be wondering about him in the context of beds at all. The restless curiosity stirring awake inside her would best stay where it was. She had come to Bayou Beltane tonight because something bound her and Drew together. She had wanted his passion, but she knew now that it would be a mistake.

"I don't know how we're going to read the diary," she

said, clinging to the most obvious thing that bound them together. "It's so dark in here."

"After a while you get used to the dark," he assured her, lifting a round mirror from a nail on the wall and carrying it to the table. He propped the mirror on its frame and glanced at Katherine. "Should we get started?"

She pulled the diary from her tote, handed it to him and reached back inside for her dictionary and the notebook in which she recorded the translations. "I still don't see why your father would have tried to steal the diary."

"Maybe tonight we'll find out," Drew said, opening the book to the page marked by the ribbon. He pulled his chair around the table to sit beside her, then adjusted the mirror and the lantern. And began to read, haltingly, hesitantly, patiently.

Next to him, Katherine leaned toward the lantern and wrote down every word he read.

"'*L'ENFANT EST NÉE,*'" he said, then translated. "'The baby is born.'"

Several hours had passed. Night had drawn tight around the cabin, blacking out the windows, muting the shrill song of the crickets. The lantern burned bravely on the table in front of Drew and Katherine. He'd been right; she'd grown used to the lack of light.

She'd grown used to Drew's voice, as well, his low, husky baritone murmuring passages, stumbling over them, wrestling with the French, struggling with Great-Aunt Patrice's contorted, inverted penmanship. Katherine had grown used to the sight of his wrists and elbows, exposed where he'd rolled up his sleeves, and the thick shock of hair that fell stubbornly across his brow. She'd grown used to the scratching of her pen on the lined pages of her note-pad.

For some reason, their dark, cramped quarters seemed

conducive to translating a diary. In the gloom, Drew could read Patrice's hyperventilating prose about her lovemaking with Judge Alvarez, and Katherine could remain reasonably poised. Maybe it was because, with only the lantern's limited illumination, Drew couldn't see her blushing. Perhaps the absence of light protected her. Perhaps the primitive nature of the cabin stripped away the need for false courtesy, leaving little room for bashfulness.

Or perhaps the same impulse that had compelled her to drive across the river to Bayou Beltane tonight had drained her of her inhibitions. Let Drew read whatever her great-aunt had written. She and Drew were archeologists on a dig, searching for what lay beneath the layers of words. Somewhere in the pages of Patrice's diary they would find the relic they were seeking, the irreplaceable shard of terra-cotta, the ancient utensil, the ultimate bone.

"'Neville wants only to make love. I want to talk about the baby,'" Drew read, his voice filling the still air. "'He says no, he will not talk until he has first loved me. I can think of nothing else except that my sister, Lorraine, may have a child. But Neville will not talk. So I let him have his way with me.'"

A chill wrenched Katherine's shoulders. Had her great-aunt Patrice actually given her body to the judge in order to get a baby for her sister? In other passages, Patrice had clearly enjoyed making love with Neville. But in this excerpt, the act seemed so brutal and self-serving that tears burned Katherine's eyes.

"'He is *fâché,*'" Drew recited. "'Angry. He is *très fâché* because I cannot think of anything but the baby. He turns my back to him so he does not have to see my face.' What a bastard," Drew muttered.

"I don't think there's any point in trying to comprehend the dynamics of their relationship," Katherine observed. "The whole thing was so—I don't know."

"Cruel."

"They used each other," Katherine pointed out. "She wanted to get that baby, so she let him do what he wanted."

"He's still a bastard," Drew said, tilting the book and peering into the mirror. "'When at last he is done,'" Drew read, "'he holds me in his arms and tells me this woman whose family he knows has given birth to a little girl. The woman's father wishes for Neville to find a home for the baby.'" Drew swore under his breath.

"You don't know it's the Delacroix," Katherine reminded him. Her neck was stiff, her hand cramped from scribbling so many pages of translation. "You still don't know that the woman who gave birth is your aunt Mary."

"Alvarez had a long association with my grandfather, my whole family. They were all thick as thieves, Katherine. Everything else we've read points to this."

"Except for the fact that you don't know Mary ever had a baby."

Drew scrubbed his hands through his hair, shoving it off his face. As soon as he lowered his hands, the hair tumbled back onto his brow. He ignored it and resumed his perusal through the mirror. "'When Neville is done with sex, he always talks. On and on. *Incessant.* I let him talk. I know that now he has had me, he will tell me everything I need to know about the baby.'"

Drew paused to let Katherine catch up. Her pen darted across the page, capturing every word.

"'He tells me he still thinks of the trial, even though it has been over for six months now.'" Earlier that night, they had read several diary entries concerning the murder trial over which Alvarez had presided, the trial of a man named Rafael Perdido. Drew had told her what wasn't in the diary: his grandfather had defended Perdido against the murder charge, and it was the only murder case he'd ever lost. "My cousin Shelby has a bunch of old files on that case," Drew had informed her.

"I know. Annabelle suggested that I talk to her. But when I did, I had no idea what that trial would have to do with my aunt's diary."

Katherine still wasn't sure she could see the connection. There had to be something more than the coincidence that Neville Alvarez, who had presided over the trial of a murderer Philip's father had defended, had had an affair with Katherine's great-aunt. If she and Drew could find that connection, they would know not only whether Aunt Claire was in fact a Delacroix, but also, maybe, why Philip had sent Jackson to her home to find the diary.

"'Neville has done so much for the brother,'" Drew repeated, locating his place in the text. The lantern light gilded the page, reflected off the mirror and skimmed Drew's face. A day's growth of beard roughened his jaw and his shirt was rumpled, but his eyes were steady, sharp and focused as he studied the words in the mirror. "'In some trials, he says, it is up to the judge to bring the proper verdict. That murder trial was very hard, but he made it go the right way. For Neville's good deed, the brother says he will hold his silence. He will not reveal what he knows about Neville and me.'" Drew snorted. "Well, Lord knows this can't be about my father. Surely a fine gentleman like him would never stoop to blackmail."

"Drew." His bitterness washed over her. She wished she could console him. But she could think of no way to do that without touching him, and she couldn't touch him. Not in this darkness, in the close intimacy of his cabin.

"And Alvarez. He treats your great-aunt like—"

"Like she let herself be treated."

"And then he *made* the murder trial go the right way? I'm a lawyer—I know how the system works. The judge is supposed to help the jury bring in a proper verdict. He doesn't bring in the verdict himself."

"You're saying you think Alvarez was corrupt?"

"That's the implication." Drew was thoughtful a moment, a line creasing his brow. "The one murder trial my grandfather lost. He was a damned good lawyer, Katherine. He didn't become the most successful lawyer in Bayou Beltane by losing big cases. This one probably cost him his life. He died of a heart attack not long after the guilty verdict was handed down. Maybe he knew something was crooked. Alvarez had been his friend, a guest in his house. Maybe it broke his heart to lose a case because his friend had betrayed him."

"I think you're overreaching," Katherine said gently. "Patrice might have simply phrased things badly. She might have meant that it was a challenge for Alvarez as a judge to see that justice was done."

"He says he did a good deed by bringing in this verdict. If he did the good deed for my father...it would imply my father wanted my grandfather to lose the case."

"Drew. You're reading things that aren't there." But she wasn't convinced he was wrong.

He shot her a quick, enigmatic look, then lifted the diary back toward the mirror and resumed his translation. "'The girl's father asked Neville to find a home for the baby. I tell him my sister, my sister, please. My sister and her husband, who would so love this baby. Neville says the girl, she is...*abattu.* Depressed?'"

"Do you need the dictionary?"

Drew shook his head. "'She is depressed. She has lost everything, and now she is depressed because her father is forcing her to give up her child.'"

"That can't be your aunt. She was a society woman. She wouldn't have wanted to keep an out-of-wedlock child, would she?"

"If she loved the father, she would have wanted to keep the child. It sounds like my grandfather was as big a bully as my father. I guess he had to come from somewhere."

"You're inferring an awful lot—"

"It's in here," he said, jabbing a finger at the diary. His voice was low but fervent. "It's in here, Katherine. You just don't want to see it." He scrutinized the page reflected in the mirror. "'Neville says this girl's brother is not a man you wish to cross. He has seen us and threatened to talk to Neville's wife.' See?" His grin held no triumph. "That's my father."

"It still doesn't say—"

Ignoring her, Drew pressed on. "'I tell Neville, if this girl will give my sister her baby, the baby will be wanted and loved and well cared for. And finally Neville agrees. He says he will arrange it. He will make the adoption happen. I am so happy, I tell him to thank this noble young woman, this selfless mother. I want to know her name, to thank her myself.'" Drew paused, taking a deep breath, and turned the page.

"'He says he will tell me only that her name is Mary.'"

Drew lowered the book, leaned back and closed his eyes. Katherine heard the faint hiss of the propane heater, the river's sluggish current throbbing against the piles of the dock outside his cabin, the silence of night itself. She heard his slow breath and her own pounding heart.

Mary Delacroix was Aunt Claire's mother.

"It's okay," she said.

"Yes." He sighed but didn't look at her. "It's okay." His voice seemed to catch on something in his throat.

He looked on the verge of coming apart. She had to reassure him. If only he knew Aunt Claire, he would be proud to call her his cousin. He would be thrilled. And maybe his aunt Mary would be pleased, too, to know how much her gift had meant to Katherine's grandparents, how very much they'd loved their daughter—*her* daughter.

Cautiously, Katherine covered Drew's hand with hers. He opened his eyes and turned in his chair until he was facing her. He didn't look thrilled, or proud, or even remotely pleased. His eyes were bleak. "My entire life has been built on lies," he whispered.

"No. You mustn't think that."

"I believed Aunt Mary was a saint. I believed I could somehow win my father's love. I believed that, no matter that his marriage had failed, he had loved my mother in his own way, and he'd felt some sort of a commitment to his family. I believed I knew who I was—"

"I know who you are," she said, squeezing his hand as if that would make him more willing to accept her words. "You're a strong, brave man. You've been dealt blow after blow, and you're still standing. Nothing can destroy you, Drew. Not your father. Certainly not this." She let go of him and reached for the diary.

Before she could touch the diary, he caught her hand and closed his fingers tightly around it, as if to protect her from a hazard. For a long moment, he stared at their linked hands, his fingers twining through hers. Then he lifted his gaze to her face. "When I met you, Katherine, I hated you. You were asking all the questions I was too cowardly to ask."

"I could ask them because the answers didn't pose a threat to me," she pointed out.

He moved his thumb gently against her wrist. "I also hated you because..." He inhaled sharply. His eyes no longer looked lost as they searched her face.

"Because why?"

"I wanted you."

Her gaze locked with his. She couldn't have broken away

if she tried. She couldn't have pulled her hand from his if her life depended on it.

"I've always gotten what I wanted—except when it was something that truly mattered. Those were the times I never got what I wanted."

"I want you, too," she heard herself admit. She wasn't sure where her voice came from, why her confession of yearning had broken free. She couldn't remember having thought the words before she spoke them. They just emerged, the truth she had been seeking all along. It wasn't about her aunt's lineage, it wasn't about an adoption or a murder trial. It was about *this,* her own lineage, the spark of innate passion her mother had endowed to her, her own bloodline burning in her veins. The flare of desire that wasn't right but couldn't be wrong.

His gaze still holding hers, he rose to his feet and pulled her out of her chair. Minutes seemed to stretch into hours, seconds into eternities as he brought his arms around her, as he urged her body against his, as he lowered his mouth to hers. And then time became meaningless. The world stopped spinning. Life and night and Katherine's consciousness condensed into heat, texture, sensation.

He kissed her gently, then fiercely. He caressed her mouth, then took it boldly, filling it with his tongue, thrusting and retreating and thrusting again until she no longer remembered how to breathe and no longer cared.

"Katherine," he murmured. "Katherine..." But she wasn't sure she heard him, wasn't sure he'd actually spoken. She could feel his voice, taste it in his kiss, understand it in the way his fingers dug into her hair and held her head steady. She knew his longing because it was her own.

They clung to each other, lips and hands and bodies. They stroked and groped, their fingers frantic as they tugged a shirt, tore at a button, searched for new skin to bare, to taste. Katherine had never before been possessed by such a deep, driving hunger for a man. It was a reckless thing, an insatiable need, and she abandoned herself to it. It was dangerous, it was the wildness that had destroyed her mother, but she had to know it once. Tonight. With Drew.

He lifted her sweater over her head, slid her skirt down her legs, swept her bra away. He buried his lips in the hollow between her breasts. His hands were large but deft, wasting no motion, arousing her even as he removed more and more of her clothing and his. Her own hands shook as she pulled at his shirt, fumbled with his belt. Every time her fingertips brushed against his skin, she wanted only to stop everything, to learn that part of him, to memorize the texture of his shoulder, the curve of a lower rib, the fine golden hairs dusting his chest.

She was scarcely aware of him stripping off her panties, pressing her down into the bed, shedding his jeans and sinking into her arms. She was aware only of his quiet groans as she moved her hands over the smooth expanse of his back, his gasps as she grazed his jaw with her lips, her own shuddering sighs as he made love to her breasts with his teeth and tongue. She was aware of his fingers on her belly, caressing, delving lower, gliding between her legs to ready her and discovering that she was already wet and aching.

He murmured something, her name again, perhaps. It didn't matter what he said. She heard him, heard a prayer in his words, a plea. And then he plunged into her, deep and hard, again and again until her body convulsed and the wildness consumed her.

It wasn't until much later, when time came to mean something again, that she realized he had used no protection.

She was her mother's daughter after all, she thought as the last tremors faded and the heat burned down to a glowing warmth. She kept her legs wrapped around him, her body not yet willing to lose him. He was heavy on top of her, his breath uneven, his mouth nestled into the sensitive skin below her ear. One of his hands rested near her head, and he twisted his fingers absently through her hair.

She was her mother's daughter. Not caring. Obeying her body and ignoring her brain, acting impulsively, wanting something so much she didn't give a damn about the consequences.

The only consequence that worried her was that she'd failed to protect her heart. Somehow, she had let herself fall in love with Drew. And he was definitely not the right man to love.

HE DIDN'T WANT TO LEAVE her, even after he went slack and only her arms and legs, locked around him, were keeping him inside her. She had beautiful arms, as pale and graceful as a ballerina's, and legs as strong as a long-distance runner's. They held him tightly, and he couldn't bring himself to pull away.

Her hair was softer than he had imagined. Her mouth was softer. Her skin, her sighs, the soft, soft curves of her body. Katherine Beaufort had always seemed such a solid, rigid woman—but oh, she was soft. As soft as silk, as soft as warm butter, as soft as a wistful Cajun lullaby.

He still wasn't sure who or what he was, where he'd come from, where he was going. But right now, on the ancient iron cot in his cabin, he was sure of this: he and Katherine belonged to each other. For this one night, in this one place, they belonged together.

Her arms gradually relented, and he lifted himself off her, bracing himself on his arms. "Are you cold?" he asked.

"No." Even her voice was soft, a sighing whisper in the darkness.

He gazed at her. Not just her face, her lips moist and her eyes both sleepy and bright, but her body, tall and slim and firm, her breasts spread round against her ribs, her nipples dark and taut, her waist delicate, her hips barely wide enough, and her legs, her thighs, the nest of hair between them...

She was the most beautiful woman he'd ever seen.

He dragged his gaze back up to her face. She was watching him, her smile pensive. "I was too fast," he apologized, sensing that something was wrong. If she wasn't cold, she might be sore. Or not as fulfilled as she would have liked. Or resentful, or regretful, or—

"No, you weren't too fast."

"Too hard."

She brushed her fingertips over his mouth to silence him. "You were perfect."

"Fat chance of that." He shoved the blanket down under her body and then pulled it back up over them both. She might not be cold now, but once she cooled off she'd learn the limits of that gas-powered space heater.

"You were, Drew. Perfect."

"Then why are your eyes full of tears?"

She touched her own eyes, as if she didn't believe him. "I don't know." She lowered her hand until it collided with his, between their bodies. He immediately captured her hand and brought it to his mouth. He kissed her fingertips and tasted her tears on them. Then he pressed his lips to her palm, and she sighed. "I didn't know I could feel so much, Drew. It's a little—unnerving."

"I could make you feel more." He wanted to make her feel things she'd never felt before. He was already feeling things he'd never felt before, feelings he'd never experienced with his family, or with other women, or with anyone he had ever loved. He'd never felt so...safe. So accepted. So strong and healthy.

"There were passionate women in my family," she said. "Like my mother, and my great-aunt Patrice. But I never...I was never like them, Drew. I tried so hard not to be like them."

"I know who you are," he murmured, echoing the words she'd said to him before they'd made love. "I'm not my father. You're not your mother."

"Maybe I am." She closed her eyes and sighed again, sounding uncharacteristically helpless. "We didn't talk. Tonight, I mean. We didn't talk, or think. All I knew was that you hated me—and I'm sure hate comes pretty close to what I felt for you, too."

"We don't hate each other, Katherine." He pulled her closer, close enough for her body to press the length of his. Her knees brushed his thighs, her breasts rubbed his chest. His arousal built, fierce for her again.

No, this wasn't hate. Not by any stretch.

"Are you sure?" He heard a smile in her voice.

"I'm sure." He eased onto his back, bringing her with him until she lay the length of him. She rested atop him, smooth and satiny, her hair spilling down into his face like spring rain. "What we have," he whispered, caressing her shoulders, her sides, the fullness of her breasts, "is nothing like what your aunt did with Alvarez. Nothing like it at all."

"You don't think so?"

"I would want to see your face," he said. "Always. I would want to watch you when you came."

She closed her eyes and let out a hushed moan. Even in the feeble lantern light he saw the flush in her cheeks, the flutter of a pulse in her throat. He felt her nipples grow harder, her hips tenser. He supposed it was possible for a man to have sex in anger, so *fâché* he wouldn't want to see his woman's face. But he couldn't imagine it with Katherine. He couldn't imagine ever looking away from her.

He arched against her and she gasped. Her legs moved and she rolled her head back, exposing the lovely, pale skin of her neck. He slid his hands up from her breasts to touch her throat, the nape of her neck, the skin behind her ears.

She opened her eyes. Her breath came in small, tight gasps. "I'm scared, Drew," she confessed. "Feeling these things frightens me."

"I know." God, how he knew. But he'd spent most of his life running from the things that frightened him, hiding from them, denying them. And it had done him no good. So now, tonight, he would run *toward* what frightened him, hurl himself into the heart of it. If he couldn't escape his fear, he would embrace it, take it, turn it into a strength.

Bringing his hands down to her bottom, he guided her against him, onto him, down around him. He felt his fear overtaken by pleasure, knowledge, a comprehension so deep it transcended explanation. He gave himself over to her heat, her texture, the exquisite sensation of loving her. This time more slowly, more carefully, this time savoring every moment of it, every measure, every cadence. This time he was patient, controlled, feeling the changes in her, the quickening, the astonished cry, the frenzied grip of her fingers on his shoulders, the soul-deep pulse of her climax, the way her teeth dug into her lip and her breath escaped her in a ragged groan.

The heart of it was where he wanted to be, and so he went, carrying every fear and every hope he'd ever known. He went, with his eyes open, seeing only Katherine, following her down.

CHAPTER ELEVEN

A CHILL MORNING MIST hovered above the water as they motored slowly down the river toward the Willow Island Swamp Tours dock. Katherine should have been starving, but she wasn't. She should have been panic-stricken that she'd given so much to Drew last night—so much of herself, body and soul—and he'd made no promises, sworn no oaths, offered no assurances that what they'd shared had meant to him what it had meant to her.

But she was neither hungry nor panic-stricken. She felt only a strange serenity as she gazed at him. He was seated in the stern, working the tiller to guide the boat between lily pads and reeds. His eyes were surprisingly alert given how little he and Katherine had slept, and his mouth was relaxed into a smile that she would have interpreted as a sign of contentment if she didn't know that their trip back to Bayou Beltane was a trip back to trouble.

Trouble notwithstanding, she had her own contentment. Sometime during the long night she'd shared with him, she had come to discover her own roots. Her search for Aunt Claire's mother had apparently reached its conclusion. But along the way, Katherine had also found her own mother. She'd located her connection to that woman, a child torn from her own parents too young, desperately hungry to experience love in the only way she could.

Katherine had lived with the love of her grandparents and her aunt, but never with her mother's, not the way she'd ached for it. Yet her mother *had* loved her. She'd called her Kitty-Kat. "Come, Kitty-Kat, come sit in my lap, darlin'," her mother would say, and Katherine would climb into her mother's lap. She would inhale her mother's sultry gardenia scent and toy with the curling ends of her long, fire-tinged hair. "Would you like me to sing you a song, Kitty-Kat? A lullaby so you'll fall asleep. Here's the only lullaby I know, child. It goes like this..." And her mother's voice, low and throaty, would croon, "The woman, she drinks from the river.... The woman, she drinks from the rain, and the man drinks his bourbon, and he drinks the tears..."

Drew had given Katherine's mother back to her. He'd given her her mother's long-forgotten song, and he'd given her her own long-buried passion, the part of herself she'd always feared—and feared still, yet was learning to accept. He had given her the ability to let go, to fling herself beyond the fear, to ride it to the other side. And to face whatever consequences came afterward.

If Drew never gave her anything more, she would be grateful for this.

Dawn was silver in the sky, pearling through the fog as Drew steered the boat into its slip at the dock. Katherine tried to remember the words they'd spoken before leaving the cabin that morning. They'd been quiet but not strained. "Here's your sweater," he'd said. "There's an outhouse down that path. I'm sorry there's no plumbing."

"An outhouse is fine," she'd told him. "Here's one of your socks."

He'd taken the sock from her hand, then taken her hand and pulled her to him. Clad only in his jeans, he'd wrapped his arms around her. Despite the cabin's chill, his naked chest had been hot against her cheek, against her lips as she'd kissed it. She'd felt him grow hard as he rocked his hips with hers. He'd whispered her name. Guided her mouth to his. Kissed her so deeply her womb had trembled.

Whispered her name again, and then groaned and stepped away.

He'd wanted to make love to her, she knew. But sooner or later they were going to have to leave the cabin and rejoin the world. He was opting for sooner.

By the time they reached his car, solitary and beaded with dew as it sat in the lot adjacent to the dock, the early morning sun was high enough to burn a few holes through the mist, and reality burned a few holes through the mist of emotions wrapped around Katherine. She waited until they were in the car and Drew was revving the engine, then asked, "What are you going to do?"

Gravel spit from the tires as he cruised out onto the road. Trees drizzled leaves onto the asphalt, flat brown parchments fluttering down, brushing against the car's windows and clinging to its hood. Focused on the empty road and the brightness of the sky above the horizon, Drew said nothing.

"Drew?"

"I'm going home."

Home? Where might that be? She almost believed his dilapidated cabin on the bayou was the closest thing he had to a home.

He must have read her mind. "Belle Terre," he said.

Katherine recalled the night he'd come to New Orleans and told her that Philip had admitted to being Jackson Boudreaux's father. Drew had said then that he didn't know where his home was—but it wasn't Belle Terre. "What about your father?" she asked. "Won't he be there?"

"Yes." Drew's expression was grim but determined, the stoic countenance of a child presenting his hand to a nurse to have a cut scrubbed with antiseptic. He was expecting pain and assuming it was necessary.

But a wounded child was allowed to have someone holding him, offering comfort through the ordeal. "I'll come with you," she said.

"No."

She dared to lay her left hand over his right, which rested loosely on the gear stick between them. "It's going to be a difficult encounter, Drew, and—"

"No kidding." He shifted gears. She refused to remove her hand.

"If you're going to talk to him about your aunt Mary's baby, I should be there. That baby is my aunt Claire."

"I'm going to talk to him about the lies, Katherine. *All* the lies. I've only just begun with him. I need to know the rest."

"Your father may not know what the rest is," she argued. "It was your grandfather who convinced Judge Alvarez to arrange the adoption of Mary's baby—"

"Oh, Lord, no." He chuckled bitterly. "That's barely the start of it. There's much more. And it's hidden in that diary of yours, Katherine. It's in there, between the lines. Alvarez set up that murder trial. He fixed it so my grandfather would lose. And my father was up to his ears in it."

"The diary never said—"

"It's in there." He spoke with such certainty she couldn't refute him. "My father told me about Jackson. Now he's going to tell me why he sent Jackson to steal the diary. The answer is in there."

"Then I should be with you."

Drew sighed, then shook his head, his gaze remaining on the road. "No."

She relented, letting her hand slide from his, forcing her will to yield to his. He needed to do this alone. It wasn't just about his aunt Mary. It wasn't even just about his father's efforts to corrupt a judge, to turn that judge in some way against Drew's grandfather, the Delacroix patriarch. Drew had to see his father alone because it was about *them,* one father, one son and a host of betrayals. If Katherine accompanied Drew, it would no longer be about a father who had systematically broken his son's spirit and a son standing up to his father and healing that broken spirit rebuilding it and reclaiming it.

"Take the diary, then," she said.

At last Drew glanced her way. "What do you mean, take it?"

"I don't want it anymore. You should have it with you when you see your father."

"If he knows I have it, he'll try to get it from me."

"But you won't let him." She had that much faith in Drew.

Drew sent her another swift look, then slowed as the car entered the outskirts of the tiny downtown district. Bayou Beltane was still asleep. The shops and business buildings were dark. No lights glowed in the storefront windows; no parked cars lined the curbs. Dawn fog hugged the streets.

He drove slowly toward the building that housed his father's law firm. Only the emergency exit light glowed inside the entry. He coasted past the door, turned the corner and cruised by the lot where Katherine's car waited. "Let me go around the block," he said, continuing past the boarded-up window of his office and around another corner. "I want to make sure no one sees you."

"I'm sure no one's following me," she said, remembering her anxiety yesterday evening.

"If they saw your car, they could be lurking somewhere around here, waiting for you to show up."

"Well, it wouldn't do anyone any good to find me if you've got the diary in your possession."

"They wouldn't know I had the diary."

"Then I could be a decoy. I could lead them astray."

At that he smiled, a remarkably sexy smile. "Woman, you could surely lead a man astray," he murmured, turning the last corner to satisfy himself that no one was spying on her abandoned car. He steered into the lot and braked to a halt next to her car. ''Where will you go?'' he asked.

Where *could* she go, after last night? Would she ever be able to find her way back to the life she'd known before? She doubted it, and she couldn't bring herself to care. Last night's passion had led her to an entirely new future, one she had never planned for. One that might not include Drew Delacroix, one that might include a child conceived in rapture. Whatever her future, she swore to herself that she wouldn't regret the night that had given rise to it.

''If you don't want me to stay,'' she remembered to answer him, ''I'll go back to New Orleans. I've got a business to run.''

He leaned across the console, and she tilted her face to receive his kiss. Instead, he looped his arm around her and drew her into a hug, tucking her head against his shoulder and pressing his lips to her hair. ''Don't make me kiss you,'' he whispered. ''If I do, I'll want to make love to you again.''

His words turned her on as much as a real kiss might have. She extricated herself from his embrace and busied herself digging the diary and her notebook out of her tote. She remained hunched over the bag until her fingers stopped trembling and her cheeks no longer felt feverish, then straightened up and handed him her precious possessions. ''Be careful, Drew.''

''Don't worry.''

''And be kind.'' At Drew's frown, she elaborated. ''He's your father and he's old. No matter what he did... Maybe he had a good reason.''

Drew appeared unmoved. ''He's a son of a bitch.''

''He's your father.'' At Drew's skeptical frown, she added, ''Don't become him, Drew. He's lost his soul. Don't you lose yours.''

His gaze reached into her. She saw dread in his face, and determination. "Don't worry," he murmured, lowering his eyes to the leather-bound volume she'd entrusted to him. He ran his fingers along its ridged spine, reminding her of the way he'd run his fingers along her wrist, across her breasts, the way he'd dug his fingers into the curves of her hips when he'd surged inside her. He had magical fingers, fingers that cherished what they touched.

Her great-aunt's diary would be safe with him. So would the truth contained in its pages.

She could only pray that Drew would be safe with himself.

HE DROVE UP THE LONG driveway to Belle Terre—and skidded to a halt when he saw the scorched grass. Something had been burned on the lawn directly in front of the broad stairs to the front veranda.

Scowling, he shut off the engine and climbed out of the car. The circle of charred grass was no more than three feet in diameter. Several burnt twigs and carbon-caked chunks of wood lay in the circle, cold and black. Soot stained the white paint of the lower porch steps and reached up the closest of the pillars like skeletal black fingers.

This was the second ceremonial fire that had been set at Belle Terre in the past year. And only recently, the stables at Delacroix Farms on his uncle Charles's estate had been torched. The evidence for that arson had pointed to Flora Boudreaux. Was she trying to torch Belle Terre, too?

Drew bounded up the stairs to the porch, unlocked the door and stormed into the front hall. "What happened?" he bellowed, his voice echoing against the vaulted ceiling three stories above the marble-floored foyer. "What the hell happened out there?"

Scampering footsteps approached down the hall from the kitchen. Then Magdalena, the new maid, appeared in the foyer, waiflike and pale, carrying a tray laden with a teapot, a porcelain cup and several slices of dry toast. Her eyes seemed to pop out of her face when she saw Drew. "Mr. Delacroix!" she whispered. "Oh, thank God you're here!"

"What happened?" He gestured behind him in the direction of the front door.

"Oh, it was ghastly! So frightening! Your father was terrified. He's in his bedroom. It was so terrible and I thought he had a heart attack, I was so scared—"

He cut her off by wresting the tray from her shaking hands and hurried up the circular stairs to the second floor, where his father's suite of rooms was located. Steam curled out of the teapot spout, the sharp, bitter aroma of a strong morning brew. His father normally preferred coffee. But then, nothing was normal this morning.

Outside his father's sitting-room door, Drew hesitated. He wanted to remember what, besides the remains of a small bonfire in the front yard of his father's house and the maid's near hysteria, made everything different.

Katherine. Her passion. Her heat claiming him, her soul welcoming him, her trust so profound in their lovemaking and even more profound afterward, when she'd given him the diary.

He wasn't worthy of her. But last night…last night she'd let him believe he was.

Her abiding faith in him gave him the courage to rap against the door with his toe. "Come on in, Magdalena," his father hollered from within, "and that tea had damned well better be hot, or I swear I'll fire you before you can blink."

Balancing the tray in one hand, Drew twisted the beveled-glass doorknob and shoved open the door. "I'd suggest you avoid using the word *fire* this morning," he said dryly.

Philip cringed. He was seated in one of the Queen Anne

chairs by the window, clad in a silk robe, a woolen lap blanket spread across his knees. His complexion was chalky, his eyes rimmed in red and underlined in blue shadows. Patriotic coloring, Drew thought irreverently as he stepped into the room and kicked the door shut behind him.

"What are you doing here?" his father barked.

Drew thought of a million caustic replies but said nothing. He had to save his ammunition for the main battle, not waste it on distracting skirmishes.

He brought the tray over to the pedestal table next to the chair where his father sat. Close up, he could see that his father's cheeks had a gray undertone, as if all the blood in his face had drained from his skin and pooled in his eyelids. His hands trembled visibly as he reached for the teapot. Before he could risk splattering the tea and scalding himself, Drew lifted the pot and poured some tea into the cup.

"Why are you being nice to me?" his father asked, suspicion sucking the life out of his voice.

Drew ignored the question. He considered sitting in the matching chair across the small, linen-covered table from his father, then thought better of it. He wanted to remain standing, towering over his pale, shrunken father. "What happened outside?"

"That bitch Flora," his father muttered, then took a sip of his tea. "She wants me dead."

Drew paced to the ornate fireplace, laid with unlit logs, its rococo mantel topped with framed photographs of Philip posing with various luminaries from Louisiana's political and business worlds: Philip shaking hands with the governor. Philip hoisting a beer mug with a billionaire petroleum executive. Philip arm in arm with a justice from the state supreme court. Philip accepting a plaque from a hospital CEO. Philip holding a thirty-pound bass on a hook. That poor bass was probably the only honest creature in any of the photos.

"What did Flora do?" he asked his father.

"She set another bonfire, that's what she did. Scared the bejeezus out of me. The woman is insane. She should be committed. As soon as I'm feeling up to it, I'm going to make some calls and have her put away."

"You had a *relationship* with her, Dad," Drew reminded him, unable to rid his voice of acid. "She bore you a child. If that didn't mark her as insane, I don't see how you can be kicking up a fuss about her little voodoo games. She left a doll for you at the office yesterday, by the way."

"What?" Philip's eyes bugged out and the skin below his cheekbones sank. His lower lip quivered and the cup rattled in the saucer he was holding. "A doll?" His voice was a mere rasp of sound.

"With a long, sharp pin piercing its heart. She threw it through my office window by mistake, but it was obviously intended for you. It was wearing a bow tie."

Philip lowered the cup to the table, closed his eyes and murmured an incoherent prayer. "She's insane, Drew. I want her committed."

"Why is she doing this to you, Dad? She obviously loved you once."

"She used me."

Drew snorted. "Who used whom, Dad? She carried your child. She raised your son."

"She wants my money. She wants Jackson to have it. She thinks I'm not doing enough for him. Damn it, I'm doing everything for him. Everything!"

More than you've ever done for me, Drew thought, although he didn't say it. "So, what happened? She set a fire outside the house?"

"Scared me senseless. It was like a witch's blaze. A circle of flame. She'd soaked a pyre of sticks with gasoline and ignited it. Made a big explosive sound, and it was burning everywhere. I feared for the house, Drew. This house that I grew up in! My father's house, and that blasted fire burning so close to it... When the fire was finally extinguished, there was another doll at the center of it, burnt to a crisp. That's what she wants for me, Drew. She wants me dead and burned. She's trying to kill me." He pressed his hand to his heart and swallowed. "The doctor's been in. He wanted to take me to the hospital. My blood pressure, my pulse rate, palpitations, angina...I wouldn't let him. If I'm going to die, it'll be in my own damned home."

"You aren't going to die, Dad. You wouldn't. It would make too many people happy."

Philip glared at him. For all his alleged weakness, his eyes were as sharp as lasers. They stung. "What are you doing here, Drew? I thought you'd gone off to have a tantrum. Are you over it?"

"Actually, no," Drew drawled. "I'm still in the thick of it." He leaned against the mantel and stared across the room at his father, enjoying the sight of Philip hunched over in his robe, too shaky to lift a cup of tea. "I've got proof about Aunt Mary's daughter."

He hadn't known his father could grow paler. "Mary's what? What the hell are you talking about?"

"Her daughter. The baby your father made her give up. The baby whose adoption Neville Alvarez arranged."

"Are you insane? How dare you accuse Mary of such a horrible thing."

"I'm not insane, Dad. And I adore Aunt Mary. She's a good woman, and I won't hurt her. It's what *you* did that interests me."

"What did I do?" his father whined indignantly. "I made a good home for you. I kept you when your mother walked out on you—"

"She walked out on *you,* Dad, not me."

"She walked out on all of us, but you had a home with

me here. I saw you through school and I took you into my law firm. I've tried to treat my daughters fairly, tried to steer them in the right direction—though God knows, they've defied me every step of the way. But I've been damned good to you. And I helped Jackson get on the police force. I help him on the side. Why his mother is trying to kill me, I can't begin to imagine—''

''Dad,'' Drew cut him off. He didn't want to listen to his father ranting about Flora. He wanted to find out the truth. ''Who was the father of Mary's baby?''

''Mary never had a baby! I don't know what you're talking about!''

''Liar.''

His father peered up at him, fear mingling with fury in his gaze. ''Even if such a terrible thing were true, what makes you think I'd tell you anything I knew?''

''To save your own neck,'' Drew said calmly. ''I've already informed Jake that Jackson broke into Katherine's apartment to steal her aunt's diary. Jackson's going to be arrested, and he's going to talk. His job is on the line. His mother wants you dead. Do you think he's going to keep his mouth shut just to spare you?''

His father flinched. ''I've got an election coming up! Jackson can't do that to me!''

''Not only can he, but he will.''

''Then—then you'll defend me, Drew. You're my son, you're a lawyer. I can't count on Joanna, but you—''

''I don't defend liars,'' Drew said, his voice as level as his father's was spiky, ''so you'd better start speaking the truth. Who was the father of Mary's baby?''

''She never had—''

''All right,'' Drew interrupted, unable to stomach his father's protestations anymore. ''Who was Mary's lover?''

"Perdido," his father whispered, lowering his gaze to his lap, a posture of defeat.

"Rafael Perdido?" The man convicted of murder in Neville Alvarez's courtroom. The man Philip's father had defended. The last case Philip's father had ever taken. The case he'd lost, the loss that had broken his heart. "Aunt Mary loved Rafael Perdido?"

"It was a long time ago," Philip muttered, fidgeting with the blanket and shaking his head. "Leave it alone. No one wants to dredge it up."

"Is that why you went after Katherine's great-aunt's diary? You thought she was trying to dredge it up?"

"I don't know what that girl is trying to do. But she ought to mind her own business."

"Aunt Mary's baby is her business. And Aunt Mary is my business, and yours." He leaned forward, arms crossed, feet spread in an aggressive stance. "So what exactly happened? Did Perdido lose his murder trial because he was Aunt Mary's lover and you wanted to get rid of him?"

"What are you talking about?" his father rasped. "Perdido was sleeping with half the women in Bayou Beltane. And he murdered one of them. Thank God it wasn't your aunt Mary. He was obviously an evil man, and he paid the ultimate price for his crimes. I'm only sorry Mary got caught in his trap."

"Why, if Perdido was so evil, would your father defend him?" Drew asked. "Why would he defend a man who had defiled his only daughter? And why was it necessary for Judge Alvarez to fix the trial?"

"Fix the trial?" Philip sputtered. "What are you talking about? Where is this crap coming from?" He started to push himself to his feet, but he was too frail, his legs wobbling, his hands unable to bear his weight as he leaned

against the arms of the chair. He sank back down, once again looking defeated despite his angry gaze.

"You know where this crap is coming from, Dad," Drew said, feeling stronger and more certain with every minute, his energy stoked by every feeble protest his father attempted. "Katherine's great-aunt's diary. It's all in there, Dad. Why else would you have sent Jackson to steal it? There's dynamite in that diary, and it's going to explode bigger than any fire Flora Boudreaux could build in your front yard. And it's going to bring you down."

"That diary is nothing but the fantasies of a neurotic old woman. Nobody with half a brain would believe the stuff in there. I just wish Katherine would get rid of it and spare our family a great deal of embarrassment."

"Not our family, Dad. You."

"And your aunt Mary. Do you think she wants the world to learn that she had a child out of wedlock?"

"It was a long time ago. No one would care anymore. No one except that child, who grew up to be Katherine's aunt."

"When a child is adopted, when the adoption is sealed, nothing good can come of unsealing it. If Katherine had concern for anyone but herself, her own absurd curiosity—"

"This isn't about her, Dad. It's about you."

"Nonsense." Philip harrumphed and attempted to lift his cup once more. Drew heard the rattle of the cup against the saucer in his father's tremulous hands.

"Why did you tell Jackson to break into Katherine's apartment?" Drew pressed him.

Outrage flushed Philip's face. He set down the cup without drinking and stared at Drew, hatred deepening the creases that lined his face. "Why do I tell him to do anything? Because he does as I say, and his price is cheap. I can't count on you. I can't trust you. You're still the sniveling, sickly little boy who can't do anything right. That diary will destroy my campaign, and where the hell are you? Not helping me salvage the campaign. Not helping me get reelected."

"On a platform of lies? Why should I help you?"

"Because you're my son, damn it! But you're as bad as your sisters. The lot of you, failures. Joanna, a traitor, working for that lily-livered brother of mine instead of her own father. And Annabelle—another traitor, taking up with Jake Trahan, a nobody from a family of trash who thinks he's going to make his career by destroying me. And now you! Badgering me about this diary when you ought to be out there getting me reelected. I've got that idiot Flora pulling her voodoo stunts and making me crazy, and my own son would rather slip a knife between my ribs than do what I tell him to do. Go ahead, then, Drew—find yourself a nice, sharp blade and have at me. I'm not that easy to kill. Ask Flora. Ask your mother. Ask any of them. You come at me with a knife, Drew, and I'll pay Jackson enough to go after you. You give that boy enough money, and he won't care if he suffers a nick or two. Why not let him lose a little blood for me? Why not give him the chance to show a true son's loyalty? If he did, maybe I'd give his mother what she wants, and then she'll leave me alone. She'll get a name for her son. A name and an inheritance as befits the son of Philip Delacroix."

Drew stood in stunned silence. At first his father's tirade wounded him, but after a while he grew numb to it. This man was not his father. A father would never speak like that to his son. A father would never spurn the love of a son who'd wanted nothing but to see his love returned.

A knife was being slipped between ribs in this room, but the knife was in Philip's hand, and the ribs were Drew's.

He couldn't remain here. He couldn't let Philip see the blood, the massive hemorrhage. He refused to stay and let his father destroy him.

He turned without a word and exited from the sitting room, closing the door behind him and understanding that he had closed the door to his past, to everything he'd ever believed, everything he'd ever trusted and hoped for. He closed the door and walked away.

CHAPTER TWELVE

EARLY MORNING WAS NOT a peaceful time at Annabelle's bed-and-breakfast. Katherine realized as soon as she arrived that she shouldn't have come, but Annabelle refused to let her leave. She insisted that Katherine sit in a corner of the kitchen and nurse a cup of coffee. "Once things settle down, we'll talk," Annabelle promised.

Things weren't going to settle down for a while. There were pastries to serve, fruit to slice, boxes of cereal and pitchers of milk to display on a buffet table in the dining room. There were vats of coffee to brew and tea to steep, orange juice to squeeze, loaves of whole-grain bread to arrange in attractive wicker baskets beside the toaster.

Tucked behind a table, safely out of Annabelle's path, Katherine sipped her coffee and watched her friend fly like a frenetic bird around the kitchen, timing the oven, monitoring the supply of plates, rolling the linen napkins into attractive pink logs, which she stacked on a tray next to the silverware. Everything had to be just so, and then Annabelle had to carry it into the dining room, where the inn's guests swarmed, some too bleary to conduct a civil conversation while others chattered with far too much energy for the early hour.

Katherine watched Annabelle work, but she felt herself at a remove from the bustle. She didn't even have to close her eyes to escape from the high-energy universe of Annabelle's kitchen. As if by some mental trick, some emotional tic, she was without any effort able to transport her mind back to Drew's cabin, to his bed, to his arms.

She wanted to believe he was strong enough to survive his confrontation with his father. She also wanted to believe he was strong enough to come back to her after the confrontation, to accept her love and return it. Maybe that was hoping for too much.

"Are you sure I can't help with anything?" she asked for the third or fourth time as Annabelle blew past her, carrying a heaping basket of warm muffins to the dining room.

"I've got it all down to a system," Annabelle assured her. "Just keep out of my way."

So Katherine kept out of her way. She closed her eyes and relived the sensation of Drew's hands on her skin, his lips loving her, the sleek muscles of his legs, his powerful arms locking her against him, his body deep inside her. She wouldn't let the sensations make her self-destruct as her mother had. She wouldn't let them drag her down into a deadly current and let it sweep her away. But she could relish the memory of them, couldn't she?

"All right." Annabelle's voice broke into her meditation.

Katherine opened her eyes in time to see her friend flop onto a chair next to her at the kitchen table. She hooked her sneakered feet over a rung under the seat, rolled back her head and sighed. In her hands she cradled a mug of coffee.

"Are you okay?"

"I'm a damned sight better than you," Annabelle said with a grin. "What happened to you? You look like you didn't spend much time sleeping last night."

"I didn't," Katherine admitted. Annabelle must have reached her conclusion based on an accumulation of evidence: the weariness in Katherine's eyes, the rumpled day-old clothes, the unbrushed hair, the fever that warmed her cheeks whenever she thought of last night. Hiding the truth from Annabelle wasn't going to do any good. "I spent the night with Drew."

Annabelle's chair scraped the floor as she jerked upright. Her eyes agog, she set her mug on the table and searched Katherine's face.

"It's not what you think," Katherine assured her.

A quizzical smile crossed Annabelle's face. "What do I think?"

Katherine wasn't going to waste time discussing the more erotic aspects of the time she'd spent with Drew. What mattered was not then but now, not the love but the truth. "I'm frightened for him, Annabelle. He's gone to Belle Terre to have a showdown with your father."

Annabelle swore softly. "All by himself? He should have let me come along. He's going to need moral support."

"He doesn't want moral support. He believes that—I don't know—whatever is going to happen, it's all between him and your father. Just the two of them. He feels as if he's been more deeply betrayed than you or your sister."

"Only because he let himself be betrayed," Annabelle said, her tone more sympathetic than her words. "He chose to stand by Dad through thick and thin, and now I guess he's finally realized that with my father, affection runs pretty thin."

"He's hurting."

"I don't doubt it." Annabelle ran her finger around the rim of her mug as she thought. After a minute, she eyed Katherine with sly curiosity. "So, you spent the night with Drew, huh?"

Katherine took a deep breath, determined to keep the conversation focused on what was most important. "We spent the night working on my great-aunt's diary. I trust you to keep what I'm going to tell you to yourself for the time being. We found evidence in it that your aunt Mary gave birth to a baby who was adopted by my grandparents. My aunt Claire is your aunt Mary's daughter."

Once again, the chair legs thumped against the floor as Annabelle started in her seat. "Oh, my God. You're joking, aren't you?"

"No."

"My aunt Mary?"

"Yes."

Annabelle looked so stunned, Katherine wasn't sure how much more to tell her. There was plenty more to tell, but she wasn't sure she dared. She watched as Annabelle turned to squint at the sunlight pouring in through the window. "Your aunt Claire?" she finally said, her voice scarcely above a whisper.

"Yes."

"Which makes us—what? Second cousins?"

"Thanks to adoption, I guess we are."

"Oh, God. Aunt Mary. I can't believe it."

"Maybe the diary is full of lies," Katherine suggested, although she didn't for a minute believe it. If the diary had been full of lies, Philip Delacroix wouldn't have feared its contents enough to attempt to steal it.

"Did it—did the diary say who the father was?"

Katherine shook her head. "Not as far as we'd gotten in it last night. There are still more entries to translate."

"So—so right now..." Annabelle seemed to struggle with her thoughts. "Drew is going one-on-one with my father over this?"

"Yes."

"That's not good."

It's worse than not good, Katherine wanted to say. Drew intended to go one-on-one with his father over more than just Aunt Mary. The betrayals had been as thick as fudge:

not just Mary's baby but Philip's own unacknowledged child, Jackson Boudreaux, and the diary's insinuations that Philip had had something to do with Neville Alvarez's handling of a murder trial. Those frequent references to Philip's having known of Alvarez's illicit affair had been creepy, too.

Yet how could Katherine tell Annabelle that Philip might have been blackmailing Alvarez sixty years ago? How could she explain that Philip had had some inexplicable connection to a corrupt judge? How could she reveal that Philip had fathered an illegitimate son who currently did his dirty work for him? She was Annabelle's friend, and she couldn't find the nerve to tell her.

"I don't know if Drew can handle this," Annabelle said. Her gaze narrowed resolutely on Katherine. "Look, I'm not going to ask you what happened last night. I'm not going to ask how you managed to get Drew to see the light about my father, or what courage you pumped into him to make him think he ought to take on the old man without any backup—"

"I wanted to go with him," Katherine told her. "I didn't want him to deal with Philip alone."

Annabelle sighed. "And he said no," she guessed. "He's always been a loner, determined to do things his own way in his own time. But my father...damn it, Katherine, my father can be vicious. Especially if Drew turns on him. He went crazy when Joanna abandoned him, and nearly as crazy when I did. But we're his daughters. Drew is his only son."

No, he's not, Katherine almost blurted out. Philip had another son.

"You're worried, aren't you." Annabelle tapped her fingers nervously against her cup. Her nails made tiny clicking sounds on the porcelain. "I don't blame you. I'm worried, too."

"That's why I'm here," Katherine said, glad not to have to explain any more than she already had. "What can we do?"

"If Drew decides to dive into a bottle—"

"He won't do that," Katherine said with certainty. "He isn't drinking anymore."

"He told you that?"

"He said drinking didn't work, so he saw no reason to continue." Katherine found reassurance in that thought.

Annabelle looked far from reassured. She pursed her lips and rolled her eyes. "All right, so if Drew doesn't drink, he might do something else—I don't know what. Freak out. Lash out. My brother keeps so much locked up inside him, I can't begin to guess what he'll do." She thought for a minute, then said, "Maybe we ought to go out to Belle Terre and make sure he and my father haven't killed each other."

"You don't think they'd be violent, do you?" Katherine asked, wishing she could laugh off Annabelle's concern.

Annabelle's sober stare warned Katherine that she found no humor in any of it. "If we're going to go up to Belle Terre, we should stop downtown and bring Jake with us, just in case."

Just in case Drew and his father had indeed become violent. Just in case they were right now locked in mortal combat—or beyond combat, too late to be saved.

Katherine nodded and tried not to succumb to anguish. Soliciting the help of Annabelle's husband, Bayou Beltane's chief of police, appealed to her for more reasons than just to keep Drew and his father from throttling each other. If Philip had committed illegal acts—whether sixty years ago or today—having an officer of the law on hand might prove necessary.

If. If Philip had bidden Jackson to break into Katherine's apartment, *if* Philip had interfered with some long-ago murder trial, *if* Philip had attempted to blackmail a judge over his mistress... If even one of Drew's suspicions carried the unshakable weight of truth, then God protect him. Katherine suspected that Philip would be like a cornered beast, teeth bared and claws unsheathed, willing and ready to fight anyone who stood between him and his goals. And there Drew would be, directly in Philip's path, so confoundedly brave and so vulnerable.

"Yes," she said. "Let's get Jake."

THE POLICE STATION was as small and low-tech as the town it served. The building had electricity, of course; it had computers, telephones, central air-conditioning and a modest fleet of state-of-the-art cruisers. But a town the size of Bayou Beltane didn't need much more than that.

Katherine could see the entire squad room from the front door. She followed Annabelle to the desk closest to the door, where a clerk in a crisp blouse and gray skirt was busy sorting files and documents. Annabelle marched to the desk and asked the clerk whether Jake was available.

"He's in the interview room," the clerk said. "Would you like to wait?"

Katherine pictured Drew and Philip lying unconscious on a floor in their house, their hands wrapped tightly around each other's throats and their faces purple from lack of oxygen. She reflexively shook her head. No, she would not like to wait.

"It's kind of important," Annabelle told the clerk. "Any way you can get him to come out for a few minutes?"

"Well, he's interrogating someone," the clerk said placidly. "Why don't you all go on down to his office? I'll send him right down as soon as he's done. I'm sure he won't be long."

With a reluctant nod, Annabelle beckoned Katherine to follow her through the squad room and down a back hall.

At the end of it stood a door, the top half of which held a window that had Chief of Police painted on it in plain block letters.

One side of the hall also held a window, the glass tinted a silver-gray, which made Katherine suspect it was actually a one-way mirror. Curious, she glanced at the glass—and saw a room on the other side. Boxy but well lit, the room seemed crowded by the long table that took up most of its floor space and by the three large men positioned around the table.

"There's Jake," she whispered, nudging Annabelle, who stopped and peered through the glass.

Annabelle frowned. "He's got Jackson Boudreaux in there with him and he's not in uniform. I wonder what Jackson's done."

Katherine pressed her lips together to keep from blurting out exactly what Jackson had done. She studied the three men through the one-way mirror. Annabelle's husband, tall and authoritative, leaned across the table at a man hunched in a chair, his head in his hands and his face impassive. She searched for a resemblance to Drew in his blunt features but couldn't find any. His eyes were too dead, his mouth too grim. He was wearing a blue denim jacket with metal buttons running down the front.

She remembered the metal button Drew had found in her window frame and felt a surge of bile in her throat.

The third man in the room leaned against the far wall, his arms folded across his chest. He had on a nondescript suit, and he was apparently just listening while Jake and Jackson discussed matters. Katherine wondered whether he was Jackson's lawyer. But if Jackson was being questioned about some dirty deed he'd done on Philip Delacroix's behalf, Philip would have hired a top-notch attorney for him, wouldn't he? Someone who could afford a more intimidating suit.

"Has Jackson been in trouble before?" she asked carefully, keeping her voice low.

"He's trouble, any way you slice it," Annabelle murmured. "Jake couldn't believe Jackson was still on the force when he took the job as chief. He's my father's errand boy. He runs through money and he runs through women. I don't think he's committed a single decent act or kind gesture in his life, but he's smart, too. He's always covered his tracks, and Jake's been waiting for him to make a slip. He doesn't deserve the badge he wears."

He's your brother, Katherine wanted to scream. "Why do you suppose Jake's interrogating him?" she asked.

"I can't begin to imagine. But as I said, if Jackson was involved in something for my father, it's bound to be corrupt in some way. Let's go wait for Jake in his office." She turned from the glass, and Katherine reluctantly turned, as well.

The door to the interview room opened and Jake stepped out. "Annabelle," he said, sounding both pleased and surprised.

Despite her own agitation, Katherine had to smile at the obvious love that flowed between Annabelle and Jake. It connected them and spilled over, warming and brightening the narrow hallway. She backed away as Jake wrapped Annabelle in a swift hug, then released her.

He turned to Katherine, frowning slightly. "Jake, you remember Katherine Beaufort, don't you?" Annabelle said.

"Yeah." His frown deepened. Katherine pressed her lips together and nodded, not as unnerved by his reticence as she would have been under other circumstances. Jake's frown wasn't intended for her, she knew. It had to do with Jackson Boudreaux. "I wasn't expecting you—but since you're here, let's go to my office." Jake pivoted abruptly from Katherine and hurried ahead of the two women to the office at the end of the hall.

Annabelle sent Katherine a perplexed look, but Katherine said nothing. Her mind remained on the man in the interview room, his cold, flat eyes, his thick hands. Those hands had been inside her bureau drawers, fingering her lingerie. They'd pawed through her jewelry, rummaged around her kitchen cabinets, emptied her closets. Another surge of bile nearly caused her to gag. As soon as she entered Jake's office, she scouted out the nearest chair and sank into it, then gulped in a deep breath of air and prayed for her nerves to settle down and her stomach to stop churning.

Jake circled his desk but didn't sit. His gaze narrowed on Katherine. She sensed Annabelle's building confusion but didn't address it. Sooner or later, Jake would tell his wife what she needed to know.

"I've got a detective up here from the New Orleans P.D.," Jake informed Katherine. "Jackson has confessed, if that's what you're here for."

"Confessed to what?" Annabelle's voice seemed to come from miles away.

"Did he tell you why he did it?" Katherine asked Jake. "He didn't steal anything. I reported that to the cop who answered my call down in New Orleans. Did Jackson tell you what he was after?"

"What are you talking about?" Annabelle broke in.

Jake ignored his wife. "He's told us an awful lot, actually," he informed Katherine, "once we offered him a suspended sentence for cooperating with us. He said he was operating at Philip Delacroix's behest, and that he was searching for your great-aunt's diary because Philip feared that it might incriminate him."

Katherine blinked at the tears beading her lashes. Jackson's confession ought to have made her feel better, but it only upset her.

"He's told us more than we bargained for," Jake went on. "Seems Philip also had him tampering with some racehorses. Jackson's got what you might call a cash-flow problem, and Philip has been helping him keep his head above water—in return for which Jackson has been dirtying his hands on Philip's behalf."

Like a loyal son, Katherine thought bitterly. "Has he told you anything else?" she asked.

"In particular, what?"

Katherine wasn't going to tell Jake what she lacked the courage to tell Annabelle. Let Jackson tell them, or Philip. Or Drew, if he was able. "I don't know," she said vaguely. "Are you going to arrest Philip?"

Annabelle erupted. "Arrest my father? For what? Drew's probably murdered him by now, anyway. That's what we came here for, Katherine, remember? And what is this about a police detective from New Orleans?"

"We're still taking Jackson's statement," Jake said, then turned to acknowledge Annabelle. "As of now, no one's going to arrest Philip." He mulled over his wife's statement, then asked with a slight lift of his eyebrows, "Should I be issuing a warrant for Drew's arrest, too?"

"We came here because Drew thinks—because that diary of Katherine's..." Annabelle took a deep breath and started again. "Katherine and Drew found passages in the diary indicating that Aunt Mary had an out-of-wedlock child sixty years ago. And Drew went raging off to Belle Terre to do heaven knows what to my father, and we thought you might help us out. It would appear that you've got other things on your mind." She glowered at Katherine.

"Jackson broke into my apartment on Monday," Katherine told her. "He was looking to steal the diary."

"What?" Annabelle gaped at her.

"Drew figured out Jackson was the one who'd broken in. He found a button..." Katherine sighed as a crushing weariness settled over her. Too much was happening, too much emotion pressing down on her, weighing against her heart, her mind. She couldn't explain everything to Annabelle. The mere thought of trying to explain made her want to weep.

"Go home," Jake said gently. "The police down in New Orleans already have your statement and the photographs of what Jackson did to your apartment. We don't need you here. You'd be better off getting away from all this."

"Are you going to arrest Philip?"

"Election Day is next Tuesday," Annabelle interjected. "I don't know what's going on here, Jake—and you know I'm no cheerleader for my father. But for God's sake, how can you arrest him less than a week before the election?"

"Annabelle—"

"It would kill him," she pointed out. "He'd just keel over and die."

"That would be redundant if Drew's already murdered him," Jake said dryly. "But I'm not going to do anything that might cause anyone to keel over. I'm going to finish pumping Jackson for anything he can give me against Philip, and then I'll follow procedure."

"Jake." Annabelle's voice quivered with anguish. "Aunt Mary had a baby and my family's hidden the truth for sixty years."

"Your family thrives on hiding the truth," Jake said, even more gently. He crossed the office to Annabelle, drew her into his arms and gave her a reassuring hug. "I want to know everything about your aunt Mary and her baby, but right now I've got to deal with Jackson Boudreaux." He gazed across the room at Katherine. "I'll probably need the diary as evidence," he said. "Do you have it?"

She shook her head. "I gave it to Drew."

Jake let out a long, steady sigh. Her answer clearly didn't please him. "All right. It's not important."

"You just said it was evidence."

"And when I'm ready to put together a case for the D.A., I'll need that evidence. Are you sure it's safe with Drew?"

No, she wasn't sure. "He went to see Philip," she reminded him.

"He wasn't going to give the diary to Philip, was he?"

"I don't think—no," she said with all the conviction she could muster. "He wouldn't. I entrusted him with the diary. He wouldn't break my trust."

Annabelle appeared skeptical. Even Jake arched an eyebrow. But Katherine had seen Drew last night. She'd seen his honesty, his decency. "I trust him," she said.

Jake decided to let the subject drop. "Maybe you ought to go home now, Katherine. There's nothing but trouble here."

She didn't need him to tell her that. But driving back to New Orleans wouldn't take her away from the trouble. It would follow her there. It would be waiting for her, ensconced in her home when she arrived. It would shadow her to work. It would hang like a scented cloud in the air around her, and she would inhale it with every breath.

"Will you take care of Drew?" she asked, immediately regretting her choice of words. She'd meant that Jake should keep him safe and protect him from the perils of his father and the pain the truth might inflict on him. But Jake could as easily answer that he would take Drew into custody if he had harmed his father, fraying the threadbare fabric of Drew's life by locking him away behind bars.

"I'll take care of Drew," Jake promised. "You take care of yourself, Katherine."

That would be impossible as long as she didn't know where Drew was, how he was, what would happen to him. But she doubted that staying in Bayou Beltane would make Drew's life any easier right now.

"All right," she said, rising and willing her legs steady beneath her. "I'll go home."

DREW PULLED OPEN EACH drawer in his desk one final time. The pencils and embossed memo pads he would leave behind. The bag of cough drops, the sterling-silver letter opener, the tray of sorted paper clips and rubber bands. The empty flask bottle he tossed into the trash basket.

He closed the drawers, then glanced behind him at the credenza. Some of the drawers were empty, others full. He'd been careful not to remove any files that belonged to the firm. Only those that related to his own private business and his personal clients had been packed. He was leaving, but he was going to do it as legally as he could.

Two cardboard cartons and a smaller shipping box stood on the floor beside his desk, all of them full. He scoured the credenza drawers one last time to make sure he'd taken everything to which he was entitled, then crossed to the boxes and taped them shut. The two large cartons contained files and records. The third box was filled with plastic cases of computer disks holding the data of all Drew's professional activities over the past decade. While packing, he had stripped his computer's hard drive of anything but its basic desktop software. All the files, notes, records of depositions and details of contracts had been methodically deleted.

He gazed around the office. It looked pretty much the same as it always did, but Drew's view of it had changed. He saw things more sharply, as if through corrective lenses. The furnishings were swank enough, the room quite pleasant except for the broken and boarded window. But it had been stripped of anything personal, anything that might signal that Drew Delacroix had once been there.

Perhaps Drew had never really been there. He could find no memories in the room, no echoes of his life—nothing but a kiss he'd shared with Katherine, and a shattered window, and a bolt on the door separating his office from his father's. This wasn't his place. He was Philip's son in name and in blood, but not in spirit or soul. He had no idea where he belonged, but it wasn't here.

His sigh spread through the still air, as if the entire room were sighing. They were saying goodbye to each other, Drew and his office, Drew and his career, Drew and the life he'd tried so hard to live for his father's sake. That life was gone, and he couldn't locate any grief within himself. Only a resonant emptiness.

It took him less than five minutes to haul the cartons out to the parking lot. It took him significantly longer to wedge the cartons into his compact car, but he managed to squeeze one of them into the undersized trunk and the others onto the passenger seat. The receptionist accepted his vague explanation—"I've got to run a few files across town"—without probing, and his father wasn't about to show up at work, not while he was playing the feeble-hearted invalid back at Belle Terre.

Drew's first stop was the bank. He rented a safe deposit box and locked his computer disks there. Then he drove the few blocks to his uncle Charles's law offices. Straining under their heft, he lugged the two boxes of files inside and dropped them onto the floor beside the receptionist's desk. "Give these to my sister Joanna," he said.

"What are they?" She scowled at the cartons. "You can't just dump these boxes here!"

"Sure I can. Make sure Joanna gets them. Tell her I'll be in touch as soon as I can." Before the woman could question him further, Drew stalked out of the office.

He returned to his car and headed south through town, away from Uncle Charles's office, speeding so Joanna couldn't chase out into the street after him to ask him what the hell he was doing. As he passed intersection after intersection, he tried to clear his head. The car seemed much lighter without all his files in it—without his past, without his father's sins and his own guilt and rage. It was just

Drew and the steering wheel, the leather seats, the motor and the tires…

And the diary. Pulling to the curb on a quiet block, he unlocked the glove compartment. There sat the worn leather-bound book and Katherine's notes, still safe with him.

He was not alone in the car, he acknowledged. His past was still with him, his family's past, his heritage. It lived in the flimsy pages of the diary, in the coded French script.

And more than his own legacy was in the car. Katherine was there, too. Katherine, with her blazing hair and her burning passion. Katherine with her relentless questions, her insatiable curiosity, her mule-headed determination to find out the truth.

Katherine. From the moment he'd met her, she had made him crazy—with anger, with fear, with lust. If ever he needed her, it was now, to help him get through the rest of his life, or at least the next minute of it. He didn't know where to go, what to do, how to exist. He had cut himself off from his world, and he was more frightened than a man facing the gallows. A condemned man knew where he was going, at least.

He wanted to go to her. But he couldn't. He had run to her before, but he'd realized then that he couldn't expect her to set his universe back on its axis. He had to find the strength to make things right without leaning on her, begging her for help, looking for her to repair all the damage his past had inflicted on him. He was going to have to discover his own salvation if he was ever going to be the man she deserved, the man he wanted to be.

He had no idea where to begin, or how. Dread gripped his shoulders like an ogre's hands and shook him so hard his eyes blurred. When at last he could breathe again, his gaze settled on a store across the road. A convenience store, its windows filled with signs advertising assorted brands of snacks, cigarettes, soda pop and beer.

They would sell bourbon there, he thought, steering into the parking lot.

CHAPTER THIRTEEN

"YOU'RE RIGHT," KATHERINE muttered, watching from her post behind the rolltop desk as an impeccably dressed middle-aged woman walked out of K & D's Antiques after having spent a good twenty minutes in mental debate before deciding not to buy the armoire. "That piece is haunted."

Dionne shrugged and wiped the brass handles on one of the drawers with a scrap of chamois. "I'm beginning to think I'll go into mourning if we ever sell it. I've gotten used to having it around, seeing it every day."

"It's taking up a lot of space," Katherine pointed out. "And we've got to turn a certain amount of profit per square foot. You sat through all those business classes with me."

"We do turn a profit, thanks to the Depression glass in the other room." Dionne stopped polishing nonexistent fingerprints on the armoire and sauntered back to the desk. "You're taking up a lot of space, too," she chided with a smile. "Either you tell me what's bugging you or I'm going to lock you in the storage room and put something more profitable in your place."

Katherine sighed. Fatigue settled in her heart like a black hole, dense and devoid of light. Part of her exhaustion was last night catching up to her, but mostly it was a result of the emotional white water she'd rafted through that morning, and the constant anxiety that just around the bend she would have to navigate even more dangerous rapids. "I told you,'' she murmured to Dionne, ''nothing's bugging me.''

''What you told me is that you found the part of that crazy old diary that said your aunt Claire is actually a Delacroix.''

''Okay. So I told you.'' Katherine bit her lip and looked away, ashamed of herself for snapping at Dionne.

Fortunately, Dionne didn't take offense. ''You came to work an hour late—''

''I called to warn you,'' Katherine reminded her. She'd phoned from the police station before leaving Bayou Beltane.

''And you've been moping ever since you got here. And I'm your friend, and you're not coming clean with me.''

''I know.'' But how could she tell her friend that she'd spent the night in Drew Delacroix's arms and fallen in love with him, and now she was beside herself with worry over what might have happened to him that morning when he'd gone to see his father? How could she tell Dionne that she'd given herself body and soul to a man whose life was in such a state of upheaval that he'd probably misplaced those two precious gifts and forgotten all about them by now?

How could she tell Dionne that no man had ever made her feel what she'd felt last night? No man had brought her that kind of pleasure—a pleasure so exquisite that all she had to do was close her eyes and it revived deep inside her, low and sinuous, a dark pulse of longing as essential as the beat of her heart. No man had ever shorn her of all her defenses and left her not even caring that she was defenseless.

The phone rang. She flinched, then stared at it, sending a silent prayer heavenward that Drew would be at the other end of the line. She had never given him the shop's phone number, but he could find it easily enough. And he *had* to call her, if only to let her know he was all right, to reassure her that he and his father had been able to review their situation dispassionately, and that Drew had made it through the conversation without bleeding to death.

At the second ring, Dionne gave Katherine a bemused look, reached over the desk and lifted the receiver. "K & D's Antiques," she recited, then listened. Katherine couldn't swallow; her heart was pounding in her throat. "Well," Dionne said, "we don't have much trade with that sort of thing. You might be better off bringing it to a costume dealer, someone who specializes in antique apparel. Or maybe even a museum. But thanks for trying us." She handed the receiver to Katherine, who hung it up. "Someone got his hands on a bunch of nineteenth-century Mardi Gras masks."

Katherine nodded dully. She hated the phone for not having carried Drew's voice to her.

Was he all right? Would anything ever be all right again?

"Maybe you'd feel better if you went to visit Claire," Dionne suggested.

"No. I don't think she's ready to hear any of this." How could Katherine break the news to her beloved aunt that she really was Philip Delacroix's niece? Claire would *never* be ready to hear that.

"Well then, what are you going to do? Sulk for the rest of the day?"

"I'll try not to." Before Dionne could prolong the conversation, Katherine forced a smile and hit a button on the computer to call up the billing accounts. Only a couple of days remained in October; she might as well start entering the figures for the month. Neither she nor Dionne enjoyed the bookkeeping aspects of their job, but she'd gladly work on them if it would keep Dionne off her back.

The door opened, and one of their regulars swept in. Terence Guillaume was among the most highly respected interior designers in the city; a significant percentage of the mansions in the Garden District had benefited from his artistic touch. He often browsed the city's antique shops looking for inspiration.

"How are my two favorite young ladies?" he exclaimed, opening his arms to Dionne, who returned his hug and exchanged cheek kisses with him. "You look marvelous, as always. And Katherine, my sweet, how are you?"

"I'm fine," Katherine said, attempting another plastic smile.

"She's wretched," Dionne argued. "She's in a funk."

"Then we must get her out of it." Terence stormed the rolltop desk with the fervor of a pirate descending upon a cargo ship laden with gold. "You don't look in a funk at all, darling. You look...sated."

"Oh, Terence, you guessed," Katherine said, playing along. "I'm sated to the point of bursting."

Terence eyed Dionne sagely, his gray eyes glinting wickedly beneath bushy white brows. "She's in love, can't you see?"

"She's as sad as a torch song," Dionne declared. "If that's love, I'm glad I'm not in it."

"What about Lawrence?" Katherine needled Dionne, eager to turn Terence's attention away from herself.

"He's what he is, and what he is doesn't lead to love, as far as I'm concerned. Now, tell us, Katherine, who's the lucky man?"

"No one," Katherine grunted, hating herself for lying yet again to Dionne.

Dionne was a true friend. She took Terence's elbow and steered him away from the desk. "If we keep badgering her, she's going to commit acts of mayhem. Let me show you these chairs she picked up a couple of weeks ago. We've had them refinished. They date to about 1910, and they're really quite charming...." She led him through the store, giving Katherine a parting look over her shoulder. Her eyes said, *You'd better appreciate this.*

Katherine nodded. She *did* appreciate it. She hoped Dionne would continue to tolerate her until she received word from Drew, until he or Annabelle contacted her and told her what was going on in Bayou Beltane. Until she did hear, that black hole in the center of her soul was going to continue to suck her in, absorbing her energy, her yearning, her hope, until there was nothing left but the blackness.

THE MOTEL WAS BLAND. Venetian blinds. Tissue-thin carpet. Fake-veneer furniture. A trite still life bolted to the wall. Antiseptic air.

Dusk came early now, bleeding the light from the sky and conveying the impression that it was much later than six o'clock. Drew wasn't hungry. A few hours ago, he'd wolfed down a sandwich without tasting a bite of it, and all through the day he'd alternated sips of bourbon with swigs of water. He was surprised to discover the bottle more than half empty.

He was appallingly sober, though.

Six o'clock. Katherine would likely be home by now. He could imagine her in her apartment, puttering around her tiny, tidy kitchen, preparing something simple but savory. Perhaps her aunt would be there with her, and they'd be discussing her aunt's astonishing genealogy. If Katherine had a shrewd bone in her body, she would be plotting with her aunt about how to get their hands on some of the Delacroix fortune.

But Katherine didn't have a shrewd bone in her body. Last night Drew had acquainted himself with everything worth knowing about her body, and while he'd found abundant stores of passion and trust, sweet, soft flesh and firm muscle, lips and hands and breasts and the throbbing darkness of her…

No, she wasn't shrewd. Shrewd didn't turn him on. And Katherine did. Just thinking about her made him groan.

Countless times he'd reached for the phone on the night table next to the bed, longing to call her. Countless times he'd touched the phone and then pulled back, changing his mind. Each time, he would instead take a slug of bourbon and return to the diary, which was propped up on the dresser, angled to face the mirror. Each time he promised himself that as soon as he finished the diary, as soon as he found the nugget of truth more true than anything else, the one single truth he had to know to make sense of everything that had happened to him in the past twenty-four hours, the past few days, the past few months—his entire life, for God's sake…

He was desperate to hear her voice. He had to know she was out there in the real world, thinking of him, caring about him. So with the sun gone from the sky and the room awash in sloping purple shadows, he reached for the phone again.

And let his hand fall again. How could he call her? He was Philip Delacroix's son. Katherine Beaufort deserved better.

Besides, he'd told her he was no longer drinking, and there he was, down half a bottle. If only the damned stuff would dull his senses so none of this mattered anymore.

He shuffled back to the diary, slouched in the chair he'd dragged over to the dresser and pushed aside Katherine's notebook. He'd filled the last few pages and was now scrawling translations on the hotel stationery. He clicked his pen and stared into the mirror, praying that he wouldn't have to read yet another tawdry description of sex between the judge and Katherine's great-aunt. The X-rated passages didn't embarrass him, but reading them reminded him of Katherine's embarrassment, her rosy cheeks, her valiant attempts to look as if she weren't as unsettled by those passages as he knew she was.

Katherine unsettled was a magnificent sight. Katherine listening to him translate an erotic excerpt was a wonder. Katherine naked in his arms was more than he'd ever dared to dream.

He focused on the reflected script and translated the French. He skipped over the amorous parts, the heavy breathing and the contorted positions. By the bottom of the page, Great-Aunt Patrice was back on track, recapitulating her pillow talk with Judge Alvarez.

"Neville doesn't wish to tell me his suspicions," she wrote in French. "I insist that we must share everything if we are to be true lovers, and my Neville is nothing if not romantic. And so he tells me about the murder trial, the one that haunts him. He tells me..."

Drew jotted down the translation, then lifted his eyes back to the mirror.

"He tells me he lies awake at night, fearful that an innocent man has been convicted."

The pen slipped from Drew's hand and hit the carpet with a dull thud. He had to get out of his chair to retrieve it, and while he was standing, it was only a few more steps to the bottle, which he'd left on the night table. He snagged it and brought it back to the dresser.

"He tells me there was such pressure to make sure Perdido was convicted. The *poursuivant*—" he flipped through Katherine's French dictionary until he found the unfamiliar word "—the *prosecutor* presented strong evidence, but even so..." Drew wrote the translation down, then perused the next words in the mirror. "In law, Neville says, to convict a murderer one must be convinced of his guilt *sans aucun doute*. Beyond a doubt. Neville tells me that he has doubts."

Drew grabbed the bottle, yanked off the top and inhaled

the sour-mash scent of the liquor inside. The aroma, once as familiar to him as the green perfume of foliage and musk outside his cabin on the bayou, now caused his stomach to rebel. He screwed the top tight, pushed the bottle away and stared at the mirror.

Neville tells me that he has doubts.

Alvarez believed Rafael Perdido could be innocent. The man Drew's Aunt Mary had made love with, the man whose baby she'd carried, the man Drew's grandfather had defended with such intensity that the loss had broken his heart and his spirit...that man may well have been innocent.

Innocent.

If Perdido hadn't committed the murder for which he was convicted, then who had? And why had Alvarez, despite his doubts, seen to it that Perdido was found guilty of the crime? Why had he arranged the secret adoption of Perdido's child? Why had he told Patrice so much about the baby her sister would adopt and raise, the baby who was now Katherine's aunt Claire?

If Perdido hadn't committed the murder, who had?

In a fit of desperation, Drew held his breath, opened the bottle and gulped a mouthful of bourbon. Then he turned his gaze back to the mirror. Behind the book he saw his own reflection, his jawline dark with stubble, his hair disheveled, his eyes bloodshot. He looked worn and ragged and obsessed to the point of dementia. He looked like a man in dire need of a gentle touch, a kind word, a woman's love.

Alvarez thought Perdido was innocent, Katherine. He wanted to shout it out loud, wanted to dial her number and scream it over the phone. No, he didn't. What he wanted was to have her beside him, jotting the translation down in her own demure script and reassuring him that she was as shocked as he was, but that they'd get through this—whatever it was, whatever it meant—together.

He resumed reading the French words reflected in the glass. The room grew darker, and he flicked on the lamp on the dresser. The light burned his eyes, but he kept going.

More erotic scenes. An excerpt recorded before Perdido's murder trial had begun, in which Alvarez told Patrice how he'd manipulated the roster of judges so he would be able to preside over the trial. More sex, and then a passage in which Alvarez told Patrice he could not give her up, even if his wife found out about their affair. She hadn't found out yet, but if she ever did, Alvarez would refuse to give Patrice up. No one pleased him like Patrice. No one made him feel so manly, so virile.

Drew groaned. He didn't need to feel manly and virile. He needed only to feel Katherine, her arms around him, her hair caressing his cheek. And he'd better get over that need, because as long as he continued guzzling booze and sinking deeper and deeper into the morass of his family's dishonorable past, he would not allow himself to get near her.

He read on. The shadows grew longer and then stopped growing as the sky lost the last trace of daylight and night descended quietly over the motel. Drew heard the scratch of his pen across paper as he wrote down his translations. His head ached, and his gut, and his heart. But he wouldn't stop. Not until he knew what he was dealing with.

Near midnight he found what he was looking for, in the final entry of Patrice Forêt's diary.

"Neville still talks about the trial. It bedevils him, plagues him, follows him around. Even as we love each other, he cannot be a man for me today. It so troubles him, like a dark storm cloud."

Drew wrote, then lifted his eyes to the reflected French script.

"I tell him again and again, he must relieve himself of this terrible burden. I plead with him to confess his secret, to let me share the burden with him. He moans, he mutters. It is so hard for him to speak the truth."

Drew scowled. That could be the slogan for the entire lot of them, he thought bitterly: his father, Alvarez, Jackson Boudreaux and his mother, Flora...all of them. Perhaps even Drew himself. *It is so hard to speak the truth.*

"He says," Drew translated from the diary, "that a man has been sentenced to death for something he might not have done, and Neville cannot make it right."

Drew wrote the English down.

"I ask him, does he know who committed this murder? If it is too late to save the man who has paid the price for this horrid act, can Neville at least guess who was guilty of it? He says he does not know."

Drew wrote.

"He says there were three of them, three young fools, all of them lusting after Camille Gravier, the girl who was murdered. Perdido was only one of the three. The other two were brothers. Twins. Either one of them could have killed her. Neville will never know which one did it. It could have been any of the three."

Drew fell back in his chair, closed his eyes and cursed. Or maybe sobbed. Probably both.

Twin brothers. His father and his uncle Charles were twins. They'd known the man who'd died for the crime. Their father had represented that man in court. Their sister had had an affair with him.

Either one of them could have killed her.

Why couldn't it have been Perdido? The creep had knocked up Aunt Mary, back when such an act was considered a crime against society. Just because Drew's grandfather had chosen to represent Perdido didn't mean the guy was innocent. Maybe old Hamilton Delacroix had represented Perdido as a favor to Mary, because she loved Perdido.

Sure, why not? Alvarez's interference was irrelevant. Perdido might damned well have been the murderer.

Either one of them could have killed her.

Not Uncle Charles. He was a hard man but a good one, stern but ethical. He'd always been fair, always honest. Some of Drew's cousins had chafed under his occasionally autocratic rule, but Charles Delacroix was incapable of evil. He couldn't have killed anyone.

That left Philip.

Drew waited for the arguments against such a possibility to flow into his mind, just as they had in the case of his uncle. He waited for his logic to begin listing all the many reasons his father could not have committed a murder sixty years ago. Reasons hobbled in, slowly, lamely—but when Drew assessed each one, he realized it argued for the other side.

His father was corrupt. He engaged in sub-rosa dealings with power brokers. He wheeled and dealed. He'd nearly ruined Annabelle's life, forcing her to marry her first husband because that marriage would reflect better on himself. He'd fathered an out-of-wedlock son who performed petty crimes for him. He had wounded everyone who'd ever dared to come close to him: Drew's mother, his sisters, even his housemaids. And his son Drew.

Why not Philip Delacroix? More than anyone, he could have done it. Philip, who was mentioned several times in the diary insinuating himself into Alvarez's business—after which Alvarez fixed the trial so Perdido would be found guilty.

"No," Drew groaned out loud. Why didn't the bourbon soften the edges of this for him? Why didn't it cushion him so his pain wouldn't be so acute? Damn it—why couldn't he drink enough to convince himself that his father had had nothing to do with this woman's murder?

He stood so swiftly the sudden force of his motions knocked the chair over. He didn't care. He kicked it on his way to the bed, sank onto the mattress and lifted the phone.

Katherine. He'd found that final, ultimate, appalling truth, and he needed to tell her. He needed to hear her voice, to feel her assurance that just because he was thinking such ugly thoughts about his own father didn't mean he was a contemptible human being—or a bad son. Just because he could imagine his father taking the life of a young woman so many years ago didn't mean Drew was worthless.

He brushed his hands over the molded plastic of the receiver, then grabbed up the phone and hurled it against the wall.

What could he say to Katherine? "I am the son of Philip Delacroix. I'm the child who wanted only one thing in my life, and that was Philip Delacroix's love. He was like a god to me, and I wanted his love more than anything. He is evil, and I am his son."

No, Drew wouldn't call her.

It took all his energy to sit up, to swing his feet to the floor, to trudge across the room to the dresser, where he'd left the bottle of bourbon. He carried it back to the bed, drank a long gulp of it and closed his eyes. The song drifted softly through his head:

My woman, she prays to Jesus.
My woman, she prays to the Lord.
And I drink my bourbon and drown out her prayers
And nobody utters a word.

CHAPTER FOURTEEN

KATHERINE GAZED at the television, which was usually stored inside a cabinet she'd bought as junk and had refinished into a presentable piece. It wasn't an antique—if it were, she would have put it in the store to sell. But it kept her television set out of sight when she wasn't watching a show, allowing her living room to look like a living room rather than a den.

Tonight was election night, and Katherine had tuned to a local news broadcast. The outcome of various campaigns mattered to her, she told herself as she tucked her legs under her and settled deeply into the cushions of her couch. As an American, as a Louisianian, as a resident of New Orleans, surely she had an interest in who won where.

Like hell she did. Nothing mattered to her, nothing at all. Not since Drew had disappeared.

Three days ago, she'd received a call from his cousin Shelby. "I can't begin to explain what's going on," Shelby had told her. "I just wanted you to know that Drew gave me your aunt's diary."

Katherine's pulse had jolted into overdrive at the mere mention of his name. "He gave it to you? When? Where is he? What is he—"

"Katherine, I'm sorry. I misspoke." Shelby had sighed. "He didn't actually *give* it to me. He left it on my desk for me to find. He left all his work files one day for Joanna, and then, a day later, he must have broken into the office or bribed the night janitor, but somehow he got in overnight and left the diary and some notes that I believe are his translation.''

''Yes.'' Katherine's heart had continued to hammer. Her hands, wrapped around the receiver, had trembled. ''He and I were translating the diary.''

''I've read through his translations. It's...it's unnerving, to say the least.''

''Where is he?'' The hell with the diary, she'd wanted to scream. The hell with the translations. The only important issue was Drew—where he was, *how* he was.

''That's just it, Katherine. I don't know,'' Shelby had admitted. ''Nobody knows where he went. He just left the diary in my office and disappeared.''

''Why? What could have made him run away? Did his father threaten him? I need to know, Shelby.''

''I wish I could tell you. There's stuff in his translations, all right—some pretty wicked stuff, but it's family business, and given the legal ramifications, I'm not at liberty to tell you right now.''

''It was *my* aunt's diary,'' Katherine had reminded her. ''I trusted Drew with it, but it's *mine.*''

''Yes. You trusted Drew with it. And now...Katherine, I'm sorry, I wish I could discuss this with you, but until we figure out just how to handle this, I can't. I'll keep you posted.''

''Keep me posted if you hear from Drew, too,'' Katherine had demanded. But no one had kept her posted on anything since then. No one had heard from Drew.

He was gone. Katherine had considered searching for him—as if she would know how to conduct such a search. But why bother? If he wanted to be with her, he knew how to find her.

''The polls are just closing here in Louisiana,'' the anchorman reported, looking as credible as a wax figure in a museum as he sat behind a desk, framed by a back projection of red-white-and-blue graphics. "We'll be reporting the results of our exit polls in just a few minutes. But first, an analysis of the reasons behind the low voter turnout from our panel of experts...."

Katherine closed her eyes and nestled deeper into the cushions. Her neck was stiff, her eyes scratchy, her throat parched. Where was the panel of experts that could analyze why a man would disappear? Where were the experts who could explain why a woman would fall in love with a man who was so obviously destined to hurt her?

The experts yammered at one another, all evidently quite fond of their own voices. After a few minutes of blather, the broadcast cut to a commercial. Too restless to sit, Katherine unfolded her body, stood and prowled to the kitchen. She rummaged through the cabinets for something to eat, found nothing that tickled her appetite and prepared herself a glass of iced tea. She took her time, slicing the lemon with precision, squeezing every last drop of juice out of it, wiping the splatters from the counter. She had nowhere to go, nothing to inspire her.

"The elections matter," she tried to persuade herself. She took a sip of her iced tea, added another half teaspoon of sugar to the glass, stirred and sipped again, hoping to find in the bittersweet taste the motivation to return to the couch and pretend an interest in the news report.

"And we have what looks like an upset in the making." The anchorman's voice reached her from the living room. She moved as far as the kitchen doorway and watched as the clean-cut fellow on the screen earnestly addressed his viewers. "Across the lake on the North Shore, it looks as if there will be a changing of the guard at the State House. Our exit polls predict that state senator Philip Delacroix has lost his reelection bid. Delacroix, a senior member of the powerful Delacroix dynasty, has served in the state legislature for more than three decades. If the final voting tallies confirm our exit polls, the voters will be retiring the senator from Bayou Beltane after a long tenure in public service."

"Public service my ass," Katherine muttered, although she was intrigued enough to wander back into the living room. She settled onto the couch, took a sip of her tea and waited to hear more of the report.

Philip Delacroix had never served the public. If his constituents had benefited from his seniority in the state senate, that was only a bonus. Philip had always served himself first—in the senate, in his private practice, in everything he did.

By the time she'd arranged herself comfortably, the reporter was projecting the results of elections in Lake Charles and Lafayette. Katherine reached behind her for the phone on the end table and dialed Annabelle's number. Not to ask about Drew, she swore to herself, but to inquire how Philip was handling his defeat. Katherine would never ask any of the Delacroix about Drew.

As it turned out, she wasn't going to ask Annabelle about anything. The woman who answered the phone identified herself as a clerk at the bed-and-breakfast and, in answer to Katherine's question, reported that Annabelle had gone to her aunt Mary's house for the evening.

Aunt Mary. Katherine could actually think of the woman as her own aunt Mary, if ever Aunt Claire could bring herself to think of the woman as her mother. Aunt Claire was her own person, though, neither blessed nor cursed with curiosity. Katherine had inherited too much of her mother, after all—an unslakable curiosity, a yearning for experience, an urgency about finding a place where she would belong in the world. Katherine's mother had searched in all the wrong places, and the search had killed her.

Katherine had survived her own search so far. But her

heart... How long could a woman survive with a broken heart?

She drank her tea, closed her eyes and absorbed the rock-and-roll melody of an advertising jingle for a four-wheel-drive. Peeking at the screen from beneath half-closed lids, she glimpsed a rugged vehicle bounding over unpaved roads, splattering mud from puddles and navigating the twists and turns of a wilderness route. The scenery put her in mind of the bayou territory where Drew's cabin hugged the shoreline, rickety yet proud, refusing to collapse.

Was that where Drew had gone? How long could he sustain himself at the cabin? How long could he hide?

"We're going to switch to Jenny Cortes, our reporter based in Slidell," the anchorman announced, breaking into Katherine's ruminations. "Jenny? We understand state senator Philip Delacroix is about to deliver a concession speech."

The screen filled with the image of a pert young reporter clad in a stylish blazer and slacks and holding a microphone below her chin. "That's correct," she said. "This is Jenny Cortes, standing outside the law office of Senator Delacroix in downtown Bayou Beltane. One of his campaign aides has just announced that he will be making a statement. Here he is—just stepping outside the building right now."

The camera shifted to the front door of the building where Katherine had gone so many times, first to see Philip and then to see Drew, the building she had fled to that rainy evening when she'd come home from work and discovered that her apartment had been ransacked. Several reporters and camera operators stood in a semicircle in front of the door, which was illuminated with glaring silver-blue spotlights.

The door swung open and Philip stepped into the harsh light. He looked wan and waxy, his skin as dull as parchment paper and whiter than the cream-colored linen suit he wore. He also had on a brown bow tie, reminding Katherine of the voodoo doll that had sailed through a side window of that very building. Philip squinted in the light but managed a taut smile. An entourage of younger men stood around him, hovering protectively.

One of the most difficult moments of his political life, and not a single family member was standing with him. Katherine almost felt sorry for him—except that she knew he'd brought his isolation upon himself.

"Thank you, ladies and gentlemen, for coming here tonight," he began in a thin, reedy voice. Even his hair appeared too white. He looked and sounded like a patient recovering from a high fever. "I would like to make a brief statement of concession to my estimable opponent in this race. He ran a strong campaign—"

An honest one, Katherine thought churlishly.

"And the voters have spoken. This is what democracy means in this great country of ours. I consider myself privileged to have served the people of Bayou Beltane and this parish for so many years. I am proud of all I've been able to do—"

Like line your pockets and alienate your children, Katherine silently observed.

"And now, this campaign brings me to the end of a long political career. I will continue to serve those who wish my service, through this office and my private practice. I will always be available—"

For the right fee, Katherine supplied.

"To anyone who needs me—"

As long as it isn't my son.

"And so, I extend my congratulations to my opponent in this fine campaign and wish him well as he takes my place in the Louisiana state senate. Thank you very much."

The reporters lunged toward Philip, shouting questions. Katherine spotted a familiar silhouette beyond the tight arc of journalists and photographers, a tall, broad-shouldered man with dark hair and a posture of certainty and rectitude. As he approached the outer rim of the bright lights, Katherine got a clear glimpse of his face.

What was Annabelle's husband, Jake Trahan, doing at Philip's press conference? Had he attended as a representative of the family? Or was it obligatory for the town's chief of police to be present at such affairs? As he wove through the crowd, she spotted two uniformed officers following like an escort.

Katherine lowered her glass to the coffee table and leaned forward. Jake was wearing a blazer, a dress shirt and a tie, but when he moved, his jacket flapped open and she saw the leather strap of his shoulder holster against the side of his chest. The fact he was carrying his gun implied that he was at Philip's press conference on official business. Maybe he was serving as a bodyguard. What with voodoo threats against him and a list of enemies several miles long, Philip might have requested special protection.

And then Jake spoke. He turned his head from the microphones and kept his voice low, but the reporters swarmed around him like bees around a blossoming peach tree, aiming their mikes at his mouth, elbowing each other to get closer. "Philip Delacroix," Jake said, "you're under arrest for accessory to breaking and entering and also for conspiracy to obstruct justice—"

"What?" Philip's face went ruddy and his voice boomed. "What the hell—"

"You have the right to remain silent," Jake recited. "Anything you say may be used against you in a court of law. You have the right—"

"Obstruction of justice? Don't tell me you believe that crap Shelby is spreading about Neville Alvarez and that ancient murder trial—"

"You have the right to retain an attorney," Jake continued, as if Philip hadn't spoken. One of the police officers with him eased Philip's hands behind his back and manacled them. The cameras recorded every excruciating moment of the arrest—the glint of metal as the handcuffs were locked around Philip's wrists, the glint of panic in his eyes. "If you cannot afford one, an attorney will be provided for you by the court. Do you understand?"

"This is outrageous!" Philip howled. The reporters chattered and nattered, waving their mikes at him, but he stood above them, bellowing over their heads. "This is an outrage, Trahan! You'll regret this! You'll regret it for the rest of your miserable life! I'll see to it that you do!"

Jake simply set his jaw and led the handcuffed old man through the crowd to a police cruiser parked at the curb. In less than a minute, the cruiser was gone.

Katherine pressed the off button on her remote, unable to bear the din of the reporters' astounded voices and malicious glee. Oh, they'd gotten themselves a story, hadn't they! A big, fat, juicy scandal about the Delacroix family.

At one time, Katherine might have shared their exuberance. How fun it was to see a wealthy, powerful bully laid low. But tonight she experienced no pleasure at Philip's ignominious departure from the press conference. Even knowing that he had caused Drew such torment didn't allow her to wish for Philip's humiliation. After all, Philip was Mary Delacroix's brother, and Mary was Aunt Claire's mother.

They were family, the Delacroix. Katherine was one of them.

SHE ARRIVED at Mary Delacroix's house an hour later, thanks to the employee at a gas station in town who'd provided her with directions, insisting that everyone in Bayou Beltane knew where Mary Delacroix lived. The house—located on Charles Delacroix's estate—was charming, though nowhere near as ostentatious as her brother Philip's home. Several cars were parked in the long driveway. Katherine pulled her car up behind the last one and climbed out.

The grass was damp with early dew, the night echoing with crickets as she crossed the lawn to the veranda. A crisply dressed maid answered her ring. "My name is Katherine Beaufort," Katherine said, wishing she'd thought to change into a dress rather than racing out in a pair of old khakis, a tailored shirt and a wool cardigan. "I understand Annabelle Trahan is here. May I see her, please?"

The maid appraised her thoughtfully, then let her step into the foyer. "Wait here," she said, turning and gliding down the hall. She opened a door and a thick murmur of voices poured out.

"Katherine?" Annabelle peeked around the door and down the hall. As soon as she spotted Katherine, she shaped a tear-stained smile and escaped the room, racing down the hall with her arms outstretched. They hugged, then separated. Annabelle wiped the dampness from her cheeks with a handkerchief. "Oh, Katherine, it's a disaster. Have you heard about my father?"

"That's why I'm here. What happened? Where is Philip now?"

"Jake has him in custody. *Custody,*" Annabelle said, as if by enunciating carefully she would be able to accept what the word meant. "I can't believe it. It seems unreal."

"It was on TV," Katherine said, letting Annabelle take her elbow and steer her down the hall. "I heard Jake say your father was under arrest for breaking and entering, and then your father started ranting about Judge Neville Alvarez—"

"I know. Dad was arrested and taken to the police station." Annabelle's voice wavered, as if a sob were struggling to break free. "My uncle Charles is here, Uncle William and my cousin Justin. Shelby arrived just a few minutes ago. She has your aunt's diary, but she says she's going to have to turn it over to Jake as evidence. Evidence of what, Katherine? What does it say about Dad?"

Katherine shook her head. Apparently there was more than one bombshell among Patrice Forêt's secret jottings. That Mary Delacroix had given birth to a baby and given it up for adoption wasn't grounds for arrest. Something more was in the diary, something more than Alvarez's fixing a murder trial. Something Drew had been sensing all along. Perhaps he'd found what he was looking for in those frail yellowing pages, and the notes he'd left for Shelby explained everything.

"Is Drew here?" Katherine asked, hoping against hope.

Annabelle shook her head. "Nobody knows where he went. He left the diary and his notes with Shelby and disappeared. He's not at Belle Terre, he's not in any hotel or motel in the area.... Obviously he's not with you."

"No," Katherine said quietly. "He's not with me."

"Well then, your guess is as good as mine. He could be out of the state—or out of the country, for that matter. Or he could be lost inside a bottle somewhere."

Katherine didn't want to believe that possibility. Before she could argue with Annabelle, however, she was being ushered into a cozy sitting room filled with Delacroix family members: Philip's twin, Charles, and their brother, William; Charles's son, Justin, and Justin's daughter Shelby; and seated in a well-upholstered wing chair, Aunt Mary.

Katherine gazed at the woman in the chair. White hair crowned a face of sharp, determined features. Her shoulders were straight, her chin raised, her eyes as clear as distilled water. Mary might be in her eighties, but she was a formidable presence, exuding pride and poise, righteousness and resolve. As Katherine's gaze merged with Mary's she felt...not a blow but something just as fierce and deep inside her. A hard, round throb of emotion.

You are my aunt's mother, Katherine wanted to shout. *We are family.* But she only smiled courteously and shook Mary's hand as Annabelle introduced them.

A portable black-and-white television set droned from its perch on a wheeled cart in a corner of the room, but no one seemed to be watching it. Shelby crossed the room to Katherine, dressed in a smartly tailored suit and carrying a leather briefcase. "Katherine, I'm so glad you're here. I've been working on this with Jake—"

"Working on what?"

"The diary. I drove out here to tell Aunt Mary and Uncle Charles—"

"About my aunt Claire, you mean?"

Shelby frowned. "Who?"

"It's in the diary," Katherine said, uneasily aware that everyone in the room was leaning forward to listen to her. "If you read the translations—"

Still frowning, Shelby shook her head. "I came here because of Uncle Philip's arrest. We're trying to figure out how the family is going to handle this. That's what we're focusing on right now."

Katherine realized that Shelby couldn't have guessed the identity of Mary's baby from any of the notes she'd taken—assuming Shelby had even seen those notes. And indeed, Shelby was correct: Philip's arrest took priority right now. The fate of Mary's baby wasn't anywhere near as important.

The fate of Mary's baby wasn't so important to Katherine, either—certainly not as important as finding Drew. "You don't know where Drew is, do you?"

Shelby regarded Katherine for a minute, then turned to Charles and Justin, who stood a few feet away, observing as the two women conferred. Her gaze journeyed to Mary for a moment, and then back to the men. "Maybe we should straighten some things out," she said discreetly.

"Aunt Mary, I know Uncle Philip's arrest has given you a terrible shock, and with your heart..."

"My heart is fine," Mary snapped.

Annabelle had told Katherine that Mary had suffered a heart attack a year ago. Her heart was not fine, and her brother's arrest must have put a terrible strain on it. To learn about her lost daughter might push her over the edge.

"Uncle William and I will stay with Aunt Mary," Annabelle volunteered. "We'll watch the news report."

Refusing Mary the chance to object, Shelby swept Katherine, her father and grandfather out of the sitting room and into the hall. She closed the door and let out a long breath. "According to this diary," she said, addressing Charles and Justin, as if she assumed Katherine already knew, "Judge Alvarez believed that Rafael Perdido was wrongfully accused of murdering Camille Gravier, and from what Drew translated, he's convinced it was Uncle Philip who is the real murderer."

"What?" Katherine blurted out, but she didn't even hear her own voice over the astonished exclamations of Charles and Justin.

"Katherine's aunt, Patrice Forêt, was the mistress of Neville Alvarez, the presiding judge at the Perdido trial. And Alvarez told her everything."

"That's not what I read," Katherine protested. "Alvarez fixed the outcome of the trial, yes—but there was nothing about Philip's having committed the murder."

"You left the diary with Drew," Shelby reminded her. "He translated the last section, and he feels strongly that Philip was implicated."

"Drew," Justin scoffed. "How convenient that he's not around to share this with us."

"He shared it with *me*, Dad," Shelby argued. "He left me all his notes."

"And disappeared before anyone could question him about them."

"What is there to question? He left me what he had. Granddad—" Shelby turned to Charles "—tell me this makes sense to you. Could Uncle Philip have murdered Camille Gravier?"

Charles Delacroix looked as pale as his fragile sister on the other side of the door. "It's possible. Yes. I always wondered... We all loved Camille, you know."

"Camille?" Katherine asked.

"The murder victim," Charles said before Shelby could respond. "A beautiful young woman, brimming with fiery passion. We all loved her—Philip, Rafael Perdido and I."

"Who loved your sister, Mary?" Katherine asked.

If the question surprised Charles, he didn't let on. "Oh, I suppose Perdido flirted with her. He was a rake. He flirted with every single woman in the parish—and I daresay some that weren't single. But I'm sure it meant nothing."

"Didn't you read the rest of the notes?" Katherine asked Shelby. "Drew and I translated most of the diary. I wrote the translations in a spiral-bound notebook. The part about Mary is in there."

Shelby sighed. "I didn't have a chance to read that notebook. I read what Drew had written about the murder trial and called Jake. Who had time for anything else?"

"What's in there about Aunt Mary?" Justin asked.

Katherine took a deep breath. "She had a baby."

"Oh, my God," Shelby murmured, blanching.

Charles spoke up. "Preposterous! If that's in your aunt's diary, Katherine, I can't believe—"

"It's true. The diary also says that Alvarez arranged for Patrice Forêt's sister to adopt Mary's baby. That baby is my aunt Claire."

"Dear Lord," Charles whispered.

"How do you know this baby was adopted into your family?" Justin demanded.

"My great-aunt had no reason to lie."

"And you trusted Drew to translate this? *Drew?* He's always been on Philip's side, and he's a drunk—"

"He's not a drunk," Katherine said hotly. "Sometimes I think he wishes he could be, but he's not. And he's certainly not on Philip's side. If you can say such things about Drew, you don't know him at all."

Justin pressed his lips together and turned away. When he looked back at Katherine, his expression was sheepish. "Maybe I don't. If he wanted to hide the truth, he certainly wouldn't have given the diary to Shelby, would he."

"I'm going to have to turn it over to Jake Trahan," Shelby said. "But—"

A sudden shriek penetrated the closed door, followed by Annabelle's panic-stricken voice: "Help! Aunt Mary! Come, help us! Aunt Mary's collapsed!"

CHAPTER FIFTEEN

NOTHING MOVED. The animals must have bedded down for the winter; Drew heard not a rustle, not a peep. No breeze stirred the air. Even the water seemed stagnant, standing inert around the dock piles. Maybe the world had shut down.

And why not? As far as he was concerned, life didn't offer much promise. His family ties were severed, his career done with. He'd passed the information in the diary along to someone who could use it more effectively than he could, so he had no more purpose in exposing his father's duplicity. The only woman he wanted didn't deserve a fool like him. He couldn't even find solace in drink.

What was left for him besides this hideaway? He'd driven to New Orleans, but his car had steered itself again and again to Katherine's street, and he couldn't face her. So he'd kept driving west as far as Lafayette, where he'd spent a night in an anonymous hotel, and then headed north, and then east, tracing a big circle back to where he'd started.

The lamplight guttered and he adjusted the wick, then set the gas lamp down on the dock and leaned against one of the piles. Bottled water was his only beverage, the mist-blurred moon his only companion. The silence was as thick as death.

And then he heard it. Footsteps, tramping through the undergrowth. A twig snapped, a dry leaf crunched. This was no snake, no furry little mammal moseying along on a chill November night. Those footsteps belonged to a larger animal.

"Drew?"

He must be hallucinating. He wanted to see Katherine so badly he'd dreamed her voice, conjured it out of the oppressive night.

"Drew, are you here? Please be here." The footsteps came closer.

"I'm here," he said, feeling like an idiot for mistaking the fantasy as real. He walked up the dock to dry land and circled the cabin, squinting into the dense foliage that surrounded it. There was a narrow path out to a dirt road maybe a hundred yards from the shore, but it wasn't much, and someone who didn't know the area would be hard-pressed to find it on such a dark night. "I'm here."

He saw a flicker of light, the round shaft of a flashlight's beam. Then she broke through into the clearing beside the cabin. Her hair was tangled, a few leaves trapped in the waves, and her eyes were wide. "Thank God I've found you!" she murmured, racing into his arms.

He held her—only to prove to himself that he wasn't imagining this. But once his arms closed around her, once he inhaled her familiar scent, once he felt the seductive curves of her body and the whisper of her breath against his cheek, he knew he wasn't imagining it. Katherine Beaufort had tracked him down. She'd come to him. She'd found him when the last thing he wanted was to be found.

It didn't matter. If she found him, she'd have him. When she lifted her face to his, he knew he was lost, and he accepted his loss the only way he could. He kissed her.

Slow. Deep. Lips to lips, tongue to tongue. He'd felt all but dead, but she tasted like life itself, and once he remembered how sweet that taste was, he drank it in like a glutton.

She caressed his cheeks with her hands, dug her fingers into his hair, aligned her body with his and took as much as she gave. "Drew," she whispered breathlessly. "Don't ever run away again."

He sighed. Every cell in his body burned for her, but he couldn't have her. Not now. "I didn't run away," he said.

"Of course you did." Her voice carried more strength now, though she was still breathing raggedly. Her hands slid up and down his back, as if she were molding the muscles with her palms.

"Katherine...look at me. Look at who I am, where I came from. You deserve better. You should have left me alone."

"I can't leave you alone," she said, her eyes so bright and steady he couldn't deny her claim. "Maybe it would be easier for you if I could. Maybe it would be easier for me. But I can't."

"I'm a Delacroix," he groaned, breaking from her. "I'm the son of a murderer—"

"Shelby told me about what you'd translated in Patrice's diary. If it's true—"

"If?" He snorted.

"Nothing is proven yet, Drew. And besides, that's your father, not you."

"And what makes me better than he is?"

"Everything," she said, her tone hushed yet so resolute he could almost believe her. She tilted her face and kissed him, lightly this time. "You have to come home now."

Home, he thought bitterly. Hadn't he spent the last few weeks trying to figure out what that was, where it was, how he was ever going to find it? When Katherine embraced him, he could believe home was in her arms. But sooner or later she would let go of him, sooner or later she would come to terms with who he was, and she would leave. And then he would be homeless.

"Your aunt Mary's had another heart attack. She's in the hospital. Your whole family is there now."

His breath caught. Aunt Mary. Oh, God. She'd had a serious heart attack last year, and it had left her frail. "Is she all right? Will she make it?"

"I don't know. You've got to come back with me, Drew."

"My family doesn't want me there."

"Of course they do. That's where you belong right now—with them, with Aunt Mary."

He wanted to believe her. Wanted to so badly he felt weak from it. "What happened?" he asked, forcing himself not to let that weakness cloud his vision, not to let it confuse him. Just because Katherine was here didn't mean she would stay. Just because she'd said his family wanted him with them didn't mean they truly did. "What happened to Aunt Mary? When did she become ill?"

"Just a couple of hours ago. Drew, it's been a madhouse. Your father was arrested for the break-in at my apartment and there are other charges pending. I didn't know about the part you translated—that Alvarez believed your father might have committed the murder, but he arranged for your grandfather's client to be found guilty. I didn't know until Shelby told me. And she and your cousins and uncle didn't know about Aunt Mary's baby. We left the room where your aunt Mary was, but she overheard us through the door. She heard when Shelby told me that Philip had probably murdered Camille Gravier, and when I told Shelby that Mary's baby had been adopted by my grandparents. It was too much for her. She just collapsed." Closing her eyes, Katherine shuddered. "It's all my fault. I should have kept that damned diary to myself. If Mary doesn't make it...it's all my fault."

"No." He pulled her back to him and urged her head against his shoulder. "No, Katherine. The only thing you've done wrong is to stumble into this snake pit of a family."

"That's the only thing I've done right," she murmured, her words muffled by his shirt. "The only thing I did right was to trust you."

"Then I'll have to do the right thing and trust you," he whispered, dropping a kiss onto her hair. "I love you, Katherine. I'm not good enough for you, but I love you."

She eased away from him until her gaze could meet his. "I love you, Drew," she said, a prayer, a vow. He saw everything he needed in her beautiful eyes. He saw love, and trust, and the very essence of home.

They closed up the cabin together, hiked the winding path to the dirt road and climbed into Katherine's car. On the way to the hospital she told him she'd driven to Remy's boat rental dock. She'd found it closed and locked, but Desiree and Flora were on the dock, tying up their boat. Desiree told her how to find Drew's shack by car.

"She told me Flora was going to take her to the hospital with some herbal remedies for your aunt Mary," Katherine reported. "I offered to take them, but she said it was more important for me to find you."

"I can't believe Flora would do anything that might benefit Mary," Drew argued. "Last night, on the way to my cabin, I boated over to Desiree's. Flora was there this time. She told me my father made promises to her and hadn't kept them, promises about supporting Jackson. If only his heart was as weak as Aunt Mary's, she would have killed him with her voodoo scares."

"If she'd succeeded," Katherine pointed out, "justice wouldn't have been done. He needs to confess to what he did, Drew. He needs to be brought to justice."

"Justice." Drew snorted again. Katherine's idealism was

endearing, but he was too cynical to believe true justice could rise from the quagmire of his family's past.

The hospital's entry and parking lot were well lit, despite the late hour. Katherine parked in the first empty spot she found, and Drew took her hand as they crossed the asphalt to the door. Perhaps she thought he was holding her hand as a chivalrous gesture, but it was for strength. As long as he was touching her, he could assure himself that she was real.

The emergency room waiting area could have passed for a Delacroix family reunion. His sisters were there, his cousins, Uncle Charles and Uncle William, all of them milling about, discussing Mary's health and Philip's arrest. The moment they became aware of Drew's presence in the lounge, they fell silent.

He tightened his grip on Katherine's hand.

"Thank God you're here," Annabelle said, and then he began to breathe again.

One by one—first Annabelle, and then his sister Joanna, and then his Delacroix cousins and, lastly, his uncles—approached him, thanked him for coming. One by one, they told Katherine that Aunt Mary's heart attack wasn't her fault, that the news that her aunt Claire was a Delacroix was something they would accustom themselves to, that Aunt Mary was still the family's beloved matriarch, and that once she overcame the trauma of learning the truth, she might actually be pleased to meet Claire Beaufort, the infant she'd carried in her womb, now an intelligent, kind-hearted librarian at Tulane University.

Sooner or later, Drew thought, he would have to tell them all about Jackson. But not tonight, not when Katherine had stripped away his self-protective instincts and he was already so exposed. Emotions surged through him, rough-edged and painful. He had nothing with which to buffer himself.

Nothing but Katherine's love.

His family's love, too. Slowly it dawned on him, as the large army of Delacroix marked time in the sterile, fluorescent-lit lounge with its vinyl furniture and its humming vending machines, that his family not only accepted but actually welcomed him. They didn't seem to blame him for having defended his father for so many years, having taken his side and invested his faith in such a faithless man. Perhaps they understood his wounds; perhaps they understood his reasons. Perhaps they sympathized with him for what he'd endured as Philip Delacroix's only acknowledged son.

And perhaps none of it mattered, because Katherine was still holding his hand.

A flurry of activity in the far doorway caught Drew's attention. Justin conferred with a doctor in a pristine white coat, and then he turned and cleared his throat. It didn't take more than that to gain the attention of everyone in the room.

"The doctor has some good news for us," he said.

Drew felt his relatives release a collective breath.

"Aunt Mary is going to pull through yet again," Justin reported.

"Lord, what a night," Shelby murmured.

Not far from her, Joanna added, "One crisis down, many more to go."

"If anyone deserved to have a heart attack, it's Dad," Annabelle muttered. "I don't know why Aunt Mary has to suffer. He's the one who's committed all the sins."

"He'll suffer," Joanna promised Annabelle.

Drew smiled grimly. Philip Delacroix would never do his family the favor of being felled by a heart attack. Flora had tried her damnedest to scare him into cardiac arrest, and she'd managed to frighten him soundly—yet he was still standing, on his feet as he made his concession speech and as Jake arrested him. No doubt he'd still be standing when the rest of the family were dead and buried.

But Drew no longer cared. "Come," he whispered to Katherine, his fingers still intertwined with hers. He led her to the door and out into the hall, away from all the Delacroix.

They walked until they reached the exit, walked until they reached the night outside. The air was cool but not cold, and stars pierced the sky.

"Are you all right?" Katherine asked as they stood in the shadows of the parking lot.

"I want to kiss you," he said, and he did. The kiss warmed him, gave him courage, enabled him to believe that the rest of his life would not be as bad as the part he'd already lived. "I want to marry you," he said.

Katherine smiled up at him. "Then we'll get married." As simple as that.

"Are you sure you want to be a Delacroix?"

"I will always be who I am," she assured him. "I want to be your wife—but I'll always be me. It's taken me my whole life—and a night in bed with you—to figure out who I am. Now that I know, I'm not about to give that up."

"Even if you wind up spending many more nights in my bed?"

"*Our* bed," she said, grinning.

His smile matched hers. "*Our* bed, Katherine Beaufort." He kissed her again, then whispered, "It's taken me my whole life to figure out who I am, too. And now I know."

"What do you know?"

"I'm a survivor. I'm not my father. And I will always need you."

"I'll always be there," she promised, and he believed her.

Their hands still clasped, they strolled back toward the lit entry to the emergency room. Doctors might have saved Aunt Mary's life, but Katherine had saved Drew's. He shed his pain as if it were a dead layer of skin, and a newer, stronger man emerged, confident that there was at least one person in the world in whom he could place his faith. And he was holding her hand, and he would never let go.

concludes with

DESIRES AND DECEPTIONS

by Penny Richards

Rafe Perdido had been captivated by shy, plain Mary, but he was a drifter, and she was the daughter of the richest man in town. And Rafe had been in the woods the night a young woman had drowned. So had Mary's brothers—Charles and Philip. Now, sixty years later, they would all finally have to face the repercussions of their youthful indiscretions.

Available in August

Here's a preview!

Contract: Paternity **Jasmine Cresswell**
September '97

Letters, Lies & Alibis **Sandy Steen**
October '97

Finding Kendall **Anne Logan**
November '97

In the Bride's Defense **Kelsey Roberts**
December '97

Every Kid Needs a Hero **Candace Schuler**
January '98

Son of the Sheriff **Sandy Steen**
February '98

Overruled by Love **M.J. Rodgers**
March '98

Someone to Watch Over Her **Kelsey Roberts**
April '98

For the Love of Beau **Margaret St. George**
May '98

French Twist **Margot Dalton**
June '98

Legacy of Secrets **Judith Arnold**
July '98

Desires and Deceptions **Penny Richards**
August '98

DESIRES AND DECEPTIONS

THERE WAS A DEFINITE stir in the courtroom as Desiree made her way to the stand. Shelby shot a look at her uncle Philip. His profile, exactly like that of her grandfather's, was all that was visible from where she sat, but she saw his lips tighten and watched as he reached up almost nervously to straighten his signature bow tie.

Contrarily, the old quadroon was the epitome of composure, carrying herself with an undeniably regal bearing despite her ninety-four years of age. She seemed calm, confident and in surprisingly good health—unlike Philip, whose complexion the past few months had taken on a pasty look.

After being sworn in and stating her name, address and what she did for a living—drawing a few titters from the visitors' gallery when she answered, "Herbalist and healer,"—Desiree started answering the D.A.'s questions. He asked her if she knew any of the Delacroix family and what her relationship had been with them in the past and more recently.

After establishing that she'd known Philip all his life, Byron Calhoun proffered some papers to Desiree and said, "Do you recognize this document, Miss Boudreaux?"

Desiree looked over the papers, taking her time. "I do."

"Can you tell the court what it is?"

"It's a statement I gave to Chief Trahan on November twenty-eighth of last year."

"Have you had an opportunity to refresh your recollection of those events?"

"Objection!" the defense council called out.

"Overruled."

"Would it be fair to say that your statement is a true and accurate account of what you saw on the night of June eighth, 1938?"

"Yes."

"Your honor, let the record show that Miss Boudreaux's statement wasn't given contemporaneously to the incident."

The judge nodded.

"You know what happened that night," the D.A. continued. It was a statement, not a question.

"Yes," Desiree replied with a nod.

"What did you see?"

She looked directly into Philip's eyes. "I saw Mr. Philip Delacroix kill Camille Gravier."

HARLEQUIN®
AMERICAN ROMANCE®

HARLEQUIN PRESENTS®

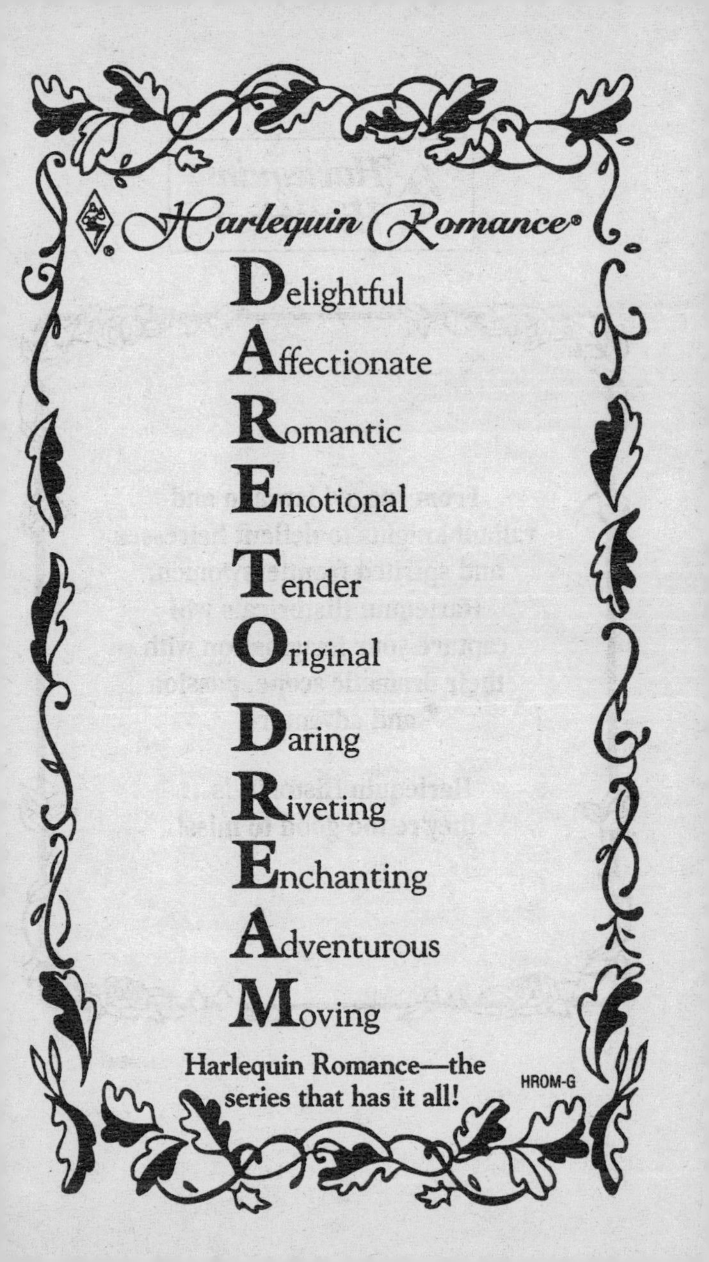

Harlequin Romance®
Delightful
Affectionate
Romantic
Emotional
Tender
Original
Daring
Riveting
Enchanting
Adventurous
Moving
Harlequin Romance—the
series that has it all!
HROM-G